ll 3

GW01080885

The Flight of the Sparrow

The Flight of the Sparrow

FAY SAMPSON

ROBERT HALE · LONDON

© Fay Sampson 1999
First published in Great Britain 1999

ISBN 0 7090 6402 0

Robert Hale Limited
Clerkenwell House
Clerkenwell Green
London EC1R 0HT

2 4 6 8 10 9 7 5 3 1

Typeset in North Wales by
Derek Doyle & Associates, Mold, Flintshire.
Printed in Great Britain by
St Edmundsbury Press, Bury St Edmunds, Suffolk.
Bound by WBC Book Manufacturers Limited, Bridgend.

To Christine

PART ONE

Chapter One

My mother's arms gripped me so hard it hurt. My eyes were
squeezed shut. I could have seen nothing even if I had not
been crushed against her chest. Under the soft, smothering wool of
her tunic her heart was beating wildly against my head. I waited,
tensed, for her to throw me from her, rake her cheeks, tear out her
hair, scream her grief. But she stood rigid as if an elf-stroke had
paralysed her. Her voice strained hoarse and hollow.

'He butchered *all* of them? Aethelfrith the Ferocious will marry
my daughter, after murdering her father and her brothers?'

I was alive. Did I not count?

Behind me, I heard how the thane's voice stumbled. I understood the reason. Wiglaf was here, alive, to confess to the queen. He
should have died before my father and brothers fell, defending
them. He would have to live with this shame for the rest of his life.

'My lady, forgive me, there's still prince Edwin.'

Her fingers clutched me fiercely but she was dumb with loss.

'And you may have one grandson left. Some say that Hereric got
away to those Britons who keep their kingdom yet in Elmet.'

'Haa!'

I struggled in my mother's hold. Her laugh was a bitter, animal
snarl.

'We need not wait for the Death-Wolf to tear us apart in the
twilight of the gods. We English can do it ourselves, here and now.

9

Angles against Angles. Woden's descendants against Woden's descendants. Children of the same wise god? And those of us who are left must find refuge with British Christians?

'They speak the truth when they call him Aethelfrith the Ferocious. I am not queen in Deira now. He will take Acha for his wife. My daughter will be forced to share the crown with her father's killer.' She stroked my hair, as though she had just remembered I was there. 'So, my little princeling, there is only you left.'

I forced myself to open my eyes and stand upright. My mother was a tall woman. I could see little beyond her but a blurred ring of appalled women and grim thanes.

'I'll fight him.'

It was the only fact I could feel sure of for the moment. I was no longer certain where I was, what time of day, what season it was on the moors beyond the door. The draught was swirling smoke under the rafters of this half-familiar hall in Catterick. York had been the centre of our world, our capital. And York was gone, carrying away Father and all those sword-swinging, swaggering brothers I had dreamed of joining. A furious warlord from the north had wrenched up the World Tree by the roots. It was spinning out of control, hurling leaves and branches at me, leaving only wreckage all around.

My father Aelle was dead. The great king of English Deira, from the Ouse north to the Tees and halfway west across Britain. If I had been old enough, I would have marched with my brothers. I tried to imagine the spear hurled with our battle-scream, the onrushing storm of the enemy, the weight of the rune-rich sword drawn from its sheath, the brute push of muscle against muscle. It would not be like training with my father's thanes, careful to do me no lasting damage. I would come face to face with snarling Bernicians intent only on my death. What must it feel like when the enemy's blade goes in and you know you have lost, finally?

But my father had not died like that. Murder. There would be no battle-maidens swooping down from the sky to snatch the hero up to Woden's feasting hall. Only the bloody huddle of a shamed, assassinated corpse.

How would Aethelfrith bury my father? It should be in a ship, the still body of the King, heaped about with treasure, launched on its crewless voyage into the grey unknown.

I was still alive.

I found my hands reaching again for the warm wool of my mother's skirt. She spoke over my head. 'So Aethelfrith has got what he always wanted. Our Deira joined to his Bernicia. One single Northumbria, from the Humber all the way north across the Giants' Wall to the land of the Picts. And poor Acha is his legitimacy. My daughter, Aethelfrith's wife.'

I lifted my eyes to her fierce blue ones. 'If Father's dead, shouldn't they hail me king?'

I felt the atmosphere in the hall change, as though the door had crashed open, letting in the bitter winter wind. But no one spoke. It took me several moments to understand their silence.

The thane Wiglaf broke it, gruff with concern. This was his last remaining duty to his dead king, before he could bare his heart to the howling gale of grief.

'We need to get this lad away before he's an hour older, my lady. If Aethelfrith knows any of Aelle's kin are left alive . . .'

I am still alive. I am still alive.

The knowledge terrified me now.

'Where can I send him?'

She was not coming with me. I was to be launched into the unknown alone.

'You are my queen. It is for you to say.'

'I have no kin in any kingdom that is safe now.'

'Young Hereric and his wife fled to the King of Elmet in Leeds. But there's a Bernician warhost between us and them. There's only the road open to the west, if we're quick enough.'

'So the English conquest has come to this? I must trust my last son to Christian Britons?'

11

'Those Christians will hate Aethelfrith the Ferocious until Asgard of the Gods falls and the Serpent of Doom rises from the depths. He slaughtered the flower of their British warhosts here at Catterick. They lost the east of their island for ever. If Aethelfrith wants to kill Edwin, be sure the British will protect him.'

'How many men will you need to get him to the coast, and a ship to Gwynedd?'

'A prince's bodyguard, my lady. A dozen warriors.'

'Lilla.' I heard my own voice break out, higher than I meant it to. 'Lilla has to come with me.'

One face swam clear out of the ring round me. Hair dark for an Angle, framing a face pale as birch bark. I caught the eager assent in his eyes. Lilla was young in my father's warband, not yet a thane, though I was determined he should be when I was king.

'To the death, Edwin. Where you go, I will go. When you come back as a man and claim your kingdom, I shall be beside you. If you die attempting it, be sure I shall have fallen first, defending you.'

I saw my mother's hands tense over her belly. 'I shall have no more sons. You must live, Edwin. Live for Deira. Live for your father and brothers. Return to avenge them.'

She was demanding that I catch the World Tree spinning on its axis and make it safe again.

Outside in the yard I heard horses waiting, ghostly as the Wild Hunt.

Chapter Two

The weapons that threatened me on the Welsh hillside were granite and slate. They struck at the pony's hooves and sent a shock through its bones against my spine. It was helpless jealousy to watch the Welsh prince Cadwallon flowing with his mount. Brown hair, black mane, streamed alike in the current of their galloping as if youth and animal were one. They raced the clouds scudding overhead, his jewellery and the pony's harness flashing in and out of the pines which darkened the mountainside. Not for me here the rolling spread of oaks in the Plain of York. No slopes of golden corn. No pigs snuffling for acorns on the margins of rich ploughland. A hard land, Gwynedd, its valleys narrower, more deeply shadowed, its mountains brooding giants. The brooks dash down headlong to the north. They breed athletic sheep.

Then we were over the pass and I was blinking in the sudden brightness thrown up by the shining lines of the Irish Sea.

Across the narrow neck of the Menai Strait lay Cadwallon's father's land. The Isle of Mon.

Nostalgia gripped my throat. The dice of exile had thrown me there, to Cadfan's court at Aberffraw. The one place in all the Welsh kingdoms that was something like home. The sandy beaches of Mon's shores. Here there was farmland. The grain silvering as the ears filled out in open sun. No slate-hung hills cast their brooding shadow over Mon. A gentle land. A loving foster-mother.

Cadwallon had long since reined up among his Welsh companions. They sat poised against that sky watching us come. A fugitive English prince, who had had to beg Cadwallon's father for protection, with twelve English warriors making a show of guarding him. The Welshmen were grinning as we approached.

'I've yet to meet an Angle who looked happy on a horse. You don't even ride them into battle, do you? Just transport. That's all you think they are. A cart with hooves.'

'I'd rather fight with two feet on the ground. You can strike a harder blow. You've nothing to brace your feet on when you're up in the saddle and your two legs hanging down the horse's sides.'

'Knees, man. Heels. You still don't understand the use of them. British cavalry, there's glory for you. Speckled herds of horses hurled on the enemy, like breakers on the rocks. You English foot-sloggers can't wheel and race and slash. We can reap like the whirlwind. And I shall have fine blades beneath me, besides my own weapons. He'll send many a man to feast the crows.'

He was tense with desire for his first battle, looking down at the dark gleam of his pony's hooves. The Welsh have the magic of words. I was still trying to learn, stumblingly, the appalling difficulty of the British tongue. Cadwallon made the language dance.

I was fifteen too. Stung into rashness I shouted back at him, 'So how is it those English foot-sloggers are pushing west all the time and driving your British cavalry back to the sea?'

It was a mistake. One of those slate-grey clouds swept across my Welsh foster-brother's face. He wheeled his pony so abruptly that the animal cried out. At once Cadwallon's face softened. His hand caressed its neck. He bent and whispered in its ear. The pony shivered with pleasure. But when Cadwallon straightened up, the scowl was back. I sensed Lilla urge his mount alongside mine.

We watched those dark eyebrows frown down at the rippling oatfields below us, the sands of Bangor, the cattle meadows of Mon.

'I should have realized. You're Northumbrian, aren't you?'

'I'm not from Aethelfrith's folk. My father was king of Deira. That's the southern half of Northumbria.'

'Same thing. Same gods. Same butchery.'

'You seem to have forgotten what brought me to your father's court. Aethelfrith grabbed the whole of Northumbria. He'd like me dead.'

'Then you could be the quarry that brings him to attack Gwynedd. He destroyed the warhost of the Britons at Catterick; we lost the east. Last year he slaughtered the Scots at Degsastan; the whole of north Britain is a beaten cur cringing at his whistle. There's only us in the west left free. If the lands beyond the Severn fall, there will be no more Britain left, only England.'

His head whipped round to glare at me. I longed for blue-grey eyes, the swing of blond hair on Angles.

'Did you know that Aethelfrith kills priests at the altar, rapes nuns?' he spat at me.

I swallowed. These were not my holy men and women. As a child, I had gone to the sacred enclosure at Goodmanham for sacrifice. I saw again the thatched temple, the spiked stockade hung with the warning corpses of polecats. I threw my little body on the ground before living pillars whose roots went deep into the earth and drank blood. I shivered, remembering the feather-caped priests, the wise women with the far sight, chanting in smoke-filled shrines to the awesome givers of life and death. I imagined what howls of anguish would shudder through the English lands if the Britons slaughtered those sacred guardians. We should be left abandoned, naked, to the gods and warriors of our enemies.

In Gwynedd, I was a guest of this Christian country. I went, out of courtesy and prudence, to the church of my Welsh foster-father, King Cadfan. The Christians knelt to their own All-Father, to their Christ-Man, hanged like Woden on a tree, to their Spirit-Bird. These were not my gods, but I did not wish to offend them.

'I suppose if your priests were cursing the English warhost in their churches, they could have been fighting as much as any warriors. Maybe Aethelfrith was afraid of their power.'

I was wondering what happens in the clouds above a battlefield, when British and English meet. Did our champions, One-Eyed Woden, Thunor with his hammer, Red-Handed Tiw, struggle against Christ and Michael and the archangels? Were the warhosts below them nothing but little pieces on the gaming board, while the real battle was somewhere else?

'But our gods proved more powerful,' I finished defiantly.

Our. One betraying word, still linking me to Aethelfrith the Ferocious, who killed my father, took my sister and wanted me dead.

'Curse you!' Cadwallon's moustache was not yet thick enough to darken the teeth of the smile he flashed out at me. 'Every time you English shed a drop of holy blood, the soil of Britain cries out a vengeance on you. Britain is a holy island. Do you know what they say? The Christ Child himself walked here. The High King of Heaven. War-leader of the angel hosts. He will avenge us.'

'I keep telling you, it's me Aethelfrith wants to kill. I'm under your father's protection.'

'In your heart you're English still. When you come to our church it means nothing to you. You'd sacrifice to the same gods as Aethelfrith, if you could. Barbarian.'

With his heels Cadwallon started to urge his pony down the precipitous slope. He was play-acting dangerously as he let the reins drop and turned round to mock me.

One hand hid half his face for the one-eyed Shapeshifter. 'Look. Woden!'

His shoulders swelled and his cheeks puffed out gigantically. He crossed his eyes and leered stupidly. 'And Thunor?'

He became a mincing woman, fluttering his hair, flaunting his necklace. 'Lady Frigg . . . a woman for a god!'

I struggled with nervous fury under his derision. My pony was following his, tilting alarmingly downhill. I had to risk freeing one hand to make the signs of protection against evil. In Deira I would have been thought a competent enough horseman, but not on this terrain, not with these reckless Welshmen who seemed to be knitted into their saddles. I clutched the reins again. Slate slithered underfoot. The pony felt to be plunging down a nearly vertical face towards the minute cattle on the flood plain below.

I heard a violent exclamation behind me. Lilla was as scared as I was. But where I went, he would go. He would die at my side, whether it was in the heat of battle or from a broken neck over a precipice. Where the track twisted sharply I got a glance at him. The angles of his face were set, white under his tan. The Britons have more blood in their cheeks than we do.

'I'm your father's foster-son.' The words were jolted out of me angrily to Cadwallon below. 'And under the protection of your country's gods.'

'One God. Don't you know that by now?'

'They sound like three to me. I didn't mock your All-Father. Take care what you say about mine.'

I meant to sound manly, princely. My voice shook like a petulant child.

'Wolf!' Cadwallon's whoop echoed round the hills and the whole wild Welsh band went plunging across the slope in pursuit of a fleeting grey shadow. My pony took off with them. I had no choice but to cling on, argument abandoned, heels sliding, hands gripping for my life in the silken rope of my Welsh mount's mane.

I shall never catch up with Cadwallon. He is always out there in front of me, taunting me.

Chapter Three

'Tell me about your father's kingdom.' Cadwallon's mother lifted her hand from stroking the wolfhound at her feet. There was more than ordinary conversational courtesy in the way she raised her eyes, hazel, intelligent, to mine.

I sensed a stir amongst the girls around her. Their skirts spread on the rugs under the rowan trees where we had come to soak up the thin spring sunshine. The girls had been busy even here, their fingers stabbing, spearing, advancing the territory of their sewing stitch by stitch. Some of them were the daughters of Cadfan, chieftain of Mon, who might one day be king of all Gwynedd. The taller ones were betrothed, but breath caught in my chest with the realization that some of the younger ones were not. With the hot self-consciousness of adolescence, I felt their eyes weighing me up. I was not merely their foster-brother, but an unmarried prince. How long had they been gossiping about me in the queen's quarters, studying my possibilities, assessing my drawbacks?

Could it happen? Had I enough dignity left, enough hope, to make the gift of a daughter a worthwhile speculation to Cadfan? A Welsh princess, bride to a fugitive English exile?

And which of them might it be? Their ring of upturned faces made me dizzy with ungovernable thoughts. I might cup these breasts in my hands in a private bedchamber, slip the tunic from those shoulders, run my hands. . . .

18

Mairi, now, blacker of hair than the others, fixing me with those huge, brown eyes and that wide warm, knowing smile. I felt my body surge with a mixture of terror and delight.

Her mother's voice called me back to reality. 'Edwin?'

'Oh, my father's kingdom? D-Deira.' My tongue stammered on the name of loss.

The girls tittered. But I would make them see.

'It starts on the banks of the Humber, our southern border with Mercia. Not good friends with us, though we are all Angles, and our longships once rowed the same sea-road to Britain. There's a great plain around York, where the corn grows thick and the forests are big with timber for our halls.' I was afraid my voice, not yet completely broken, would crack, but I felt it ring deep and warm as memories took hold. 'Any fool could see why Aethelfrith would be jealous to steal Deira from us. His Bernicia's a grim land, bleak, bony, steep.'

'Like the mountains of Gwynedd?' asked Mairi, looking over my shoulder towards the mainland. I was unsure about the innocence of the solemnity in her big brown eyes.

'We have moors in Deira too. But sweeter vales beneath them. York's an ancient city, the work of giants. You wouldn't believe it unless you saw it. A circle of huge walls, not earth and timber, but piled up far above your head with stones mightier than any man could lift. And towers on them climbing into the sky. Inside the walls there are the ruins of palaces and temples. Stone-carvings so big no humans could have dreamed of them, let alone made them. But that old race of giants was gone before we landed. Their stones are tumbling and trees have grown up through the paved floors. Yet you can still see what they must have been like. There's figures of them, gods and goddesses, not carved out of living wood like ours, but the hardest stone.'

The girls were all laughing.

'Have you never seen Caernarvon or Chester, Edwin? Don't you know about the Romans?' Queen Rorei asked me gently.

19

Always it was like this. My Welsh hosts made me feel like a barbarian, though we English had conquered half their island.

'I've heard of them,' I heard myself blustering. 'But what are Romans to the English? Where are they now? Have they got great dragon-headed longships hung with shields, like ours? Or a warhost of thousands of spearmen? Can they fight the Picts and the Irish off when they come raiding our good farmland?'

'All that and more, once. The Romans had legions upon legions. An empire across Europe, from Jerusalem to Spain. It is not all lost. They left us roads and cities. They brought us Christ on his Tree.'

I did not want to argue with her. She was a courteous lady, who had opened her home and her heart to me.

Less confident now, I fumbled for the British words. 'There are Britons still in Deira, outside the cities. They didn't all run west when the English came. Up in the dales. . . .' I managed a smile for Mairi, meeting her eyes across the circle. 'Yes, we have valleys like Gwynedd's too, where the hills run down from the dragon's spine they call the Pennines. Close little dales with rushing brooks and sheep jumping across the rocks to find good grass. There's a little British kingdom tucked away there still. Elmet. We haven't taken it from them yet. That's where Hereric hid.'

'Your brother? I thought you were the only son left.'

'I am. Hereric is my brother's son. My nephew.' I grinned at Mairi, acting the hurt, brave prince. 'Only he's older than I am. He has a wife.'

I saw the Queen nod, as if satisfied. Personal tragedy plays no part in diplomatic liaisons. But Mairi's eyes grew wider yet, and softer, staring into mine. She was three years younger than me, her body only just beginning to hint at a woman's shape. But it would not be long. The dark curls seem to nestle knowingly into the hollow of her neck. Against the white skin, her rose lips curved into a pursed O of sympathy. Surely it should not be difficult to make them soften under mine.

'So should you have one soon,' Queen Rorei said, startling me with the closeness of her thoughts to mine.

So I had not imagined it. There was more to this interrogation than idle chatter on a sunny afternoon, out on the slope above the orchard at Aberffraw. Blood began to pound in my temples. If the Queen of Mon wanted to know about my kingdom, my inheritance, my family, it must mean she thought I was not without hope. Aethelfrith's bloodlust might still be thwarted. Mairi. . . .

The wolfhound bounded to its feet barking. The girls were scrambling up on to their knees, heads turned, faces alight for the entrance of a more exciting figure than me. Cadwallon and his friends came bursting out from the stable yard. He crossed the grass with that swinging stride that made you see a sword at his hip and a shield on his shoulder, even when he went unarmed. He had ridden on his first cattle raid when the year turned.

'I might have known you'd be sitting with the girls, Edwin. How's your embroidery coming along?'

The wolfhound hurled itself on the Welsh prince, so that he could not see my face.

'Edwin has been telling us about Deira,' Queen Rorei said. 'It sounds a fine, rich kingdom.'

'But it's not a kingdom any longer, is it?' Cadwallon snatched up a withered apple from the basket between his sisters. His teeth bit into it, too close to my face, and he waved the result under my nose. 'Just a province now. Barely half of Northumbria. Wild Bernicia in the north, soft Deira in the south, they say. All one for Aethelfrith the Ferocious.'

I kept my eyes on Cadwallon's apple. The hurt of his words was like a physical lump in my throat. It was as if I had tried to swallow that bite myself and it had stuck. At last I muttered. 'Then a Deiran has as much right to be king of it all as a Bernician.'

There was soft burst of clapping. Mairi was applauding me.

'He'd need a warhost behind him, boy.' Cadwallon peered pointedly past me. I was not quite alone. Most of my men were back in the yard with the Welsh lads. Lilla, as always, had stayed with me. I felt his strength.

I clung to the last threads of my dignity and walked for the gate. I needed the cool breeze and the silence on the hill.

I heard Queen Rorei's voice scolding behind me. 'That was unkind. The boy has lost everything for this while, at least. Father, home, kingdom.'

'His kingdom? He had older brothers, till his brother-in-law butchered them. Why should the Deirans ever have cried that runt for their king?'

'But Edwin has survived them all.'

I quickened my stride, out of earshot of Cadwallon's contempt, his mother's calculations. I was aware as never before of those younger girls' eyes following me, balancing my blond English looks, both menacing and exciting to them, against the low ebb of my fortunes.

Loyal as the hound to Cadwallon, Lilla followed me.

'The tide will turn, Edwin. The Queen believes so. Aethelfrith's mortal.'

'So am I. Have you forgotten why you brought me here? I'm a beggar at a British chief's court. The last of my father's sons. Almost the last male of the royal house of Deira. Aethelfrith won't sleep easy until he sees me dead.'

'These Welshmen won't betray you. They hate Aethelfrith as much as we do. He's gobbling Britain up like a ravenous wolf.'

'When my father was alive, our warhost raided westward too. We English must, mustn't we? Since our longships landed, we've dreamed of taking the whole Island of Britain, from sea to sea.'

'I wouldn't speak that dream aloud, here.'

Even in English conversation, it was dangerous. We stood side by side, exiled prince and bodyguard. We were gazing down over the busy stables and kitchens of Cadfan's residence, and out past the shore to the western light over the Irish Sea. Lilla sighed. I did not need to ask to know why. He was seeing again, as I was, the coast of Deira, the long sweep of Bridlington sands where I had run as a child, fishing boats coming in under the shelter of the cliffs at Scarborough, and out to the east, the huge grey sky over the North Sea that numbs our English souls to silence.

Chapter Four

Cadfan's family were streaming out of Aberffraw church. The breeze was blowing up from the harbour, rippling the grass around the wooden preaching cross. I stood and waited. The Welsh called us Angles heathens. Like all the unbaptized, we left the church before they began the Eucharist. I had lingered outside among the yew trees. I heard the swell of singing, the tinkling of the priest's handbell. I could not guess what mysteries the Christians were sharing without me.

They were coming now, bright in their finest clothes and jewels for Sunday. Their faces looked bright and cleansed too. King Cadfan, with that firm, slow step. You might mistake him for an older warrior than he was. And Queen Rorei, still with the spring of youth in spite of her childbearing, looking about her to see what her lively family were up to. The older daughters, some soon to be queens like their mother, the younger ones pulling the demure veils from their hair and starting to run. Mairi danced past me, her hand tugged by a smaller sister. The dark curls skipped on her shoulders. But her head turned, so that the brightness of her smile lingered fixedly on me. I could not doubt the warmth of the message in those brown eyes.

I was aware of the jangling strut of the Welsh princes past me. I would not allow my eyes to turn on them. Cadwallon's contempt hurt too much. I was as highborn as he was. If things had been otherwise, I too should have come to manhood surrounded by my father's court, his warhost, his loyal people, his priests. I should be riding to war as the king's son, not earning my mead as one of his retinue of warriors.

It was pride that made me blurt out the question to princess Anna as she paused near me. 'Is your sister Mairi betrothed yet?'

She turned her face, surprise in her eyes, ready to tease me. But it was Cadwallon's voice that answered from behind us, reading too well the confusion of thoughts I had hardly admitted yet even to myself.

'*You*? Edwin the runaway? You and my sister?' He swung round in front of me, the dancing grin showing his delight that he could rile me with a new justification. 'What could a beggar like you have to offer a princess of Gwynedd, boy?'

I was a warrior now. I had been taught to defend myself. I snapped back, 'Fortunes can change. I've got my whole life in front of me. There are spearmen still loyal to me in Deira. They'd rise against Aethelfrith if I called them.'

I had no knowledge if this was true, but I could dream.

'Oh, yes? And suppose you did ever snatch the rags of your kingdom back from Aethelfrith, do you think my father would give our little Mairi to a heathen? Do you think Mairi herself would consent to such a marriage?'

I had seen the smile in her eyes, deliberately cast over me like a spell.

'I'd be a fair husband. My wife would have her freedom. She could bring her priest to York, if she wanted.'

'To the land where they kill Christian priests, and drive their congregations into the hills? And when, exactly, is this remarkable change in your fortunes destined to take place?'

'Your mother doesn't think it's so impossible.'

'You see my father there. He doesn't look particularly busy this morning. I dare you to ask him for Mairi's hand. Now.'

He knew I could not speak for her. I was barely blooded in

Cadfan's warhost. I had no wealth but what my sword won. No scrap of comfort from my homeland, where Aethelfrith swelled with power after every battle. News trickled out of British Elmet that my nephew Hereric was still alive. Breguswith, his wife, had borne him a daughter. I felt they were all the family I had. My sister was Aethelfrith's queen. I counted her as good as dead.

I could never beat Cadwallon. My only answer was to stride away up a Welsh hill.

The eagle hovered high up, a dark dazzle against the piercing blue of the sky. It had silenced the skylarks. Seeing it, I felt the same catch in my breath. Up here on the vast sweep of the heathered hillside I was just a small parcel of skin and blood and nerves and bone, easily spotted, inescapably vulnerable. I glanced below me. I should have known Lilla would be there, following me at a little distance with his easy, purposeful stride. All this while on Mon, he had never been very far away. There was a straggle of others lower down. What could they do to save me if that eagle swooped and took on the craggy face of Aethelfrith the Ferocious, the fierce blue eyes that had ordered my father's murder? He had killed all the royal males of Deira, save only Hereric and me.

'Stop right there!'

I heard the scream of the eagle coming for my eyes. A shudder convulsed me. Then sense steadied to the sound of a woman's voice yelling at me in the British tongue.

'For the pity of Christ's wounds, you flat-footed oaf!'

Even if I had not become attuned by now to the complications of its melodies, I could hardly have mistaken the sense of her language. But where was it coming from?

I checked my stride with the shock. I had thought myself alone, except for the hovering eagle and that distant, tactful escort. Still seeing no one, I took another hesitant step forward.

She erupted in front of me, seeming to burst out from a hole in the bank. She wore a rough gown the colour of porridge, and none too clean. I could smell the sweaty wool from here. She had a big knotted staff in her hands and, for all she was dressed like a field slave, she thrust it out sideways at me, like a bar to a door.

'Not one step further, lad, or I'll thrash you over the rump for a clumsy bullock.'

My instinct was to look back, to see whether Lilla had witnessed this encounter. Though, dressed like that, she might appear to him from below no more than a sheep, grey-white in the heather.

But I found I could not turn away. This woman was less than common height. She would not have the physical strength to use that stick against a young man trained by the finest English and Welsh warriors. Yet I felt I did not have the authority to defy her.

Slowly she let one end of the staff fall, grinning at me with yellow and blackened teeth. Her head was bound up in linen, so that her face shone out with no wisp of hair to give me a clue to her age. Her cheeks flamed with a high colour, her nose too. Her eyes sparkled at me, greeny-grey as the high-curling waves swept in by the Irish Sea. She carried the glow of health, and of her own certainty. In her plain, poor tunic, she was laughing at me as confidently as the Queen in Aberffraw and all the princesses.

'That's better. Stand still.'

She skirted the semicircle of heather in front of me and came to join me where I stood. She still made no reverence to me, though she must have seen the chains of gold round my neck and the gold and garnet brooch that pinned my cloak. Still smiling, she moved her grubby hand. I thought she was reaching out to take mine. But just as I felt my own arm lift obediently from my side, she motioned in front of me with her staff.

'Look. Another stride and you'd have crushed them.'

The blackthorn stick parted the brush of heather. The eggs were speckled blue. Five, in a hollow of the peaty earth.

'It's late in the summer.' The woman's voice sang with sorrow. 'She'll have lost another clutch before this. More than one, maybe. But she won't give up trying.'

'A s-skylark?' I was stammering to find the British word.

She turned her face up to mine. I read the same compassion for me she had shown towards the bird.

'So you're the Angle? Edwin ap Aelle, from the kingdom we once called Rheged, but which you English have taken from us for your Northumbria.'

'You British still hold the west. Carlisle, Penrith.' The straightness of her stare at me was an accusation.

'*Men went to Catraeth wearing gold torques. Only three escaped the slaughter.* That's Catterick to you.'

'I know the song. The bard sings it often in Cadfan's feast hall.'

'And you are thinking how our bards always glory in tragedy.' Her grin flashed at me and was gone. Her keen eyes darkened like the sea before a squall. 'The British have lost too much. And Christ is wounded with every stride your English warhost takes across our island. Do not crush the skylark's eggs, Edwin ap Aelle, either now or once you are king.'

I started as though her staff had struck me. My next words were barely audible. 'I shall never be king. Aethelfrith has taken it all. He wants to kill me.'

'The eagle would kill the skylark if it could. But God's sky is wide and her song is not silenced for long. If we suffer for Christ, our wounds are the seeds of our resurrection.'

'We shall all be silenced in the end. Even the gods won't live for ever. When the Doom-Wolf comes, fire will engulf the world and the sky will fall.'

She leaned both her hands on her staff and stared at me, her grey eyes very searching and steady.

'To be so young, and not have hope.' She shook her head. Compassion had smoothed the laughter crinkles now, but when I looked at her mouth, it held the teasing of a smile.

'Edwin? Are you all right? Who's that you're talking to?'

I felt an unwillingness to break the link with this confident woman, even as I moved my eyes away from her to look round. I had known it could not be long before Lilla came running to monitor any encounter of mine with a stranger. Wiglaf and others of my bodyguard stood behind him, tall, military men. They had acquired the habit of squaring of their shoulders more aggressively than they might have done at home, to counter the mocking superiority of our Welsh hosts. There were some Welshmen in the group too. It would not do to let foreigners range unsupervised over the fertile land of Mon. Not safe for either side, given the bloody progress of English conquest over Britain. I was both guest and hostage.

'Peace of this holy morning to you, sister,' said the Welsh lad Idawc. 'Is he bothering you?'

'And the peace of God's forgiveness on all of you rascals today. No bother from him, as long as he keeps his eyes on the little marvels of creation and doesn't let his fear put a prison cage round his heart.'

The young men followed the line of her staff to the nest in the hollow.

'Skylarks, is it? In July?'

'It's never too late. Even for a young sinner like you, Idawc ap Tryffin. 'I'll hear your confession any day you're ready to take me as your soul-friend.'

Idawc's comrades laughed, like shamefaced schoolboys who have not prepared their lessons. I had been excused the classes where they learned to read and write.

'And I'll listen to sins in English too.' For the first time she spoke in my own language, staring directly at my English bodyguard.

I was jolted again. Now I was free from the spell of her eyes, my conscious mind at last took in the fact that this was no peasant woman, tending sheep on the hill. The grubby tunic, the dark bothy cut out of the hill itself and thatched with heather, contrasted with the authority of her speech, the breadth of her knowledge. I became aware that these young Welsh heroes, with their touchy pride, were giving her unquestioned respect.

But my loyal English escort had no sense of this. Garth made a lunge at her with his spear, an ostentatious threat.

'Prince Edwin takes no instructions from foreign crones.'

'What's he saying?' Idawc challenged me in Welsh. 'Is he insulting Nevyn? Let me tell you, boy, she's a holy virgin and the wisest woman you're likely to meet this side of Bangor. You wouldn't understand that, would you? Dancing round idols, you lot, aren't you? Filthy magic. You wouldn't come to church here if Cadfan wasn't a Christian king and you needed his protection. Sacrificing calves to them, you'd be, if you were at home, and worse, I shouldn't wonder. Drinking blood.'

'By the Thunderbolt! Edwin may have lost a kingdom, but Thunor's not dead yet and the power of his hammer will strike you dead.'

'Quiet! In the name of the Prince of Peace, stand right where you are, the lot of you. And if you put your hobnailed boot in that nest, Idawc, I'll brain you first.'

Nevyn was in the middle of us, staff planted so that she seemed to grow a tall woman holding it. It was an illusion. The ring of heated faces, sparking eyes, glowered over her. She was a diminutive smith in a giant's forge. But like any smith, she bore the wisdom and authority of her craft. The flames died down, the angry eyes cooled. We young men shuffled our feet and could not meet her look.

'Shame on you,' she scolded the Welshmen. 'Is this our British hospitality, to mock ignorant children, who haven't learned to tell a toy horse from the real thing? And you . . .' She turned on us, in English, now. 'Is this gratitude to your hosts? The King of Mon saved your prince's life. If this foreign crone had counselled Cadfan differently, he would not have consented to take you under his roof.'

Lilla muttered, 'We English honour our wise women too. My apologies, Mother.'

'No harm's been done, even to these eggs. But watch how you walk.'

We thought she had dismissed us. I moved to go. Her voice arrested me.

'You. Edwin ap Aelle.' I felt she was reaching out to hold me, though our hands never touched. 'Come back, if you like. The honey from this heather is sweet for bruises. Bruised hearts as well. I live here for the silence. But I don't get so many penitent pilgrims that I've no time to listen to their troubles.'

'You heard my men. I'm not one of your Christian pilgrims.'

'I know that, boy. That didn't stop people pouring out their troubles to my Master. He's the best listener.'

I found her words disturbing. There was no sacred shrine here, that I could see. No chapel, or grove of trees, or standing stone. I did not think she could be a priest. I looked down at the church of Aberffraw, where Cadfan's court worshipped, with the tall cross outside its door. The thought that even up here on the hillside I might speak to her Master, as well as to her, unsettled me.

'You're generous.' I pulled out the garnet cloak pin and knotted the cloth back on my shoulder. 'Here, Mother. For the insult my man gave you.'

It made me feel better to be acting as a prince should, handing out gifts to those who pleased me. I was no longer quite destitute. Since I rode with Cadfan's warband, I was taking my share of the booty. Still, it was an oddly high price to set on the honour of a woman dressed like a field slave, living in a hole in the hill.

She laughed briefly. Her grimy hand reached out. This time our flesh touched. Strong fingers curled round mine and crushed my fist over the points of the jewel I offered.

'Courtesy's a delicate flower. I won't say I'm not accepting your gift. But not for myself. If you've riches to spare, and a troubled conscience, give it to God's poor. I'll count my honour well satisfied.' Her grin grew broader at my expression. 'The poor. You know, boy. Those folk who freeze in winter and starve before the harvest's in. Did you never notice them?' And now a more sympathetic smile flickered like an eel across her lips and danced up into her eyes. 'Or have you been so shut up in your own grief you think there's nobody suffers more than you do?'

Blood heated my face. I felt my own hand grip the brooch now, as though I held a weapon.

'It's easy for you to mock me. A fatherless fugitive. An exile in constant danger of my life.'

'Oh, I wasn't mocking, Edwin of Northumbria. In the name of the Prince of the Poor, I'm deadly serious.' But the laughter was crinkling her eyes as I turned my face away. 'Deep peace to you, body and heart, boy. And hope. These eggs will be hatching in a week. Come back and see the chicks. But tread carefully.'

Chapter Five

I did return to the hermit in the heather. There was solace on the slopes above Aberffraw from the goad of Cadwallon's tongue and the disturbing speculation of Mairi's brown eyes. Lilla came too, and the two of us would sit with our arms round our knees staring out over the western sea while Nevyn talked, and listened to us. She filled our hungry hearts with stories.

She told us of the Philistine army threatening the sheep runs of Israel, of their armoured giant Goliath and the lad David in his shepherd's tunic, defeating him with a pebble from a sling. I dreamed that I was that young David, and Aethelfrith Goliath. But then I pictured the Philistine army, marching to conquer the little kingdom, and I feared that this was the English advance across Britain and the hero David must instead be the British prince Cadwallon.

She told me how David married the King's daughter Michal. She chanted songs of the deep love between David and the King's son Jonathan. What was this woman trying to tell me? That I could heal the enmity with Cadwallon, be embraced by my foster-brother?

Then she told us of King Saul, hurling a spear at David as he sat playing his harp, of the jealous rage that drove the shepherd-hero to hide in caves. How could I not think then of Aethelfrith, poisoning Hereric in Elmet, now surely plotting to kill me?

She showed us Saul slain on the battlefield and David anointed king.

'And he was the finest King of Israel there ever was,' she said catching my eyes with her bright robin's gaze, 'until the Christ came himself.'

But her meaning still teased me.

She read the stories of Christ to us from her holy book, the gospel of St John, though she knew every word by heart. It was a smaller book than the glorious volumes laid on the altar of Cadfan's church. They were brilliant with purple and blue and crimson ink, the covers bound in gold. Hers, for the most part, was plainly written in a small neat hand, an everyday companion. Just the title page was wreathed with an interlace pattern of fabulous beasts, dragon-headed, sharp of claws, fantastically contorted. In and out of each other's bodies they twined, till it made me dizzy trying to distinguish where one began and the other ended.

So her pattern of stories flickered in my head. David and Goliath, David and Saul, David and Jonathan, David and Michal.

What did she intend me to understand? Angle against Briton, Angle against Angle, love between Briton and Angle?

She told us of Christ the King, tying a towel round his waist to wash his twelve followers' feet. And one of his own betrayed him.

I was not safe, even here.

I went down towards the shore past King Cadfan's stockade with my thoughts in tumult. There was a flicker of colour on the grass at the top of the dunes. The young women of the court were playing ball in the wind. I stopped at a distance to watch. It was not hard for me to pick Mairi out in her crimson tunic. The dark ripples of her hair were blown about her shoulders. She was more womanly of figure now. She no longer skimmed the sand with the butterfly lightness of a little girl. But the slight awkwardness with which she bent to retrieve the ball, the deliberate swing of her breasts as she tossed it back, stirred me with more painful longing.

There was a muffled thud of hooves on the sandy grass behind me. I turned and saw Cadwallon. I felt myself flinch, as always. There was no hope I could escape his bitter wit now he had caught me so evidently watching his sister. But his eyes were flashing with news more important than the chance to taunt me. He tossed his spear in the air and caught and flourished it.

'At last. All my life I've been getting ready for this. I'm only surprised it took him so long.'

'Aethelfrith's invading Gwynedd? To kill me?' Two surprises rang like horncalls in my head: that I knew beyond the slightest doubt what Cadwallon meant, and that my own fate was bound beyond separating with the fate of this British land in the coming battle.

'You?' The gold chains over Cadfan's practice-mail jangled with his bark of laughter. 'You think Aethelfrith the Ferocious is marching on Gwynedd for the sake of some lank-haired youth who's escaped his butcher's knife? It's our country he wants. He doesn't care a damn about you.'

'He killed my family. He took my kingdom. I'm still my father's son. And now Hereric's been murdered. We have to stop him before he gets to me.'

'We have to kill him because he wants Gwynedd. That English devil isn't going to wash the blood from his sword until he reaches the Irish Sea. You Angles are all the same. You mean to finish what you started when the longships came. Rob us of every inch of the Island of Britain. Well, it stops here. They'll never cross the Dee, not if the sands run red with every drop of British blood.'

I took a tremendous breath of the salt air. 'This will stop when Aethelfrith dies, and I am king of Northumbria. I'll kill him myself.'

Cadwallon nudged his pony alongside me. His eyes were blazing. I feared him more than ever. Nothing that Cadwallon said to me had ever been innocently meant. 'You're serious? You'll go to war with us, Edwin? Angle against Angle? Side with the British against your own kin?'

'You call the man who murdered my father my kinsman? What do you think? That I'd take your father's hospitality all these years and not pledge my spear to him when this land was in danger? That I'd let that devil redden the waters of the Dee, the way he did the Yorkshire Ouse? The Welsh are my brothers if they stand against Aethelfrith. But I claim the honour of running my own blade through his breast.'

I really meant it. Cadwallon hooted with laughter. 'You? You don't stand a chance, boy. You've never won a horse race against me yet, have you? You'll be miles behind when it comes to the charge. It's our own country we're defending.'

'You don't know what it feels like to lose everything you love, for all you sing about it. He hasn't killed your father. He hasn't snatched your sister for his wife. He hasn't seized your home. That's why I'll get there first.'

'You couldn't even stay in the saddle.'

'You'll see.'

'And do you think I don't know what reward you'd ask from Father?' Cadwallon's eyebrows rose to a great height, till they tangled with the fall of his hair. He was looking past me, across the grass of the low cliff's edge to the sand dunes where the girls were leaping. I felt the blush burn more than my cheeks.

'If Aethelfrith dies, I shall have all the reward I want. My own kingdom.'

I had not known from how deep in me the truth would be hauled. Cadwallon looked at me keenly. Then a grin splintered his black moustache.

'And if you do kill that ogre, Cadwallon's your true blood-brother as long as he lives. But you won't beat me to it.'

He dropped the reins and grabbed me in a hug that nearly dragged me headlong under his horse's hooves. He was more powerfully built than I was. My heart was thundering in my bruised chest against his mailcoat. Was he mocking me still?

Cadwallon's grip was fierce, squeezing me to his broad chest. He kissed me passionately on both cheeks. This at least he understood, love for one's country, loyalty among brothers. I struggled against

36

the confusion to know which country was mine. Northumbria of my birth, Gwynedd of my adoption? Was Cadwallon giving me his blessing to marry his sister and enjoy both? The east could be mine, the west his, united through Mairi. Struggling to free the arm crushed against his jostling mount, I stumbled and dragged him with me from the saddle. He was nimble footed. He leaped lightly on to the turf. I thought my clumsiness would have angered him, but he rocked with laughter and threw an arm round my shoulders again.

I stood, feeling the warmth of his body pressed against mine in unfamiliar friendship. I could not speak for emotion. All my boyhood I had imagined this, the two of us united, Cadwallon accepting me. I was surprised to find I was looking down on him. He had dark curls, so like Mairi's. I realized I was slighter in build than Cadwallon but had grown taller. There had always been such a storm of passion swelling in my foster-brother, he had stridden through my imagination as a giant.

I dared to dream that he might soon be more than a foster-brother.

The pony whickered. Cadwallon vaulted back into the saddle and urged it into a canter, with a wave to me.

I started to walk towards the beach, my heart singing. The air was brilliant. The lines of surf were rolling east towards me, like the white horses of the sea-prince Manawydan whom the Welsh bards sang of. The gulls were circling over the sands, wings feathered against the sunlight to catch the breeze. I would hold this scene always as paradise. The gentle island of Mon, the land of Mairi and Cadwallon. My beloved sanctuary in the western sea, until I rode home to claim Northumbria.

From the other side of the hill rose singing, deeper voiced than the bird-calls or the laughter of the girls. The monks of Cadfan's royal church were chanting their midday psalms. I heard it as a benediction. The wind stung tears from my eyes.

I stumbled down on to the soft sand below the dunes.

My cry of alarm shattered the peace, sending the oystercatchers skittering away over the lines of seaweed. My arm was fast in a strong grip.

The man who had leaped to his feet to stop me did not look like an assassin. Now he was straight and steady, he stood taller than me, lean to the point of gauntness. His hair had once been fiery red but it was mingled with white now. He had eyes more green than grey, piercing as a gull's, yet there were lines creasing the corners of his eyes and mouth which might have meant laughter. Just behind him, three rocks crouched round a crystal pool left behind by the tide.

He let go of my arm. He was almost as plainly dressed as the monks, though his long tunic was grey, while theirs were oatmeal white. I noted that the cloth was good weaving and the border discreetly embroidered with blue crosses. And between us at our feet, tumbling on her hands and knees, was the creature I had nearly stumbled over. A little girl, scarcely old enough to walk steadily. She was dressed gorgeously enough for both of them, with hair in flaming waves, as his must once have been. It burned over her short mantle, which was bright green woven with threads of blue, so that it had something of the shimmer of water when she moved. Her little tunic was daffodil yellow, ribboned and embroidered with gold. Her arms were wet and sandy. Yet you would not have mistaken her for anything but a princess.

'You frightened all the little crabs away,' she accused me. 'And I've been sitting still as stone for such a very long time, watching them. They were eating some fish we gave them. Two of them had just started fighting over it. And then you came.'

'I apologize, my lady.' I bowed to her affronted majesty. 'But you were being such a very silent stone that I didn't realize you were here. Only now I see you, this gentleman in grey could be a rock, but you're much too bright and beautiful for a stone. I think you must be a jewel washed up from a mermaid's cavern.'

She scowled up at me under her red eyebrows, mistrusting me.

'I'm not a jewel, silly. I'm Rhiainmelt and I don't live under the sea. And he isn't a rock. He's Grandfather.'

The lines in the man's face carved themselves into a slow smile. His British voice was deep, but less musical than the accents of Gwynedd. 'Rhun, son of Urien Rheged, who was once King of the Men of the North. Now I'm content to serve the King of Kings, as a priest in the realm of God.'

'Edwin, King Aelle's son, and foster-son to Cadfan of Mon.'

'The Englishman from the northeast.' The lines of his smile did not relax, but they deepened into something like irony. 'You must know, then, where my father fell. On the sands in the east of the land you call Northumbria, facing the island of Lindisfarne, which to us is Ynys Metcaud. But for his death, we would have driven the English back into the sea.'

'We are both warrior people, English and British. The gods favour the bravest fighters.'

'You mistake me. It was no battle took him. He was murdered by our own side.' The smile lingered, one-sided.

'So was my father.'

A silence fell, save for the distant calling of gulls. The knowledge of northern Britain lay between us, like the body of a woman over whom men fight. Then Rhun reached out over the little girl's head and we clasped arms.

'Edwin is rightful king of Deira, and shall be so one day.'

The assertion from the dune above me told me Lilla was within arm's reach, monitoring this meeting.

I turned up to him and grinned my acknowledgement. 'Lilla, Byrtferth's son. If I should ever be king of Deira and loyalty were properly rewarded, he would be my thane.'

'Exiles need good friends.' Rhun saluted Lilla and turned back to me. 'I laid down royalty by my own choice to become a priest. But you and Rhiainmelt have much in common. She should be growing up as princess in a Rheged that stretched from coast to coast.'

I looked down at the child gazing at me with solemn eyes. 'So we are both fugitives from Aethelfrith the Ferocious?'

'No,' said Rhun, and the lines about his mouth cut deeper still. 'It was your father overran half her land.'

Lilla leaped down to the sand, his hand ready on his knife.

'No need for that, lad. I'm a scholar, not a soldier now. I'll leave it to others to avenge her wrongs.'

'I've fought for Cadfan in his border raids, when it's Briton against Briton. I'm a loyal foster-son. Now when the warhost of Gwynedd rides against Aethelfrith, you can be sure I'll march with them.'

'You'll defend the Christian remnant of Britain against the heathen English invader?'

'I'll honour my bonds of gratitude to Cadfan and his God. I'll kill my father's murderer.'

'Not your God? Cadfan's foster-son all these years, and you've never been baptized in the name of the Trinity?'

'Edwin is English. He is a prince descended from Woden the Wise,' the sharpness of Lilla's defence surprised me.

'So was great Aethelbert of Kent, who was baptized by Augustine. Now Redwald of East Anglia has knelt to Christ.'

I stood silent. The hairs on my neck prickled to hear my name joined with this roll-call of powerful English kings.

Out of sight on the grass above, the laughter of Mairi and the other girls came to me. At my feet, little Rhiainmelt was turning over the spoil of bladderwrack, revealing a swarm of secret insect life. Rhun bent and picked up a spiral shell, examining the beauty of its opalescent interior.

'Edwin ap Aelle, they tell me you and your friend Lilla climb the slopes above Aberffraw often. Outside her hut, you talk for hours with the hermit Nevyn. Nobody hears what you say but God. Over and over again you go back to her. Why, Edwin? Why does a heathen English prince talk with a British holy woman so long?'

'If you know so much, hasn't she told you what we talk about?'

His answer lashed me with anger. 'My information is not from

Nevyn. No soul-friend would discuss such confessions with anyone but her God.'

I found I feared this man, gazing at me with such steady, keen eyes. Rhiainmelt was staring up too, her hands full of shells. I knew that, if I spoke my thoughts aloud, it would be like venturing out from this beach to round the headland. Half of me was longing to discover the unknown coves beyond. But the tide might sweep in. I might not be able to get back to safety.

'I ask her questions. She tells me stories.'

Rhun was still watching my face. 'And what is your part in this story, Edwin ap Aelle?' Those sea-grey eyes unsettled me. I felt him unfastening my bonds of prudence. 'You will be riding to war soon, lad. Not some hotheaded cattle raid or a border skirmish meant to keep the neighbours respectful. It's real war this time, against Aethelfrith the Ferocious. The Church will fight to defend you with prayer. But many warriors will lie on the borderland of Gwynedd, spilling their lifeblood. Where is your own hope of victory over death?'

'The Valkyries carry off our heroes to Woden's high feasting hall.'

'Until the Day of Doom, when even Woden will fall.' The solemnity in Lilla's voice shocked me. I took a step forward, and felt the tide-pool swirl coldly round my boot.

The little jewelled Rhiainmelt held up to me a curved shell as yellow as her dress. Her green eyes stared, huge and solemn, waiting for my response to her generosity. I bent, feeling the enormous effort it needed to bring a smile back to my lips. The clutch of memory brought a rush of warmth to my exiled heart. This morning, Cadwallon my foster-brother had hugged me for the first time as though he really meant it. I had become a part of these people.

'Thank you, Princess Rhiainmelt. Edwin of Deira humbly accepts your gift.'

Chapter Six

We walked the path to the river in solemn silence, as though we were walking into an ambush. Lilla was at my shoulder, the other nine of my bodyguard ranked behind. I stopped on the track between the gorse bushes and turned to them.

'Are you certain you wish to take this step? All of you?'

I was younger than any of them. I had been a small boy when I fled, though I saw myself as a mature man now. These soldiers had guarded me all these years, had taught me the ways of an English warrior, and the sagas of the English gods. They were fewer than they had been. Two had died protecting me from my own rashness in Cadfan's cattle raids.

I watched some faces, disciplined to unflinching loyalty, crease darkly. Anxiety, like a bubble of marsh gas, surfaced momentarily. It was no light thing to abandon their fathers' gods, though here in a Christian land we must live under the protection of the Christians' Lord. Still, these were warriors hand-picked for their courage. The voice of the thane Wiglaf spoke out, as he would lead any charge in my cause.

'Where you go, my lord, we will follow. I swore that oath to your father before he died.'

'The vows that matter today have still to be made. I won't force any of you.'

'I'll make those vows gladly. To a greater king even than Edwin's father.'

Lilla's voice, above all of them, rang out confidently that day. For myself, I had fallen slowly under the spell of Nevyn's clear certainty, her undaunted hope, and now the challenge of Rhun's grey-green eyes. I believe Lilla travelled this road more willingly than I did.

There was a rumble among the men, louder than the distant fall of water.

'We will serve our prince.'

'And our prince's Lord.'

We walked forward round the bushes.

'I'd have thought such a great thing would have been done in the chieftain's church,' Wiglaf muttered.

But this was how Rhun believed baptism should be. This river was his Jordan. And mine now.

The waterfall dropped over a ledge of slate, straight down into the shadowed coomb. It might have been a fluted white column, the last survivor of a Roman ruin. No sunlight danced on the deep pool under the thickets of overhanging oak. The rush of the water drowned out the voices of the people at its edge waiting for us. Cadfan and his queen and those of his family who remained at home. Mairi was there, and my heart raced, betraying the worldly hopes I carried to this baptism. Rhun, of course. His angular body in his priest's robes was crouched at the pool's edge. I was glad to see Nevyn beside him. She had put on a clean tunic, pale as a sheep after shearing. Or had she washed the only one she had, in my honour? And little Rhiainmelt, Rhun's small, bright granddaughter, was kneeling on a boulder. The intense flame of her hair was softened in the water, where the shallows turned golden brown over the stones and threw back a darker mirror of herself. She looked more than ever like a fairy child. Something hurt in my heart. Must the English and the British always be at war over this island?

The priest looked up, his eyes bright as a boy's. 'Look, Edwin, there's a mighty salmon here, under the ledge. A prince of a fish. I doubt it can get any further up the stream than this.'

Fay Sampson

I came and stood beside him on the flat boulder. The pool into which the river was tumbling looked green at its centre, deep, cold. I saw my own shadow darken the water, cutting out the sky. 'Or a pike?'

'I've seen enough fish in sixty years to know the difference. Be sure that this is a salmon stream.' He smiled at me gravely. Then he stared down again at all our quivering faces in the pool. My body-guard were ranged behind me. Their English faces were grim, as though this was a real death we were facing, not a ritual one. Only Lilla's shone.

'Your men are all determined to make this pilgrimage with you?'

'They say they have followed me everywhere since my father was killed. They won't desert me now.'

Rhun stood then, looking straight at my warriors and not at me. 'You are prepared to take these vows, each man for himself? All of you?'

'Aye.'

'We've pledged our word.' There was a note of defiance in Wiglaf's voice.

With a suddenly businesslike air Rhun stood up and wiped his wet hands on his skirt. Rhiainmelt too scrambled from her knees and shook out her muddy tunic. Her eyes danced expectantly as she watched her grandfather.

'Where are your sponsors?'

Cadfan stepped forward from his waiting court. He was richly gowned to honour my conversion, even if it was done in this rustic setting, not in his royal chapel with the incense sweet, the candles glowing and the comforting wink of gold on the altar.

'I've fostered him since the boy came to us, no higher than my wolfhounds. The Queen and I have prayed for this. Nothing could give me more joy than to stand godfather to Edwin today. And we have Welshmen enough for all the English here.'

He gripped my hand. He meant it as a welcome to his Church. But I was more afraid than he knew. It felt like a farewell.

44

'I've been his soul-friend long enough. I'll see him through this as well.' Nevyn knew, better than anyone, the stumbling passage of my doubts. The black and white patchwork of her teeth grinned in acknowledgement. 'I'll witness his oath, be his mother in the faith to keep him going forward, and drag him back on to his feet when he falls.'

'It needs one more.'

Cadwallon was not here. I had not allowed myself to admit it until then.

'I asked my foster-brother.'

It had been reckless folly. I had put myself at Cadwallon's mercy. At this crucial point of my life, I risked the scornful laughter that had made a mockery of all my boyhood. I had so longed for the Welsh boy's approval.

Cadwallon consented. He even hugged me again. Yes, there was laughter. He teased me that I was doing this more for love of Mairi than of Christ. And yet I had felt a new warmth. I truly believed he was welcoming me as his brother at last.

I scanned the ranks of Cadfan's family and little court. I caught the warm gleam of sympathy in Mairi's brown eyes. I could not look at her steadily. Cadwallon had not come.

Rhiainmelt's red-gold ringlets bounced as her head spun round. A whistling was breaking towards us through the brambles up the steep valley. Snatches of song danced with the rushing stream. There was the crashing of confident men breaking past twigs and briars on a path too narrow for their swaggering stride. Cadwallon and his companions leaped down through the greenery with the grin of those who expect the rest of the world to rejoice or tremble at the sight of them.

And I could still not quell the clutch of nerves in my belly at the appearance of my foster-brother.

'So you mean to see it through?' His hound's grin mocked me across the pool. 'Or are we just here to tickle a wily old salmon, while your English warhost marches up on us? And Mairi too, as beautiful as ever. Or are we about to see you plight your troth to the gorgeous Rhiainmelt? Would you like me to be a witness to that?'

Rhun looked sharply from the young Welsh newcomers, lounging on the rocks now with the insolence of their leader, back to me. 'Does Cadwallon really not know why he's here?'

I kept my dignity. I was a prince, even in exile. It was hard not to sound haughty to cover my nervousness. I was preparing to risk more than Cadwallon would ever have to. He was born a Christian; I was not. This was my free choice, a daring bid for freedom against all the awe and terror of our English gods. He would not know the fear of breaking the rites of his ancestors. I had begun to hear them howling round the house after nightfall.

'Of course he does. Prince Cadwallon of Mon has agreed to stand my sponsor in the Christian faith. To witness my baptism.'

I must not lower the challenge of my eyes across that pool. He must respect my courage.

'Is this true, Cadwallon ap Cadfan? You'd jest with your brother's soul?'

Even Cadwallon was silenced, but not for long. He laughed defiantly. 'An English Christian? Doesn't that strike you as a bitter joke? After all they've done to us?'

'It is not easy to forgive the English,' Rhun agreed. 'But in the name of the crucified Christ it can be done. If the Roman mission in Kent can convert the English, the British of Gwynedd and Mon can do the same. Will you still stand sponsor to Edwin or not?'

His eyes grew merry. 'Me, his godfather? I can see from the look in his eye he's wishing he could punch me on the nose.'

'You promised. You've thrown down challenges to me often enough. Now take mine.'

His dark eyes studied me. I tensed for another volley of scorn. King Cadfan had not intervened. He would not, even if I challenged his son to physical combat. He never had. We two young men must battle this out between us.

46

Little Rhiainmelt waited, huge-eyed. I dared not look at Mairi.

A sudden avalanche of laughter echoed off the rocks. Cadwallon leaped at me across the pool from rock to precarious rock. 'You win ... brother!'

He caught me to him in a dangerous embrace. I felt the warmth of his chest without a breastplate, the strong curl of his black moustache against my mouth as he kissed me. He drew back grinning and looked sideways at the chilly green of the water on whose lip we swayed.

'Shouldn't we be doing this in front of the whole warhost? Or do you not want too many witnesses? Suppose Aethelfrith wins this battle and my father and I are killed? Who will be left to cry traitor if you run back to the winning side and throw yourself at the feet of your English idols again?'

Rhun's voice rang out with keen authority. 'Hold your tongue, Cadwallon. If Aethelfrith the Ferocious defeats Gwynedd, which God and all the archangels forbid, Edwin, more than any of us, is a dead man. You both stand in peril of your lives and your immortal souls. Do not play games with God.'

'I made you two brothers,' Cadfan said. 'That should be enough.'

'What are we waiting for, then? That water's not going to get any warmer.' My foster-brother's arm was round my waist, steering me to the edge.

He helped me take off my clothes.

I was the first. I must lead my people.

The English and the British stood around that thundering pool, while the priest and I waded out into the shock of cold water. Above the deluge, Rhun shouted Christ's challenge to me. The promises I mouthed were lost under the roar of the falls. I felt his grip on my waist, the strong clasp of his hand at the back of my neck. The pool heaved, and the water came over my mouth, my eyes. I was sinking. He buried me in a watery grave.

I thought Cadwallon had won. I feared I was never going to rise.

At last, out of my helplessness, Rhun hauled me up to gasp new life. The sky was brilliant in my eyes, though the sun could not reach the river where I was standing. The wind caught at my wet chest. I had broken with my father's gods. I was reborn a Christian.

My sponsors, Cadfan, Nevyn and Cadwallon, helped me up on to the rocks. I shook the water from my eyes. Nevyn rubbed me dry.

That tiny, dispossessed British princess came staggering up to me, carrying the folded white of my new baptismal gown. Her solemnity was marred by the bramble that reached out to pluck at one hanging sleeve so that it trailed behind her through the mud.

Only when I was robed, feeling like a newly sceptred king in this almost-pure white linen, did I dare to look steadily at Cadfan's family. I saw Mairi's face swim towards me like the clouded silver of the moon. Her eyes were dark and very serious.

Cadwallon led me to her. I could hardly breathe. Now there was nothing to hold us apart.

'Kiss your brother, Mairi. He's truly one of us now. We're going to have two triumphs to celebrate tonight. Edwin's baptism and Mairi's betrothal.'

I heard myself gasp. Could it be this easy, after all this time? All the years of our growing up together, when I was terrified she would slip away from me before I had anything to offer her? I had not dared to speak for her yet. Had they only been waiting for this, my baptism into her faith?

My arms went out to take her. She was blushing darkly, her eyes lowered in confusion as her lips avoided my eager mouth to find my cheek more chastely. Her hair smelt of daffodils.

Cadwallon watched us, his face dancing. 'Have you heard the news, Edwin? Mairi is going to marry the prince of Powys.'

Chapter Seven

I rode with the warhost of Gwynedd when it clashed and jingled its way under the Roman walls of Chester. I could never see the old fortifications without a catch in my heart for lost York. It was less hurtful to turn my head and watch the lazy loop of the Dee reflecting our grey ringmail, the cloaks of scarlet and tartan and spring-grass green. The breeze sent jewel-points sparkling on the crest of ripples. Swans moved with swift but stately ill-temper upriver from our approaching horses.

The sagging grandeur of such masonry no longer awed me. I pushed to the back of my mind my nurse's tales of giants. Still, I could not imagine humans who might make such a city. I would not say such a thing to King Cadfan or Cadwallon. I had lived and fought too long beside these Welshmen who dreamed of old Rome.

'We have giant walls like these in York too . . . so Lilla tells me.'

Cadfan's teeth flashed through his curling moustache in a bitter grin like his son's. 'They're not your inheritance, though, are they, Englishman? Even if you get to be king, you still won't know what they stand for. Of course you'll see them, from the east to the west. This was all one land before you English came, Britain . . . and the Church of Britain. It was all ours once.'

'Under a Roman emperor?'

He wrenched his horse's head away.

Peasants stopped work to cheer as we passed their fields. The people of Chester were flocking out to welcome us. Craftsfolk were waving their tools. Milk-skinned Welsh girls turned up their earth-hued eyes in admiration. Dogs barked excitement.

There was singing coming towards us. The deep chant from the throats of hundreds of men. It checked our warhost on the river-bank. The king held up his hand.

'Our other army,' said Cadfan, with a satisfied smile. 'The monks of Bangor-in-the-Wood.'

They were coming into sight now around a bend in the Dee. Still distant, they might have been a flock of sheep winding along the water meadow. Yet the sound of their chanting carried powerfully before them.

I had seen monks on Mon, as well as the secular priests of Cadfan's court. I knew them for scholars, arguing wisdom in the king's councils. I knew them for fanatics too, sleeping on pillows of stone, praying up to their waists in water, scourging themselves with nettles. Some were hermits like Nevyn, living in the country-side unafraid of wolves and bears after dark, fearing only the assaults of devils.

Cadfan saw them as reinforcements, warriors to match his spear-men.

The white flock had become a marching column, swinging as they intoned a psalm. Even without armour or weapons, they were a formidable sight. Each carried a tall staff. A leather satchel held what little they needed. They were lean from fasting, dark skinned from work out of doors in all weathers, the pallor of their hundreds of long undyed tunics startling against our royal confusion of colours. As they approached, I felt myself trembling at the steadi-ness of their eyes on us. Men like that saw visions.

The abbot stopped before the King. He was a tall, spare man, with a mane of light brown hair swept back from his skull, the front half of which had been shaved completely. He carried a crooked staff, like a shepherd. I felt his authority. Some of these men were princes before they took their vows, as well as abbot-princes in the Church.

'I have brought what you asked. Two hundred warriors of God's host. We will do our part for Britain. Bless your weapons for victory in the morning and give you absolution with the Saviour's blood. Then, let the heathen Aethelfrith strike. The monks of Bangor will stand strong over the battlefield and curse the enemies of God.'

'I'm grateful, Dinoot. Christ is our champion. We'll roll the darkness back together, my troops and yours.'

Abbot's crook, King's sword, lifted to salute each other.

I left the warriors of Gwynedd setting up camp below the walls. The monks had settled themselves in the shelter of the willow trees, bending shelters out of the supple, living branches.

I walked upstream, along the river. This was the way Aethelfrith would come. I was walking to meet my destiny. Hereric my nephew had been poisoned in Elmet, leaving a widow and two daughters. I was the last of my father's male line.

The flood plain was broad here, room for the largest of armies. The King of Powys and his warhost were already here. A ridge of low hills guarded the east. Is that where the monks of Bangor would stand to hurl their incantations against the invaders? The British must surely deny that high ground to the English.

The word rang discordantly in my head. I was English.

If I were king in Deira now, instead of Aethelfrith, would I come marching west? I winced away from the treacherous thought, the might-have-been, the conqueror I was not. I looked over my shoulder. It was a reassurance to see Lilla following. Someone was, would always be, loyal to me. Lilla was English and an exile, like me.

He halted, because I had, waiting to see if I would beckon him forward to join me. He understood both my need for loneliness and that an English prince must not be left alone, especially since that prince was now Aethelfrith's only rival.

I walked on. My nerves were strung too tight for talk. My eyes were still on that ridge Abbot Dinoot had claimed.

'If I were Aethelfrith, I should want that hill,' I said aloud to the rump of a bolting hare.

'If you were Aethelfrith, you'd be dead before you took a step further.'

I leaped like the hare. I did not need to turn to know that Lilla would be racing to close the gap, but too late to prevent my assassination. My long knife was in my hand.

The man who stepped from under the willow branches confused me. He held no weapon. Over his shoulders he wore the same hooded undyed wool cloak as the monks. But it parted to show a breastplate marked with the dents of old battles. Burnishing had not been able to remove the last traces of rust. The leather of its buckles looked stiff and cracked. His face was marked with age too, furrows grained down it like weathered wood. His head was shaved in front like Dinoot's, with grizzled locks behind.

Out of this sternness, his teeth flashed in a grin. 'You're safe enough for the moment, boy. If I'd wanted to kill you, there'd have been a spearpoint in your belly before you'd seen me move. You wouldn't even have had time to say "Amen". I've forgotten more about war than you've dreamt of learning. I was Brochfael, once king of Powys. But I left it all for love of God and a touch of gout. It's my grandson Selyf will command Powys tomorrow.'

Pain seared me at the name. Mairi had gone to Powys as a bride. Britain could never now give me my heart's longing. I would fight for her still, but with the dull, dead grimness of a duty owed.

Brochfael's smile flickered over Lilla's panting face, his drawn knife, beside me now. 'Good lad. I like to see loyalty. But you'll need to be quicker than that.' With a rustle like a swift footstep in dry grass, his sword was out. It sliced through the air between us, so that we leaped apart. Too late, Lilla's blade rang against it and was struck aside. Brochfael looked hugely pleased with himself.

'Well, there. It's a temptation, isn't it, for an old monk who thought he had put his toys away for good? I'll be up there with the brothers tomorrow, chanting psalms of doom on the English with the best of them. *Trample under foot those who come lusting after tribute. Scatter the nations who delight in war.* But let the cursed English come near the monks of Bangor-in-the-Wood and they'll have me and my boys to teach them a sharp lesson. *God will shatter the heads of his enemies, the hairy crown of him who walks in his guilty ways.* I'll protect them with more than prayer.'

The grey veteran peered closer. He seemed to see us truly for the first time. It struck me then that the eyes of his mind might not be as sharp as his soldier's instinct. He was an old man.

'Where are you from, boy? You don't look like a Briton, though I watched you coming out of Cadfan's tent.'

Always this difference. Always I had to explain myself, the blond Englishman in the British camp.

Dawn lit the flood plain of the Dee, where the river circled Chester. The coming sun made our army appear huger than it was. Gigantic shadows stalked our heels. We waited with our eyes fixed on that radiant east.

This was the way my sister's husband would come on us, out of Deira, following the dales up from York, over the Pennine passes. The names were still grief to me. This was the homeland I had been too small to remember securely. But I could dream. Wiglaf and my exiled bodyguard had been true to their country. They had filled my boyhood with sagas of English heroes, English victories, our English land. They kept my dream alive.

If this day, with this British warhost, in the name of this British God, I could defeat Aethelfrith. . . .

The column of monks was marching away from us, starting to climb the ridge, past the Welsh cavalry already poised on its lower slopes. I heard a snatch of their singing.

'*They boast of chariots and horses; but we boast in the name of the Lord our God. They will collapse and fall; but we shall rise and stand upright.*'

Their psalms of vengeance faded in the distance, rising higher with the sun. At my left shoulder a deeper voice took up the chant.

'Let them be like chaff before the wind, with the angel of the Lord driving them on. Let their way be dark and slippery, with the angel of the Lord pursuing them.'

I looked sideways in surprise.

Lilla's face glowed under his helmet. 'They were singing it all night, keeping vigil by the river.'

'You should have been asleep. This will be a hard day's work.'

We were far from the sea, but there was the sound of the sea all around me. Not the soft sands of the Dee, but a monstrous grinding, as of waves over shingle. Metal on metal, voices sharp with suppressed terror, loud with anger and battle-boast.

I knew terror, though I must not show it. I was no longer a boy. I and this shield-wall of Englishmen around me had earned our British mead and our seats in Cadfan's feasting hall at Aberffraw. We had fought for him in skirmishes on the Welsh mainland, in cattle raids, in tribal feuds on the borders of Gwynedd. Today would be different. Our terror was in one name. Aethelfrith the Ferocious.

The sea was shifting around me, horses' heads tossing. Young British princes were trotting needlessly through the ranks, brooches glittering, hair flowing, spears commanding. My eyes went up to the sky, walled in by hills. The crows were noisy, like gulls behind a fishing boat. They must know. Whether it was British or English, they would not care whose guts they gorged on.

There was a line of white high on the ridge now, among the heather, like a crest of spray flung up from this grey sea of soldiers. I let my eyes dwell on it with a grim hope. The monks of Bangor ranked around their cross. Brochfael would be stiffly proud with his spear and chain mail, released to be the royal warrior once more and defend them.

But the monks would defend us. A king needs shamans as well as warriors, aristocrats of sacred magic, doorkeepers to the gods. I had sworn my oath to the British Christ and his Father and the

Spirit they call the Wild Goose. I was fighting for this land. The Christians' God would protect it.

'I wonder what it's like to go into battle on horseback.'

I returned with a shock to the practicalities of warfare. Lilla was eyeing Cadwallon's cavalry. We had dismounted from our own horses before we took up position. Lilla's eyes were watchful, their blue darkened by the shadow of his helmet, the metal eyebrows, the jutting nose-guard, ears encased by cheek flaps. I must look as fearsome myself.

'I'm not Cadwallon. I'll lead you English fashion, on two firm feet.'

'They're coming.'

A tide of shadowed silver, with the sun at their backs. Less gold about them than the men of Powys and Gwynedd, fewer horses too. Cold as the North Sea that had brought both our grandfathers to Northumbria, the army of Aethelfrith the Ferocious advanced in close-set waves.

Horns bayed and screamed like bronze-tongued hounds. The sea of warriors round me began to roar. Our Welsh neighbours were jostling us hard enough to start a quarrel. A surge of movement swept us forward with it. Through the rush of bodies I could hardly see my opponents now.

The wave in front of me broke apart in red-flecked spray. The two warhosts plunged into each other. Hard-learned lessons, the monotony of daily training, swung my muscles into action. In minutes, I had lost my long spear, carried down by a falling enemy. My sword sprang out. I felt the weight of it, and the exhilaration of arms lifting it time and again. Raise and slash, swing and smash. To stop this cycle would be death. With the same grim fury, my bodyguard were killing Englishmen round me. They fought with a double determination, to preserve my life as well as their own.

It was impossible to think I could hear the chant of curses from the overlooking hill, that powerful protective magic. But I glanced up for a moment. One of the monks held the cross high over the battlefield. The sun flashed on silver.

I put my faith in that.

Cadwallon's cavalry was sweeping down on to the sandy plain to smash Aethelfrith's flank.

My brother Cadwallon.

Lilla grabbed me by the arm and flung me behind the protection of his own shield. His spear was jabbing frenziedly at three assailants. Jabbing, wrenching, jabbing, twisting, jabbing. I sprang out of my trance to fight beside him. Their death cries screamed up at me through the holes of my helmet. I heard their tortured pleas. They were screaming in English.

Two more of my loyal men wrestled me backwards from behind.

For a moment, I failed to understand. The three Northumbrians were dead. But there were too many more, coming at us all the time, heaping the plain with British dead, like seaweed on the sands.

'It's no good, prince. They're beating us. Pull back before we're surrounded.'

To my bodyguard I was their prince, their warleader. But they had sworn an oath to my father to protect me. If I fell, they would die before me. They would not desert me. Even now, I could rally them. I could charge on forward, blindly, heroically seeking my brother-in-law. They would not hesitate. I would carry every one of them to glory with me.

As they pulled me back, my glance caught the hilltop again.

I wiped the sweat from my eyes.

There was nothing there any more. No line of white-clad priests defiantly chanting. No shining cross. The monks had gone. But there was something moving lower down. I saw a detachment of Aethelfrith's warriors leaping back down the slope. Streaming from their spears like banners were white cloaks, blazoned with scarlet stains.

I knew then where victory lay. Two hundred monks of Bangor, dead in the heather. Silenced.

I had washed away the safety of my father's gods in that cold pool on the island of Mon. Not for me now the sky-riding Valkyries, swooping down to lift me away to the feasting-hall of Valhalla. Not for me the welcome of Woden and the company of English heroes. I had sided with a cross, sacrifice, failure. I was a fool, a traitor.

Aethelfrith had the victory.

Numb with the chilling loss, exhausted, I let Wiglaf hustle me away over the slaughtered bodies of the British who had been my comrades. We found horses. They were not our own. We mounted them.

'Where's Lilla?' I gasped out. 'And the others? Gyrth? Stigand?'

'Lilla was guarding your retreat. They'll follow us.'

Chapter Eight

We splashed our way homeward through the damp, gnarled, sprawling oak woods. We had found no boar. I thought of the quick, darting ponies of the Welsh hills tossing their manes while their hooves sent the slates skittering down the hill. Then I reminded myself I should be glad to be alive and on English land.

I was in the midlands kingdom of Mercia, surrounded by Englishmen. These were the remaining seven of my bodyguard, who had protected me since childhood and survived the disaster of Chester. Wiglaf, greyer and stiffer now, Lilla, always closest beside me, and five more. I could sense the relief in most of them to be talking their own language again, living in the old English way I hardly remembered. The years of the island of Mon and Aberffraw were behind us now, like a long-lingering dream.

There were newer friends to turn my thoughts from Cadfan's British court. Not far behind me I could hear my brother-in-law Cenred. He and his young men were slashing about at the tangle of ivy and brambles, though we Deirans had cut a path for them already. Only a few steps from our trail the ground fell away into soft, black hollows where collapsed trees rotted into murky pools and their branches were shrouded with moss and fungus.

Gyrth had wandered away from us, always curious to follow up strange footmarks in the mud. He called from behind a holly bush. 'Look what I've found. Traces of the giants' days, in the middle of the forest.'

We pushed the sprays aside to join him.

At first it was hard to see, for oaks had shouldered their way up through the black earth both inside and outside the outline of walls. If Gyrth had not gone closer, we would have walked past and not realized they were walls. The roof had tumbled, buried deep under generations of leaves. Ivy and swags of honeysuckle had heaped themselves over the crumbling stones. But Gyrth was pulling trails of it away to reveal the solid shapes beneath. A soft red stone seemed to warm the overgrown glade through the gloss of smothering dark green.

'Rome?'

All my small band felt Lilla's word conjure a rush of memories. The Roman walls of Chester, from which we had ridden out to defeat at Aethelfrith's hands. Caernarvon, lost to us with the coasts of Gwynedd. And before that, York, where I was born.

Lilla pushed his way past to hack about and find an entrance. I followed him. Standing beside him, it was easier to feel it as a little hall, roofed over now with oak branches. Living tree-trunks rose where pillars might have been.

Lilla wandered further in, scraping away the leaves, breaking off sweeping twigs, revealing the shape of the building. Suddenly he gave a cry and stumbled. I ran to catch him. One of Lilla's feet had broken through the carpet of debris, plunging him in knee deep. A speckled toad fled past me out of the stinking hole. When Lilla had recovered his balance, we cleared the fallen wood away. There was a square-cut basin, half filled with black muck. Under the slime we uncovered steps of marble. Lilla stood up slowly and looked around, a haunted look on his face. I followed his gaze. The shape of the little building tugged at my memory, a rectangular hall, the rounded apse to the east, the fine stones.

'This was a chapel of Christ,' Lilla said, in a low, hollow voice. 'Rhun told me the Romans didn't baptize like him in rivers. This hole was their baptistry.'

He lifted his head to where the great face of Christ might once have looked down on us with dark, grave eyes. He stood very still, his face pale, like a man on trial for his life.

'That's done with,' I told him, more sharply than necessary. 'Their King of the Universe might have been here once, but he's dropped his sceptre and run before an English warhost.'

It was true. I heard the growl of assent from Wiglaf and Gyrth and the rest. I scuffled the rotten leaves at my feet. Mildew had blackened the fragments of beams, painted plaster had long since crumbled into loam. There was no Christ left in Mercia. We had been right to go back to worshipping Woden.

Cenred and the Mercians hallooed to us to come away. An old ruined church held no curiosity for them. I was glad to step outside and find the path back to Bromsgrove. Lilla lingered after all the rest, his face turned up to leaves and sky. As we set off for home, I thought I saw his hands lift in prayer. When he caught up with us, he was silent. He lagged several paces behind me until we were clear of the wood.

We came out into pale sunlight. There was a village ahead. It looked a poor place. The thatch drooped like mangy fur. Thin children with old faces staggered under adult burdens. Down by the brook, women's voices rose. For a few moments I heard an incongruous beauty as the quick-running stream of their language sang in my ears. That pang again, of something almost recognized. This was not quite the Welsh of Cadfan and Mairi and Cadwallon, but something very like it.

Then they saw us. The song died. The women turned their faces to us, pinched, fearful. They stood up hastily and bowed respect to Cenred and the rest of us. Under their hanging hair I thought I caught expressions that were resentful, proud, angry with us and with themselves. They were British, but I was no foster-brother here. Their land was in English hands. They were powerless to say what they felt about English nobles.

After a moment's silence, one of them offered to fetch us oatbread and milk. I was relieved when Cenred declined. I knew that the women must be glad too. I had seen the thinness of their children.

We strode on, until we came over the hilltop and saw below us the halls of Cearl, Cenred's father. The others went whooping away down the path, but I stopped, staring down at the sharpened stockade, the grandly rearing gables painted with brilliant colours on the dragons' heads, the fresh thatch of reeds more golden than my wife's hair. It still took a surprised effort to realize that this was my home.

I sat down for a moment on a low rock. Lilla's shadow fell over the grass beside me.

'I feel as if I've left bits of myself all over Britain, escaping from Aethelfrith. Deira, Mon, now Mercia. It still seems strange to be back on English soil, married to an English princess.'

I must not let myself think of Mairi.

Lilla did not turn his face to me. He picked up a stone from between his feet and tossed it down the hill. 'Do you think it's true what Rhun said, if we abandon Christ our souls will burn in hell?'

'That's over. We're Englishmen on English soil. Anyway, I didn't force any of you back to the worship of Woden, any more than I forced you to accept Christ.'

I sensed him crouched, just behind my shoulder. His voice was unhappy, but doggedly loyal. 'You're my prince. I vowed to follow you. But I leave my heart outside the temple.'

We sat in silence between the birch trees, looking across the river at the King of Mercia's stronghold.

'I'm on English soil. I need the protection of English gods. The Northumbrian border's not so far from here. I should be more afraid than I was on Mon.'

Lilla spat the grass stem he was chewing. 'I miss home more here than I did in the Welsh lands. To be so close, and hear the English language. But we're still too far south. This isn't like the country I grew up in. My parents' estate was in the dales, east of York. I remember the ramparts of the Pennines, like a wall above us. The way the eagles used to drift in circles, looking for a weak lamb. I used to stand out there on the hillside and look down, and I'd see the sun catching the Ouse, and think of the day I'd ride to York to serve your father.'

His eyes were gazing north, across the rolling forests of the midlands. I was glad that he could not see me shiver. 'I feel like that lamb catching the eagle's eye. Exile didn't save Hereric's life. Aethelfrith's poison found him, even in Elmet. There's only me now.'

'King Cearl won't give you up to Aethelfrith. He'd hardly have given you his daughter if he didn't believe you had a future, would he? And you still have us, your men of Deira. I swear even Aethelfrith won't touch you, as long as I live.'

'I know.' I covered his hand with my own. The two of us were much more than prince and bodyguard. 'For friendship, I ought to say I'd rather you lived on after I was dead. But it would be a lie. I shall need your company more than ever when I'm carried aboard that ship of shields, and Woden's priests launch me out into the grey unknown.'

Lilla did glance sideways at me then. His mouth twisted and stilled. Then he forced a laugh. 'No gates of pearl, now? No city of light?' He saw my expression and gripped my hand hard. 'I'm not complaining. If I lived after you, I should be dishonoured. What kind of an Englishman do you take me for?'

'It may not happen in fair fight. It didn't for my father, or Hereric.'

'The women say it was the shock that made his wife give birth. . . . And look, here's your own wife coming to see where you are.'

A party of gaily dressed women had come out from the palace. We watched them greet the hunters. Now some of them were crossing the bridge, starting to climb the hill towards us. I saw the tall noblewoman in the lead. Coenburg, my wife. I still found it a strange word, like a lump of dry bread, hard to swallow. I could not

stop my imagination darting back to Mairi, with her teasing eyes
and the swing of her breasts as she chased after a ball. I ground my
nails into my palms. Was it my fault? If I had accepted baptism
sooner, would they have let me have her and not betrothed her to
the Prince of Powys? I should never know. I fled before I knew my
British hosts had survived the battle. Cadfan was king of all
Gwynedd now. He had made Cadwallon chieftain on Mon.

Coenburg was walking at the head of her women, panting a little
as she came up the slope. She was a big-framed woman, past girl-
hood. She wore her striped tunic loosely girdled, but it was a
matter of pride to see how her body swelled.

Lilla stood up to greet her. Coenburg was still out of earshot.
'You've been luckier than your nephew. Hereric's posthumous
child was another girl.'

'Hild, they call her, the "battle-maiden". What good is that? We
need sons to avenge my father, to win Deira back.'

'Your princess has provided one already.'

The Mercian women drew close to where we were sitting. I rose
too. It would not have been courteous to remain seated any longer.
I watched Coenburg throw back a corn-gold plait. My heart ached
for darker ringlets. It was a daily loss. It was odd to be back in
English lands and feel such longing for a people the English had
defeated.

No, that ache was all for one Briton. The rest was fury. I should
never forgive Cadwallon for what he had kept from me, the day of
my baptism. He knew Mairi was betrothed.

I called out, 'Good morning, my lady. Are you well? Should you
be climbing hills in your condition?'

'Edwin, you have a head as full of fears as a barn is fluttering
with bats. Englishwomen were carrying children in their bellies
when they rowed the longships across the North Sea with their
men.' She clasped my arms in greeting. 'You lived too long with the
soft Welsh. Must they always harp about tragedy and defeat? While
we live, let's drink and fight and conquer the world.' I saw her big

hands curved on her belly. I knew that the pressure of her fingers was speaking to my child inside her, as her strong voice was rallying its father.

'You have your own battle coming,' I warned her. 'You look near your time. Aren't you women afraid of birth, as a man is before he rides to war, until he's got a good skinful of mead inside him?'

Her eyes were blue spear-points, levelled at me. I should not have doubted her courage. 'If I die, promise me this, Edwin. Promise me, whatever happens, one of my sons will rule Northumbria. And not just your father's Deira. I want all that ogre Aethelfrith's kingdom for Osfrith. Bernicia in the north. The British lands he's conquering in the west. The Scottish borders. Drive your brother-in-law out of Northumbria soon. Become a great king.'

I had to smile. What was I, but a beggar at her father's court, as I had earlier been an exile at British Aberffraw? 'You put me to shame. I'm a fool with my gloomy talk. Yes. We'll both survive. We'll rule together at York and Bamburgh, side by side. It needs your strong spirit and my too-wise head. Pray God our son inherits more of you than me.'

I had betrayed myself with that unguarded prayer. Did she realize it was not All-Father Woden I meant in that moment?

I think she did. 'I've made my own sacrifces to Frigg, Lady of Life.'

I caught a troubled, sideways glance from Lilla. The roof of King Cearl's household temple showed above the stockade. Smoke wandered from its thatch above the carved jaws of monsters. There were sanctuaries more powerful than this, further into the oak forest. I walked in procession with my hosts to prostrate myself there, when it was my duty to do so. I offered sacrifice. I was an English prince once more, acclaimed by English warriors, back under the protection of English gods.

I stood for a long while, saying nothing to Coenburg. Then I smiled with a false wideness. 'I'll ride to Weoley Hill tomorrow. I'll pay the priest of that grove to make the biggest sacrifice the gods demand, for the safety of you and the baby, and for our future. One of our sons is going to be king of kings, Chief of all Britain, I promise you.'

Coenburg pinned me with her strong arms and gave me a smacking kiss. 'You're talking like an Englishman at last. I was afraid you had gone soft, living with those beaten Welsh dogs. What's Cadwallon of Mon? Let's spit on him. When you're king, you must seize his land from him and make him kneel to you, pay you tribute. You should be another Aethelfrith. But you must kill this one first.'

'All my life I have lived under the shadow that Aethelfrith wants to kill me.'

'In Mercia? Bah! We'll never let him touch you.'

We walked together down to the bridge, Deiran exile, Mercian princess. She was as tall as I was. I looked at her pregnant body and thought, 'I don't love this woman. But we are useful to each other. King Cearl has several daughters. He gambled this one, in the hope that my fortunes may change. Perhaps Aethelfrith will die before he manages to kill me. But neither Cearl nor Coenburg will grieve very much if I am murdered, so long as I leave her sons to claim the crown of Northumbria.'

She gave me a wicked, sideways smile. 'That's what I came to tell you. There's a Northumbrian messenger with Father now.'

I felt the blood drain from my cheeks. Words choked in my throat.

We came through the gates, and the guards saluted me like a prince. More smoke was drifting out of the door of Cearl's household shrine. The darkness within was powerful. The strength of the Ash Tree, the strength of blood, the strength of the ritual that summoned magic from the deep places. I stopped and touched the doorpost reverently, seeking protection. My hands cupped round the dark stained pillar, clasped it tight. I tried to wish myself back into the certainty with which, all my boyhood on Mon, I had stood firm against Cadwallon and his British Christ. Still, I had given in too soon.

I was English. I should have been safe here. But I was more afraid now than ever. Of the gods I had betrayed, on both sides. Of Aethelfrith the Ferocious, who had found me out.

I was not admitted to Cearl's council. It was hours before I heard the hoofbeats which told me the Northumbrians were leaving.

'They're not feasting with us. That should be good news,' Lilla reassured me.

As I entered his hall, Cearl shot a look at me under his eyebrows. He looked angry, like a cornered bear.

'I've sent them away with a proud answer. But they'll be back. I can't keep you. Northumbria has the strongest warhost in all Britain. Mercia's not ready for battle on that scale.'

I felt only numbness. The warlord of Mercia strode across the firelight into the shadows of dusk, spun angrily and marched back to me. I watched him pass from darkness into light and warmth and on into darkness again.

'I've been generous to you,' he shouted. 'Sanctuary when your British friends fell apart at Chester. My daughter to warm your bed. A son for you, and another coming.'

'I'm grateful to you both, sir.' The February chill was bitter now. My face felt stiff. I turned to see if Lilla had closed the door when we entered. His face too was white as a clouded moon. I saw Wiglaf and the rest as grey presences behind him.

Coenburg sat crouched by the flames. She held little Osfrith between her knees. With her lap spread, I could see the thrusting shape of the coming baby. This was the loss I ached for, more than anything. I knew what was going to happen. I could tell by the troubled way Coenburg looked up at me that my wife would not be coming on the run with me. She was anxious for my safety, but there were no tears. She had not risen to rush to my side and gabble of preparations, what road we should take. She was not clutching her belly in fear, like a woman near her time about to be hounded into exile. Cearl would provide her a place of safety for the birth. I would be gone before my first son could speak my name, before my second child was born.

I knew the truth already, but I could still defend my dignity.

'If the King of Mercia is afraid to give his son-in-law hearth-room, or raise a warhost to defend me, I'll take my family and pray the Hooded One will guide us to another kingdom that will.'

'Coenburg stays here. I can protect my own.'

'You'll keep my son? If I die, Aethelfrith will kill him next.'

'Oh, come, lad. You're not a fool. Do you think I can hide a pack of grown warriors as easily as a baby? There's no need to toss your blond locks back and snap your eyes at me. You look like some boy with three hairs on his chin, who's been refused a swig at the men's drinking horn. You're a grown man. You've been in campaigns. You've seen what happens to women who follow the camps. If you get yourself killed, do you think I want her raped under a hedge or holed up in a hovel in some marsh to freeze to death? Aren't you man enough to lead these murdering Northumbrians away from her? If Red-Handed Tiw ever smiles on you again, and you win your kingdom back, it'll be time enough to send for your queen and her princes.'

Osfrith was playing with Coenburg's thumb. It turned my heart over to watch him. Would that tiny, curled fist one day grasp a sword?

'You'd like your grandson to inherit Northumbria, rather than me, wouldn't you?'

'Talk sense, lad. At the moment, there isn't a bigger king anywhere on this island than Aethelfrith. Who's to stop him taking what he wants? Mercia's a young kingdom, with a small army. I'd rather he marched on some other land than this.'

'You scorned my Welsh hosts just now because they fell in their thousands at Chester. They died fighting Aethelfrith. I find more honour among those Christian Britons.'

I turned away. The Mercian thanes shouted their anger. There was heat in my cheeks now, and the flames of Cearl's hearth were not hot enough to flush them this deeply.

A smaller roar of support greeted me. I felt a warmth there too. My Northumbrian bodyguard, who had followed me wherever I went since the fall of York. They had been protecting me since I was a child who could hardly lift a sword. Now they moved meaningfully closer to me. I read the grimness in their expressions, behind the greying beards and eyebrows. Our world was narrowing. If Gwynedd had fallen to Aethelfrith's power and English Mercia threw us out, what kingdom now would give us hospitality? Yet these men would follow where I fled, close round my body like a coat of mail, die themselves before they let Aethelfrith's spears reach me.

'Where will you go?' Coenburg asked.

My wife was not a coward. But little Osfrith and the child she was carrying mattered more to her than I did. I could trust her to protect them.

'He's hounded me out of the west already. Now he's coming for me in the midlands. Where is there left? I can feel him driving me back to the eastern beaches where our longships landed. If that fails too, there's only the sea.'

'Well, then, Redwald of East Anglia is growing stronger. He might have reason to resent Aethelfrith's ambitions.'

'Northumbria borders East Anglia. If I were king there, I'd make a better friend to Redwald's land.'

My wife turned her face up and met her father's scowl. Firelight glinted on her swinging gold braids. 'Do you think Redwald might defend Edwin?'

The Mercian chieftain shrugged. He did not look as though he cared for my insult to his honour. 'He has a big warhost. But is he mad enough? This isn't a normal king we're talking about.

Aethelfrith the Ferocious. More like the Wolf of Doom. He might be killed one day, but he'll tear the throat out of whoever strikes his death blow. I tell you, there isn't a warhost in Britain that dares stand in the way of his frenzy.'

Coenburg did clamber to her feet then, supporting the weight of her pregnancy with both hands. She looked at me levelly and the firelight flashed in her eyes. 'Go tomorrow, my lord. May all the gods defend you. The chariot of Tiw speed you. The shield of Thunor be over you. The one eye of Woden guide you wisely. And Lady Frigg give you life.'

I held her shoulders and she kissed me strongly. I felt no personal warmth from her, neither grief for my going nor fear for my safety. The passion in her voice was all for Mercia, the heroic words an English queen should speak. I was only her path to power, and I had not yet proved up to the task. I was leaving a small son, and perhaps another coming, and nothing but danger for them to inherit.

There was a draughty space in my heart that should have been filled by a beloved homeland, a flourishing family. I had lost both now. It could not be much longer before I lost my life.

Cearl gave a bark of mocking laughter. 'You seem to carry a mark of doom. What if Redwald refuses to harbour you?'

I had been schooled in self-control, all those long years as an English orphan at Cadfan's court, enduring Cadwallon's taunts. I felt the set of resignation drag at the skin of my face, ageing me. It took on a blankness, a shield against loneliness.

'Then I must lose myself in their freezing fens. Stumble on until I reach the sea. Launch out into that fog, until the name of Edwin, Prince of Deira, is lost past remembering.'

My men growled, as they were bound to do.

'The name of Edwin, Aelle's son, shall never die,' Lilla shouted, too loudly. 'He's going to live to rule Deira, as his father did.'

'What's Deira now? Swallowed up in Aethelfrith's Northumbria.'

69

'Then it needs brave men to win it back. And here are seven.'

Seven, that had been twelve when we fled Catterick. But the Deirans stamped their feet, leather boots thudding on the floor of Cearl's hall. If they had been carrying weapons, they would have clashed their spears on their shields. The dark roof rang with their ritual acclaim.

'Edwin!' 'Edwin of Deira!' 'Edwin of Northumbria!' 'Hail, King Edwin!'

It was madness to let my heart beat faster, for my forehead to flush with pride, as if what these men shouted in their blind loyalty was ever possible. Their battle-cry was like a rising wave carrying me off my feet. If I lost my footing, these men's frenzy would fling my body, bleeding and broken, on the stones.

Chapter Nine

'Can this be the way to sanctuary?' I asked. 'The fog may have gone, but there's no sign of the road.'

Lilla shivered and did not answer me. He pulled his cloak closer around him against the bitter marsh wind. Good Welsh wool, we all wore, old, but still thickly felted. Those cloaks had seen us years of service, in rain and snow, through Gwynedd and Mercia. They felt like the arms of friends in a strange country. It was this English land which was a stranger to us.

Tostig muttered behind me, 'You'd think the air here had knives in it.'

'I seem to remember it could blow pretty chilly on our own cliffs in Deira. I come from Ravenscar,' Wiglaf snapped.

We were all silent a while. I, with the pain that I could not even remember the country of which I claimed to be the rightful king. My bodyguard, because they had not seen their homeland from the day they sped me away to safety. More than twenty years, and I knew Deira still lived in their hearts.

'At least we had hills you could shelter under. Look at it. It makes your soul cold.'

Level land lay all the way in front of us, fading towards the horizon. It dwindled into nothingness under a huge, pale sky. There was only the thinnest gauze of cloud left, but it drained the world of colour. The reeds stood stiff with ice, resisting the wind and hissing against it. Ice pearled the edges of the waterways but left black channels, which plopped and sucked with evidence of unseen things.

We heard the boat coming before we saw it. The creak of wood and leather, the lightest splash of drops running from a skilful oar. My men murmured and drew closer around me, with Wiglaf in front.

The pole rose higher than the reeds. The blunt bows of the craft carved curves on the slate-dark surface of the channel and brought the stern into view. A single shrouded figure stood bent as a heron, sculling one-handed with a single oar. The hooded head turned our way with no surprise. The craft changed course.

'Is that a woman?' Lilla said.

I saw a shadowed face, netted with lines, like cracked mud. I had expected the eyes to be piercing, bird-black, but they were pale, as if, like everything else, they were filmed with ice. The lips were sucked in on themselves over toothless gums. We all stepped back as the boat nudged accurately into the bank.

'Have you lost your path, dears? Or are you running away to lose someone else?' Her blue-white eyes were full on me now, though it was hard to guess how much she saw.

'I could say yes to both, Mother. I am—'

'We're trying to reach the palace of Redwald of the Wuffings,' Lilla cut in. His interruption of my identity was as quick as a sword shot out to protect me.

The old woman's laugh was like the crack of icicles snapped from a tree. 'You've been elf-led a long while, then, to end up here. Lucky the Marsh Worm didn't scent you. Fine soldiers like you wouldn't know the charm for that serpent.'

'Can you point us the road, Granny?' I let Lilla take charge while I stood silent. 'Can we make it by nightfall? Or some decent house?'

'The nights fall early, wintertime. Road, is it? The right roads here are the ones without stones. I could take you. You'd fear to cross the fen any other way. I know where the dry land is, and the track up to his fort. Redwald!' She spat into the oily water. 'May the Grey Stranger strike him dead.'

'Redwald of the Wuffings is your king, woman!' I could not stop my harsh protest. To have lost my own kingdom was wound enough. To deny the mystery of a ruling king was blasphemy. My escort stiffened in anger too.

The woman looked up at us, from where her stooped neck thrust her head lower. 'The land and its king must be one. You should know that, Prince.'

This boatwoman saw too much. I saw Lilla shudder.

'Then surely she who wishes the King dead curses the land too,' I retorted.

'The land is never without a king, is it? If one falls, there's always another.'

'Redwald could have you hanged for a traitor.'

'Then you won't be needing my ferry to the King's fort.' Her chapped fingers, livid through the mittens, tightened their clutch on the oar.

Wiglaf cried out, 'No, Mother. We know it's the way of commoners everywhere to grumble at their betters. We'll take it as a joke and say no more. How many can you take?'

'Five of those who eat at kings' tables. Our sort come lighter.' She looked us over shrewdly.

'How long before you come back for the other three?'

'If they're lucky, there'll still be enough light to see them up the track. And what's it to gentlemen like you if I have to take myself home by starlight afterwards?'

'Can we trust her?' Lilla whispered. He was making the sign against the evil eye.

I must lead them. I was their prince. I made to step down from the bank into the blunt-bowed craft. It was a bigger step than I had calculated. The boat rocked violently, splashing us with icy water. The woman cursed.

In a moment Lilla dropped more lightly beside me, steadying me.

'I don't like it. I'd back five of us with steel against all comers. But we've no weapons against demons.'

Still, I saw him finger something under the neck of his tunic. I had suspected for a long time that Lilla kept his cross.

'Too late for that. Christ isn't going to help us out of this watery wilderness.'

'Christ!' The woman spat again, thrusting our boatload violently out from the bank. 'That's not a name for English tongues. English land needs an English king, Prince. We know our own.'

The barge rode perilously low in that death-cold water. The woman's breath moaned as she propelled us deeper into a maze of snaking channels. I sat huddled amongst my silent thanes.

'This would be a fitting place to lose my life. Drowned, along with my land and my family and all my hope.'

Fire. It blazed up into the pale blue of the sky, till the colour of the flames was lost and the air quivered with heat. The logs were leached of sap so that the smoke soared thin and white, while ash drifted like snowflakes from the cloudless sky. Cold faces were turned to the smell of the ox roasting richly as the cooks heaved on the spit. The mere rang with the strike of bone skates and hissed where the young men swept the curves of their dangerous races and the women sang as they crossed hands and zigzagged past.

I let out a shout. 'Tostig's down.'

'Another broken leg?' was Wiglaf's first question.

'You have all the gloom of a professional bodyguard.'

'A fall on this ice could mean the end of a warrior's career. There are not so many of us left that you can afford to lose one more Northumbrian.'

I put on my broadest smile to tease him. 'My turn next.'

He was no longer a young man. His face stiffened. 'You're my prince. I can't stop you.'

'You shouldn't want to. If we can beat these East Anglians at their own sport, so much the better for the honour of Northumbria.'

'Is that the only contest left to win you glory?'

'You believe there could be real war, still?'

'It's the only way for you to win your father's crown back.'

'What quarrel has Redwald with Aethelfrith? Unless I'm to be the cause of war. Do you think Aethelfrith knows I'm here in East Anglia?'

'He's ears everywhere, and an arm long enough to reach into other men's kingdoms. If war doesn't come soon, it could be too late.'

'You mean, like Hereric?'

'No one's safe from treachery. Least of all a prince in exile.'

'The Doom Wolf's really on your shoulder today. Let's see if I can make you laugh.'

A roar of cheering saluted the end of that race. I stood up, the skates strapped to my boots. Lilla held my unsteady arm while I balanced myself.

'It's not a fair contest. They've been doing this since they were babies.'

I launched myself out on to the mere, feeling exhilaration rise in my throat as the speed took over. There was risk, there was the joy of daring overcoming fear, there was the challenge from Redwald's sons and foster-sons, his young warriors, the heroes of his body-guard, and a few of my own men.

We were streaking down the broad now, the sun flashing on the crystals in our wake, wild geese taking off ahead with furious clattering of wings and a startled honking. We men yelled as if it had been a hunt. We were without weapons. Only the ice was our adversary, and then only if we fell. As long as my body obeyed its laws, it was a wonderful friend. I had a sudden, piercing vision of the fairy women of the Britons, radiantly beautiful, but ambivalent, dangerously promising glory or destruction.

A shout from the shore told me someone behind had fallen. I was

going to disappoint Wiglaf, though. There were too many men straining ahead. I could never win through their bodies to take the prize.

The cheering was rising to a huge peak as I flailed my limbs
towards the finishing line. It could not be meant for me. There
were not enough Northumbrians to will me on. Someone came
sweeping past me. A chequered skirt of red and yellow. Two thick
fair plaits tossing like cable ropes as the skater swung from side to
side. Flashes of gold on warmly wrapped arms. Striped stockings
above her boots. The tall form of Redwald's queen, Witburg,
stormed past the men I was struggling against.

She swept beyond the judges and swung in a great arc, threaten-
ingly close to the crowding spectators. As I rushed up in her wake
they were laughing and yelling. She was not the first past the
marker. She would claim no prize from her amused husband. Then
I was over the line too. Witburg pulled up in a flurry of powdered
ice in front of me. I almost overbalanced. I should never become as
practised as these eastern marsh dwellers.

'You're a brave man,' she said. Her eyes were direct, her smile
wide for me. 'You haven't been long here, but you risk your bones
to make sport for us. And you stayed on your feet.'

'I confess myself beaten by a fair champion, lady.'

'Never mind. You deserve a hero's portion of that ox.' She seized
my arm and towed me strongly towards the bank. Lilla was waiting to help me off with my skates.

'So you live to fight with four whole limbs. If we ever get to
fight.'

Witburg stood listening. She lifted her eyebrows, making her
speedwell eyes wider still. 'You sound as if our East Anglia is too
tame for you, Lilla.'

'I didn't intend to be ungrateful, Lady. You've honoured Prince
Edwin, when the King of Mercia was afraid to keep him.'

'Redwald is made of tougher stuff.'

'I know that, Lady. Only Aethelfrith still denies he's the greatest
English king.'

She stared at him very hard, in silence. 'Then, you think that Redwald should go to war against Aethelfrith?'

'It's not for me to give counsel to East Anglia's king. I don't have a seat in your Witan.'

'But if you did? It's not just for Edwin's sake, is it? You are saying it's time for Redwald to challenge Aethelfrith.'

'It would be a brave man that would make war against Aethelfrith the Ferocious. He's trampled too many warhosts into the ground already.'

'But if nobody stops him, he will become the master of all Britain.'

'He already rules land from the eastern beaches to the Irish sea. He's hammered the Scots and Picts and Welsh into submission. Where can he stretch his muscles next? If he wants to increase his power, he can only look south of the Humber.'

Witburg frowned at him for a while longer. Then her laugh broke out, loud, approving.

'You have the best of guardians, Edwin. It's not only your body Lilla protects. In his eyes, you're already wearing the crown your brother-in-law snatched from the corpse of your father. Lilla can fight with weapons of wisdom as well as his spear. He may yet make his dream come true.'

'It's a dream without substance, Lady. What can eight Northumbrians do?'

'You have more friends than seven. Redwald, these young savages are as hungry as Northumbrian wolves. Carve me the right shoulder for the champion of the race and the left for Edwin.'

It was an honour I had done nothing to deserve. I turned to the East Anglian king. He had a round, red face softer than his wife's. He took the greasy knife from the cook and sharpened it expertly. Obedient under Witburg's eye, he slashed through the roasting ox's flesh, sinews, joints, so that the juices ran, spitting on the fire. He held out a generous portion of the shoulder to me.

The meat was hot in my hand as I took it from him, the blood still running red near the bone. There was spiced ale in the cup. It fired my throat while my forehead froze. I heard shouts, cheers, jokes, laughter all around me. Here in East Anglia, I had crowds of new friends, a sleeping-place in Redwald's hall. It shut out the huge, chilling loneliness of the fens after dark. I was safe here for the moment. No one could touch me through this ring of allies, could he?

Witburg was still at my elbow. 'You think the world is cold and dead now. But in three weeks it will be the festival of Eostre. Each spring the goddess makes everything new. Come to her temple with me, and we'll make a sacrifice together. Perhaps to others besides her. The egg for Eostre, the blood for Tiw. Strong magic to change the balance for you this year. What is the matter? Are you afraid to pay their price? Life requires blood, Edwin. The old English way.'

Chapter Ten

A high fence surrounded the temple at Ipswich. The massive gates had been hauled open to the daylight. The gatekeeper sat crouched in their shadow, at once bored and watchful. A young priest, by the look of him, a stag's pelt thrown over his shoulder, furred slippers on his feet.

I approached him, a little shamefacedly. Once, so long ago, I had been a royal child in Deira. We had secular servants in my father's palace and religious servants in temples like this. I had liked the way they leaped to attention when we approached. I wished I could remember it better. Redwald's East Anglia here must be more like my English birthplace than the island of Mon had been. But I was still an exile. Folk treated me courteously, but I was of little importance to them.

The novice priest rose lazily. 'Your name and business with the gods, sir?'

'Edwin, Prince of Deira. I have come . . . I have come to make a wish to Lady Eostre and to Tiw the Red-Handed.'

He seemed not to care about my hesitation.

'The peace of the morning to you, then, sir. Pass. If you've brought a gift, the priests can offer it for you.'

I knew what he meant. Long ago, my mother would have provided me with a silver trifle to drop from my childish fingers as I passed him, teaching me the manners of a generous king's son. Now, I must wait for campaigns with Redwald's warhost to win me booty of silver and gold. Till then, I had only the little wealth I brought from Mercia. I accepted charity from the King's board. Redwald had tossed me a gold ring one evening for telling a lively tale of Cadfan's wars, which I had embroidered with adventures concerning Welsh dragons. The higher status I had got by marriage I had left behind with my wife in Mercia. Was my second child born yet? What did it matter? I was still running for my life. If Redwald's protection should be withdrawn, there were only the marshes left for me, and the grey sea.

My men followed me. I was inside the sacred enclosure now. I knew that Lilla was uneasy. Carved pillars reared in front of us. Their branches had been lopped, but they stood mightier than living trees because of the magic graven deep into their heartwood. There was a ring of darker stumps, humped like kneeling women, but for white hair they had runes painted on them, a knowledge older even than their roots.

It was a relief to turn my eyes to the more human activity busy at the huts that lined the inside of the wall. There was the steam of cauldrons and forges, the chants of doctors and dream-tellers, the squawking of cooped hens and the squeal of pigs. I was by no means the only suppliant. A trail of petitioners, noble and common, moved along those lanes, hungry to find some relief, or purchase some power.

I made my feet walk slowly but purposefully past them. My gaze was fixed now on the high-roofed hall of the gods. My face felt stiff, clenched on an emotion I must not reveal. I was sure I saw a flickering movement from the heads of the carved dragons, wolves, bears and ravens, all craning forward from the eaves to watch me come.

Another doorkeeper waited. This one was older, more experienced. He made a measured bow, calculated exactly to my status.

'Good morning, Prince.'

'Is Queen Witburg here yet?'

'No one from the court today, sir, except yourself.'

I had kept a more valuable gift back for him. A muttered charm passed me into the dusk within.

All I saw in that first moment was the central fire. It burned low, a red eye under black, charred logs. The iron hanging lamps had been fed with herbs. They gave more smoke and pungency than light. I heard a choking cough from Wiglaf behind me. But still I did not turn. There were more priests, male and female, here, moving about their work in the shadows. It took me some time before my ears distinguished their murmuring as a tangle of many subdued chants.

As my pupils widened to the gloom, separate shrines around the walls began to stand out in sharper relief. Each god had its own boxed stall, its personal altar. They demanded different sacrifices. Small flames of votive lamps glowed like the eyes of beasts. I heard the rustle of birds' wings. There would be fresh blood soon on some of these tables.

I told most of the men to wait. I caught the appeal in Lilla's eyes and ordered him follow me. We moved on forward, not quite blindly, threading the square-cut pillars that lifted the roof high. This house of All-Father Woden and his family was larger than Redwald's gift-hall, but far less brightly lit.

Abruptly I halted. My check forced a stifled exclamation from Lilla, keeping too close behind me. I heard his rapid breathing. He had seen it too.

I steadied my sight on the table in front of us. It was set against the right-hand wall, well away from the door, and screened at its sides by planked partitions hung with yellow tapestries. Yet there was a brightness about it that brought it leaping out more vividly than larger altars. Two white wax candles burned with a clear flame. The white linen cloth that covered the table was embroidered with gold. In the middle was set a gold and ivory cross.

I had a confused impression of Lilla crossing himself, genuflecting, muttering a prayer we had been taught in Christian Gwynedd.

'How did that get here?'

I was still on my feet, struggling with an emotion more pressing than mere explanation. From before my marriage in English Mercia, back beyond the barrier of that disastrous battle, one memory of a lost land came rushing back. A thundering waterfall. The shock of immersion in a pool as cold as the grave. The strong, sure hands of Rhun raising me into the light. Little bright Rhiainmelt laughing and clapping her hands. Cadfan and Nevyn embracing me, clothing me in a white baptismal garment, so soon to be blazoned with blood at Chester.

And Cadwallon, my foster-brother, kissing me. He had been laughing as he led me to Mairi. And then he told me I had lost.

And in days, all of it wiped out in death-screams and defeat. Now here I was, standing again in front of the cross, on the throne steps of the Lord I had sworn those vows to, so long ago. What was I supposed to do? I felt my own knees begin to flex, uncertainly. I had barely had time to get acquainted with the customs of Christian worship, before Chester. I felt terror rising at this unexplained presence of the crucified Christ here in English East Anglia.

I could not help myself. I started to move cautiously nearer, up one wooden step. My hand reached out and gripped the edge of that altar. At once, I snatched it back and cast a swift, nervous glance around me. Had I come impiously close to the sacred things? Was anyone watching me?

'So it's true what I heard,' Lilla muttered. 'Redwald kissed the Cross, when he went to Kent. He's still got it here, among all the blood offerings to Woden. Along with Thunor and and Frigg and the Wyrd Sisters and all the rest.'

'I didn't know.'

'He went back to Woden.'

'Like us.' Lilla stayed silent. 'But why this? Do you think he still keeps a Christian priest here?'

'In the temple of Woden?' Lilla laughed harshly. 'Can you imagine Rhun or Nevyn standing for that?'

I did not want to think of the holy woman alone on the hillside, talking to heaven. Of Rhun with his searching eyes, bringing me to the point of decision. I forced myself to stare at the cross. It was not like the ones the Britons made. Outside the church at Aberffraw a tall wooden cross had thrown its arms wide across a wheel of glory. The sun had blazed through it. For all its precious gold and crafting, this cross was starker, sterner, plainer. I saw it for what it was, an instrument of execution.

The candle flames leaned and twisted in a sudden draught. Black winds of smoke were wrenched from them. There was a roaring in my ears, as though an avenging host was advancing upon me.

The voice from behind which startled me was a woman's.

'Good morning, Prince Edwin. So you have discovered my husband's curio.'

I turned, my breath fluttering in my throat like the candle flames. I had climbed the step before the altar, but Witburg stood tall too, Redwald's queen. The flames swung dizzily, multiplied in the baubles in her braids and the bronze scissors, knife and key on her girdle. Around her thronged a pale blur of faces, men and women from the palace, the watchful priests, my own guard.

'I had not expected to find this here.'

Witburg's voice was amused. 'Redwald has been more changeable than an English warlord should be. A woman might have shown more constancy as chieftain.' She spoke her mind, careless of the listening crowd. 'It's true the interest of East Anglia once lay with Kent. And the Kentish folk turned Christian in Aethelbert's time. But what's that to us? Did Redwald need to be ashamed of what he is? He could be as great a warrior, as rich a gold-giver, as any Kentish king. As he is now. But he went to Canterbury and let Aethelbert persuade him to turn his back on the All-Father and take this foreign Christ's baptism. Is that the courage that brought us here to conquer half of Britain?'

I lowered my eyes before her contempt. The candles and the cross were out of sight behind me now. I was at the mercy of this woman's generosity. I had fled from the far west of Britain to the furthest east. Beyond East Anglia there was only the cold sea left. My life lay in her hands. But more than that, I longed for the courage of her laughter, her certainty.

'No,' I agreed. 'It was not like that with the English warships.'

'And so I told him when he came home with his cross. We English know what we are. Lady Frigg and Thunor the Thunderer are life-givers enough for us. Didn't our Woden hang on the World Tree nine days to seize wisdom? Why should we want another hanged god?'

She was not angry. Her tone spoke cheerful scorn, not hatred. She was sure of her right. She had never been brought low, as I had. She had never been a hunted exile, orphaned, landless, begging at a foreign court, in fear for her life. She had not felt the need for a saviour who stooped to those who had nothing.

I did not have the courage to tell Witburg that.

She came up the step past me, picked up the cross, as though it held no sacred awe. She looked at it idly and put it down again. 'Redwald is changeable, but he is not stupid. I showed him sense. The East Angles will never follow that track. A king must rule, for the land, not himself, by the wisdom of his Witan in council. We English do not want a foreign Christ.'

'I never knew that Redwald was baptized.'

'What difference does it make? This is a private matter now. He still offers a king's sacrifices to Woden, Thunor and all the rest, as our fathers did. The land stays safe. What harm can it do if he keeps one more table in his temple than they did? It makes him happier. And it changes nothing.'

'Then he still prays here? Does he have a Christian priest?' I heard my own voice, no more than a whisper.

Witburg laughed, supremely confident. 'Since it's here, I suppose he prays to it, and some of those who caught the Kentish fever with him. But it's not as king of his people that he does it. As for a priest, at first there was some black-eyed shaman he brought back, babbling in a foreign tongue. That one learned to keep well out of my way. He soon went back to Canterbury.'

I was walking down the step with her, back to the smoking fire. Her retinue was parting in front of us. Witburg's stride was firm beside me, leading me on towards a larger altar where the priests of Tiw were waiting. Her voice rang confident beyond contradiction.

'Well, Edwin? Suppose you were ever to seize your kingdom back from Aethelfrith. Wouldn't that be your choice? The English gods for an English nation? You'd vow your weapons to them, wouldn't you, with gold and blood?'

'Yes, you know I would.'

What else could I have said?

Wiglaf was at my elbow, handing me the offering I needed, a young black boar trussed for the priest's knife, screaming its protest.

The Queen and I rode back in Witburg's chariot. That felt strange. I found I was wishing myself back in the saddle of the roan horse Lilla was now leading. I did not enjoy being jolted about on these straw-stuffed cushions over the flinty track.

Witburg chattered of hawking and hunting to entertain me. She probed me for information about my Mercian princess. She shared my sorrow at the separation from young Osfrith and the baby I had never seen. She was generous hearted. Yet I heard the harsh strength of her voice, saw the flash of her far-sighted gaze over the huge marshlands, felt the ash-straight nearness of her body as the chariot tried to toss us to left or right. A woman like this would not bend, would not soften just for me, if East Anglia's good was at stake. I was welcome here only on her terms.

And how would Redwald treat me? I now had to picture the king I had thought so powerful, in the light of my discovery of his Christian altar. I recalled a face fleshier than those of the hard-bitten warriors who surrounded me. My host was tall, yet he had a way of stooping considerably towards people when he talked. He was gentle in his manner at court, though the skalds sang him a fierce war-leader on the battlefield. He appeared smilingly deferential to his strong-willed wife. Could I trust Redwald to stand firm against Aethelfrith? Was he strong enough to protect me? He had shifted his faith under pressure. Would he keep his loyalty to me?

Where was my own loyalty now?

We came in sight of the East Anglian palace. No rampart-crowned hill, no gale-defying stronghold on the cliffs, like the British chiefs. This was an English town rooted on flat earth. A wooden stockade, timber halls. Redwald's reputation was defence powerful enough. The rebel British were long since beaten, fled west, the few survivors crushed into the invisibility of serfdom.

Witburg half rose from her seat, bracing herself for balance against my knee. 'Oh, ho. We have visitors.' The charioteer quickened the ponies' pace and she fell back, laughing.

A brisk contingent was coming, riding down the road from the north. The pale light of winter's end glinted on their mail breastplates. The foremost carried a spear from which fluttered an envoy's pennant. The rest had their weapons couched, but looked about them keenly, as though they made no assumption of a welcome.

My mouth felt dry. 'I know of only one kingdom to the north. It hasn't taken him long to learn where I am.'

The Queen looked sideways at me with a sly smile. 'You think, like your brother-in-law, Northumbria is a single kingdom, even though your fathers ruled it as two? Well, I suppose you're right. Aethelfrith the Ferocious is not the man to share what he's seized. So it must be him or you.'

'You talk as though it could ever be an equal contest. He has the mightiest warhost in Britain and I have nothing.'

'Courage, little prince. How much did our forefathers have when they leaped ashore from the longships? The British owned everything. And where are they now? Fled to the mountains of the west and left us conquerors.'

'I don't imagine Aethelfrith is going to run west if I stand up and shake my spear. And I've nowhere left to hide from him.'

'We are not so spineless that he can touch you in East Anglia. We won't allow his spies to poison you, like poor Hereric in Elmet.'

'But suppose he threatens you with war? Would Redwald fight for me? Cearl of Mercia wouldn't.'

The wheels clattered suddenly loud in the pause. Witburg was honest. She stared ahead, laughter straightened from her face. 'Redwald will do what is best for East Anglia. I shall see to that.'

I felt despair, like an enormous stone, weighting my spirit down to depths from which I could not hope to rise. Lilla urged the horses close to the chariot. He said nothing, but his look told me he read the danger to me. The day was long past noon, the cold advancing. I felt a wild impulse to leap into the saddle and gallop back to that temple. Surely in all that multiplicity of altars there must be one god there with the power to protect me, if I made the right sacrifices. Through the increasing chill I felt the warmth of Witburg beside me, almost a goddess herself.

The chariot rolled in between the saluting sentries and drew to a halt in the yard. The visitors had got there before us. Their steaming mounts were being led to the stables. There was no sign of the embassy. Lights glowed inside Redwald's hall, though the sun had not set. I turned, and Witburg's plaits shone like a flash of sunshine.

'Keep your courage up. You shall sit next to me at supper.'

'Excuse me, Lady. I have lost the stomach for eating.' Without waiting for her permission, I walked slowly towards the separate lodge Redwald had granted me and my men.

A stout woman came hurrying past me from the Queen's quarters. She wrapped her mistress's cloak more warmly about her. I heard her say, 'Come away in. I've got hot ale ready for you. And enough in the jug to warm that poor prince too. Those Northumbrians! Giving us orders, as though we were hounds in their kennels. And your Redwald gave them a soft answer, like the good host he is.'

'What do the Northumbrians want?'

'Too soon to say, dearie. Though I do know they've brought a heavy bag they won't let anyone touch. The gossip is they've come offering him a deal of gold for our young Northumbrian gentleman to be handed over to them.'

The oath that broke from Lilla was wrenched from his guts.

Witburg stood very still and tall. Her own malediction on Aethelfrith was more thoughtful than Lilla's, but no less forceful. I shuddered, listening. She called out across the space that separated us. 'And the Wyrd Sisters do worse than that to Redwald, if he ever thinks he can sell a house-guest's life. East Anglian honour is not to be bought with gold, while I am his queen.'

Next morning, still carrying their gold, the envoys went away. But not for long.

Chapter Eleven

Spring was turning the frozen marshes into flooded lakes. Redwald and the rest of us went hunting the boar through the old brown sedges. The ground was treacherous underfoot, a crust of mud, dried in the brief sun, shattering under a boot to plunge the hunter into the mire. One step sideways in the jostling chase would send a man into chilly water. The reeds were tall, sagging, but not yet laid low. Thick brown clumps, where the deadly tusked wild boar could lurk, ready to charge in red-eyed fury on the first unwary warrior who stumbled on his hiding place.

Our spears were tense in our hands. Voices were low, guarded, yet they seemed to echo over the watery waste.

My mind was only half on the four-footed savage who would rend my guts if he could. I was glad of the solid friendship of Lilla, running just at my shoulder. He was more watchful for my immediate danger. There was a yell ahead from the men round Redwald. All of us, young and old, doubled our speed. Across the reed beds, heads bobbed, dividing left and right, throwing a ring across the marsh to head the old boar in. As the line of men was flung out, the gaps between us widened. With the danger to our quarry increasing, so each one of us became a separate target. Lilla was still not far from me.

'Stand off, man. You've left a gap on your left wide enough to drive a flock of sheep through.'

'I swore an oath to your father, never to see your life in danger while I lived.'

'Why should I care? I'd sooner die on the end of a boar's tusk than be bartered to Aethelfrith for a sack af gold. As far as my guts are concerned, they'd be spilled just as quickly, without the honour. Not even your loyalty could stop that.'

'He won't do it. Redwald will never you give up for gold.'

'It was a bigger bribe this second time.'

'And the same insulting answer.'

'Aethelfrith is a man who takes what he wants. If gifts won't work, it'll be threats next. He won't—'

'Look out!'

Lilla's spear whistled through the shaking sedge. Simultaneous yells rang out around an arc of hunters. I gripped my own spear, stiffening my arm, watching for the hurtling rush in my direction. Lilla already had his long knife unsheathed.

The sound was uncanny, a squealing so demented it seemed to pierce the ear-drums. Redwald's men and my guard roared their killing-cry. We were loosing the din from our throats to drive down terror. His speed was ferocious, his course uncertain, on legs that seemed too small for his horrific body. He weaved from side to side, spattering mud in fans that hid his next intention. Now I was closing in with the rest, willing myself step by step over shaking ground into the range of his charging fury.

'Keep back from my spear arm,' I muttered. 'He's mine.'

As though he heard, the small fierce eyes swung my way. The tusks curved cruelly before mud-spattered bristles. Cleft trotters tore the ground. I could hear the huge panting of his breath as he lowered his head. Lilla started to move.

'Now!'

The old boar leaped in the air as a flung spear tore through the armour of his hide just behind the shoulderblade. With a roar of exultation, Redwald's warriors rushed forward. The King's javelin stood out quivering as the brute scrabbled to turn, screaming vengeance. With their king's life exposed to those tusks, a dozen expert weapons found their mark. Knives flashed. Blood flew. I stared at the fallen brute, my muscles still shaking with tension. Was it over?

I had cast my spear with all the rest. I went cautiously forward with Lilla to retrieve my own weapon from the fallen carcase. One bright eye was open. It did not move.

The royal spear was left standing proudly erect in the hide. Redwald was smiling.

'One ogre the less in the marsh for mothers to scare their children with.'

I tried to steady my breath. 'Their parents will thank you for this. And they're not the only ones who have cause to be grateful to you that they can walk in safety.'

The King's grin broadened. His hand clapped me on the shoulder. 'Don't look so glum, lad. I've promised, haven't I? You're safe with me. It would take more gold than your brother-in-law's offered yet to tempt me to give you up, and I'm no more frightened of his threats than of a pig's. Do I look the sort of man likely to change his mind?'

His smile was innocent as a small boy's, immensely pleased with himself. All past changes, broken promises forgotten. Only today's success was radiant in his mind.

I made myself smile too, less genuinely. 'You've been very good to me, so far. I hope one day I can show my gratitude, when I've something to give.'

'Give your gratitude to the gods. East Anglia's rich enough.'

Redwald turned abruptly to his hunt servants, who were gutting and trussing the gigantic boar. 'Be careful of the head. I want this trophy carried whole to the table tonight, with an apple between its teeth. Let our women see those tusks and think of the flesh they might have ripped.'

'Redwald!' 'Redwald Boar-Slayer!' 'Redwald of the Steady Hand!' All around, his men were thundering praise in a rhythmic chant, thumping their spear butts on the ground.

The King nodded his head, well-satisfied with himself.

Aethelfrith's Northumbrian envoys came a third time. The baggage of bribes and threats they carried weighed heavier still.

That evening, dusk was falling around Redwald's palace. Alone in my own lodge, I saw through the shutters how the roof of the great hall stood out, the gables stag-crested against a still-pale sky. Light glowed from it, a lyre played, but there was not the loud singing, the thumping of ale-horns or the shouts and jesting that usually drove back the dark from men's minds. Outside, the trees were skeletons, their leaves hardly showing yet. Firm ground petered away into fens, their borderline treacherous in trails of mist.

An English voice came from outside. I had not called for the lamp to be lit.

'My lord? . . . Edwin?'

A light wind rustled the ragged ends of thatch. I saw the door move. It was bolted.

'It's me. Lilla. Can I come in?'

I wrestled the fastening open and stepped aside to let Lilla slip in. Then I closed it again.

'I didn't expect you back while the ale-cup was still going round. I sent you to listen. Tostig can guard me.'

'You do well to be careful. No one blamed you for not being in the hall tonight. It wasn't hard for the King to excuse you.'

'Not when he has Northumbrian envoys to entertain.'

'Edwin, the news is bad. This is the third delegation. Each time the price for your life gets bigger.'

'Redwald promised me sanctuary. He's an honourable man.'

'This time Aethelfrith's not just offering him enough gold to make a dragon's eyeballs burst. He's threatening war.'

I felt so weary of my life, it was an effort to argue. 'Redwald may not want to defend me, but he must fight Aethelfrith for East Anglia's honour.'

Lilla's hand found mine in the dark. 'If you prize honour, I don't want to tell you this. The word I hear from the king's counsellors is that he has been swayed. Whether by bribe or threat, it makes no difference. The result will be the same, for you. Redwald is either going to hand you over to Aethelfrith or have his men murder you here.'

I let out a sigh, almost of relief.

But Lilla was wanting something more from me.'Edwin! God knows we've run often enough from kingdom to kingdom. But you've got to do it. You can't stay here, even tonight. I've found out a man who really knows these fens. I trust him. The Northumbrians seized his sister in a border raid. He says he can get you away tonight, while there's moonlight. He'll hide you somewhere in the marshes where neither Redwald nor Aethelfrith will ever find you. I don't doubt Redwald will be mightily relieved if the assassins come for you and find you flown.'

I slumped down on the bed. I felt neither fear nor hope. My voice was dull.

'I've run enough. There's hardly a kingdom, British or English, I haven't been a beggar in. I've left a wife, a son and a child I've never seen, behind in Mercia. Do you want me to go on wandering to the world's end, or shiver my life out in these wet fens? I was born at a king's court in York. If I must die, then let it be here, in Redwald's palace.'

'Edwin! Redwald can't be trusted. Everybody knows that. A stronger mind can always influence him.'

'If Redwald is without honour, what's left? Some other treachery, a murderer's knife in the dark, on the run? I came to him openly and honourably for sanctuary. Sanctuary he has given me. My honour says I can't quit his court now without his leave.'

'He's going to break his promise and betray you.'

'And I am firm that I will stay.' The next words dropped from my lips, almost inaudible. 'I don't know that I deserve to live.'

Lilla hesitated, then rested his arm round my shoulders for a moment. After a while he said, 'I must go back and find what's been happening. Bar the door stoutly. Have your knife ready. Do everything you can. When they've all finished in the hall I'll join Tostig. We'll stand guard over you, tonight and every night.'

I could not help a bitter smile. 'If it comes, it will come. You can't always stand between me and death. Thank you, but if you love me, leave me alone now to the will of the gods.'

'Edwin!' I heard the pain in his voice, when he thought the darkness hid his face. 'At least ask Christ to have mercy on you.'

When he had gone, I did not bar the door after him. I stepped quietly outside into the deepening twilight. The singing in the hall had broken out at last, as though something had been decided and noise was needed to drown out thought. I sat down on a slab of stone under the eaves.

I found I was not as calm as I had pretended to Lilla. My body was tense. Anxiety churned up my imagination, wondering how the end would come. I tried to harden my thoughts with a warrior's willingness to meet the advancing weapon. Then panic pierced, and I was ready to jump up and run.

The drunken songs died. Women laughed their way warmly to bed. Men staggered past and did not notice me. I might as well not have been there, or already a ghost. There was still a light at one end of Redwald's hall. Four of my men came back, drunk. Lilla was not with them. I set Gyrth to relieve Tostig and sent the rest to bed.

I could no longer see where Gyrth stood sentry. The night was as dark as ever it would be now, and colder.

Slowly the ground brightened in front of me. A late moon was rising over the trees at my back. The hall stood out dark, save for that one glow, huger than before, and all the lanes between the lesser buildings grew brilliant. An unleashed dog came lurching round the corner and passed me by.

Wings shadowed the air in front of me and hardly stirred it. A hunting owl. When it had gone, there was still a thread of movement at the limit of my sight. Was it Gyrth patrolling? I stiffened, breath held, to identify it.

An icy dread crawled through me. This shape at last was human. Tall, cloaked and hooded. Frozen on my stone seat, I peered for some tell-tale sign by which I might recognize my doom. One of Redwald's East Anglians? Aethelfrith's man? Would he reveal himself before the death-blow struck?

My lips parted but I did not cry out. Yet he did not have the look of a warrior. His tunic, like his cloak, was long, of dark plain cloth.

A simple cloak could hide a dagger.

As in a dream, my hand moved towards the hilt of my own knife. But my fingers did not grip. The figure was closer now, calm, unhurried. There had been no warning challenge from Gyrth. It did not even occur to me that I could still cry out, leap up and run, that four of my bodyguard were in the lodge behind me.

The moon lit two points of light within the hood but showed me no known features. The voice, when it came, did not sound like an Englishman's.

'My son, why do you sit so sad and watchful on a cold stone, when everyone else is in bed and asleep?'

'What is it to you, whether I pass the night indoors or out?'

The voice took on the warmth of a smile. 'I am rebuked. It was a foolish question. All the palace knows why Edwin, Aelle's son, should be awake and troubled tonight. May I sit down?'

I shifted aside in silence. The stranger was taller than I was. Though the wool of his cloak did not touch me, I felt the warmth of the man's nearness. There was a clean smell about him, like a man who washed himself frequently, not the tang of sweat and horses.

'What would you give to someone who could deliver you from your troubles?'

I could not disguise my bitterness. 'You ask me for a reward? When all the world knows me for a runaway hounded from country to country? I have little enough gold to give away. But I'd promise whatever may one day be in my power to anyone who could save me from this.'

'Can I trust your promises?'

I started at that. The stranger might have a dagger under his cloak, but my own was out first. The voice sang smoothly on, his tongue making the English syllables flow more liquidly than we do ourselves.

'If I told you there was one who could not merely rescue you from death but restore your kingdom, overthrow your enemies, raise you to higher glory than any English king before you, what would you offer then?'

'The gratitude of a king, on a king's honour.'

'How stands your honour tonight, Edwin?'

My knife-hand stilled on the stone and my skin crept coldly. Not all my fear was for my mortal life.

That hooded face did not turn to me, nor the voice rise. Gentle but insistent, the questions probed. 'Suppose these things come true. Wouldn't you grant that whoever can save your life and your kingdom can do more still for you? Will you promise to obey his wisdom and follow him in everything?'

My answer came harshly. 'You seem very scornful of the worth of my vows. But yes, if I ever stand crowned as the king of Northumbria, I swear to put the rest of my life under the guidance of that man who helped me.'

The tall stranger rose and stooped over me. I found myself slipping down on to my knees. There was a moment's silence, then I felt his hand rest strongly on my head.

'When you feel this sign again, remember. You've given a king's oath. Honour it.'

When at last I raised my head, I was alone.

I knelt there for a long time in the moonlight, afraid to move, though it was not my life I feared for now. How was it possible for a single, weaponless human to offer me such hope?

Some yards away, Gyrth paced acrosss the track, black clarity against white. I heard him cough, plainly. Had it been just drunken stupor that made my bodyguard offer no challenge when a stranger spoke to me? Thoughtful, I resumed my seat. The stone felt warm.

Feet came pounding through the shadows. Cyrth cried out. I lifted my head but felt no terror.

Lilla burst into the moonlight in front of me. 'Edwin! Come to the hall! This calls for ale! Your changeable friend Redwald has changed his mind again. The Queen's been arguing with him half the night, the archangels bless her. She's a stronger sense of English honour than he has. She swears she'll never see her court shamed by betraying a guest for gold or buckling to a bully. Since Aethelfrith is threatening Redwald with war, he'll fight back. He'll do better than that! East Anglia's going to return the insult on Northumbria, march north with a warhost and win your kingdom back for you.'

The night was black and silver like a dream.

'Edwin! Why are you just sitting there staring? Aren't you going to cheer, man?'

I was on my feet then, but my legs seemed strangely nerveless. I staggered against Lilla for support.

An English queen, who feared nothing but Woden and dishonour? A foreign voice deep within a hood, and a hand in the dark, firm on my head? Which way should my heart go in gratitude?

I hugged Lilla. 'Get the rest up. What are we waiting for? Did you say there was still ale in the hall?'

Chapter Twelve

For the first time, I was riding to battle as a leader. Redwald was at my side. Behind us, eager as hounds loosed from their kennels, marched the warhost of East Anglia. Aethelfrith the Ferocious had loomed too large on their border. Now they were going to challenge him. Fear of his invincible reputation was heightening the excitement in every eye. We were bringing priests of Woden with us for protection, shamans of the war gods Thunor and Tiw. I looked sidelong at them, the robes of fur, even in late summer, hung about with the skulls of small predatory animals, the tattoos that made their faces dark as thunderclouds.

'Do you think Aethelfrith would dare slaughter Woden's holy men, the way he did the monks of Bangor?' The words were out before I thought how they might shame Redwald.

'He's not going to get the chance this time. These holy men know how to curse.' Redwald stared straight ahead where the track unrolled before us across the plain and the streams ran down out of the Pennines towards Deira. Every boast he made hammered home how deeply we all feared this adversary. 'Aethelfrith's stayed away too long harrying the Welsh. My scouts report he's let half his warhost go for harvest. He thinks he can't be beaten. That arrogance is going to be his undoing.'

I lifted my eyes to the land around us, that was neither Aethelfrith's nor Redwald's. The little cornfields showed like golden leaves scattered across green pasture. It was time to put the sickle in. Further south, we had left East Anglia's own fields, already white with stubble.

We crossed the Trent in a flurry of spray. The terror in the faces on the far bank told us the news would soon be flying west to the returning Aethelfrith.

'How does it feel, to be coming home at last, Edwin?' Lilla urged his horse up behind me.

I felt my eyes widen. 'Is this Deira? I thought we were still crossing Mercian territory.'

'If Aethelfrith is master here, you should be.'

I could not speak, just then. As my horse climbed the sandy bank on the far side, the shock of the soil went through his spine into mine. This was south of the Humber, but I would be a greater king than my father. I slipped down, fell on my knees, took up two great handfuls of grit and kissed it. Then I grinned shamefacedly at Lilla and the men watching me.

'I was born a prince of Deira. But I have yet to win my kingdom. If Aethelfrith stands between me and it, then I have one last river to cross before I can die where I belong.'

Redwald turned in the saddle. His bellow of laughter rang too loud. His red genial face hid his darker thoughts. 'This is no day to talk of dying. Look at it. We're on Aethelfrith's territory, and not a border patrol galloping to challenge us yet.'

For all that, he settled his helmet into place. His broad, smiling jowls were now shadowed under the iron casque. No jeweller's fancy work for the parade ground, this. The noseguard was pitted, the cheeks were fenced with metal, scrolled with bronze, His once-merry eyes were all but hidden within the dark slits. We both knew the fearsome boar that surmounted his crown was there to break the force of a descending axe as much as for royal show. Yet he was awesome. It sent a strange shudder through my heart to know I must look as terrifying. My armour set a shield between the men trusting me and my fear, my uncertainty, my terrible hope.

Every moment of that ride from then on was a gift to me. I had never felt so alive to terror and joy. The brakes of red-stemmed alders in the watery lowlands, the shout of heather on the moors, the half-reaped barley in the fields, from which the farming folk fled in horror at our approach.

No, not all. The second day a ragged band of infantry appeared, their spears and hayforks carried point downwards in sign of peace. We let them approach.

They threw themselves prostrate on the ground before me. It was not to Redwald of East Anglia they had come. Their leader was a grizzled veteran, who knew how to handle his weapon. Behind him were more greybeards, and younger men too, even rosy-checked lads with skin as smooth as girls'.

'Hail, Aelle's son. I fought for your father, twenty-eight years ago. Welcome home, my lord.'

Here, I was Edwin, son of Deira's old king. Edwin, the rightful heir. These were my father's people. They came with scores to settle, deaths to avenge, long years of injustice to overturn.

A rush of optimism swept me up. It could be done. We could defeat Aethelfrith. I could be king in my father's place, though every one of my brothers was dead.

As I rode on with head high, I found myself praying aloud. 'Please, please, Father. Make it come true.'

I felt fear then, hard as a stone in my chest. The words had escaped me spontaneously. Whom had I spoken them to? It was not the way of Woden's worship to talk to the All-Father so intimately. That needed ritual. Kings played their proper part in that drama. They did not invent the words. It was not a conversation.

It brought a piercing vision of a Welsh hillside, of a little woman in a muddy tunic who had talked like this, familiarly with her God. Nevyn had chatted with him, thanked him, pleaded with him, even argued with him when the news was hard to bear, as though she took him for her oldest friend. I felt a curious ache, as though of homesickness, for the island of Mon where I had been an exile.

'There!' cried Lilla exultantly, as we topped the rise above the River Idle. 'The old wolf's camp.'

'He's evidently heard we were coming.' Redwald's son, Raegenhere, sat up tall in the saddle, looking across the valley to the flicker of light on hundreds of armed men between the shelters of branches. His eyes, more grey than his father's, flashed eagerly out from his helmet. 'Each day that passes, he's going to snatch more of his warband back out of the fields. The quicker we strike, the better.'

'You shall lead the charge, then, lad.' King Redwald laughed with paternal pride. The sound rang hollowly between his cheek guards.

Our army came to a ragged halt, unable to stop its momentum until both sides were fully in view of each other. Aethelfrith had chosen his ground. They were fewer than they should have been, the Northumbrian warhost. But they greyed the hillside opposite, like the moving shadow of a storm.

There was the nerve-straining slowness of consultation among us, of Redwald's heralds despatched. We watched the tiny go-betweens threading the lower slopes, crossing the stream, escorted to Aethelfrith's camp. As long again to wait. Our shamans made an evil fire to choke the enemy's heart. They seized pigs from the nearest farm and poured out blood to Tiw. They hammered out thunder to Thunor on the stretched drumheads. The tassels of their fur cloaks whirled in spirals as they danced and shouted spells.

And now the slow return of our heralds, their figures magnified with each step, until at last they appeared as human faces grim with the inevitable answer.

'Aethelfrith will not grant one inch of Northumbrian soil to Edwin. His queen is Aelle's daughter. Her blood and the blood of her sons is truly royal. Aethelfrith claims the southern kingdom by right of marriage and he will prove it by spear and sword.'

'His own blood shall flow here. I shall not let it foul true Deiran soil.' I said it quietly. I looked at Redwald, and the older man nodded. He raised his hand. The horns brayed.

We were all committed so quickly. Raegenhere, Redwald's son, was already dismounted. He yelled as he shook his spear to the sky and charged. At once the hillside erupted with the war cries of East Anglia. Joined with them now was the full-blooded battle shout of Deira. I had never known that, save from the few voices of my bodyguard. It thrilled my heart to hear Wiglaf yell like this, and have his voice taken up by scores of my countrymen, storming forward all around me. The din drowned out the cries which must be ringing just as fervently from Aethelfrith's side.

Our armies closed and clashed. We few exiles had fought through so many other battles. Again, my friends were round me, hacking, spearing, slashing, yelling. But I knew they had never been so buoyed up with hope, never wielded their weapons with such energy, never felt this blaze of certainty sweeping us on. I, their rightful prince, was in the midst of them, fighting for my own land.

It could not last. As the day wore on, the euphoria ebbed to weariness. Now there was only the grim struggle to raise my weapon again and again, to kill another man, to stay alive.

We came on a pool of stillness, where the fighting had stopped. The grass was tangled with bodies. As the yells of battle shifted into the distance, it was the crows who screamed, hopping in flocks from corpse to corpse. Few men but the nobles had the protection of helmets over their fallen faces, and even helmets have eyeholes. The scavengers were going for the eyes first.

Lilla fought off a raven larger than the rest. The bird squawked and flapped reluctantly to land a little way off, still eyeing us. We found Aethelfrith sprawled on his back, with the men of his body-guard all dead around him. The helmet had slipped crooked over his face, but the wolf crest was unmistakable.

My men fell silent. We all felt that to say what we saw might shatter an illusion.

'Is it truly him?' I said, and my voice trembled. 'My sister's husband?'

Lilla had lost his spear. He leaned on his sword, panting. 'That's him. The Doom Wolf that terrorised half Britain. All that ambition, all that savagery – ravens' meat.'

'He died with his weapon in his hand. He must be in Valhalla now. Did anyone see the battle maidens of Woden swooping down to snatch him away and leave us his cold corpse?'

'I was too busy making sure it wasn't your corpse.'

Aethelfrith was terrible even in death. I drew the edge of his cloak across the bloodstained features. 'It's over.'

I straightened up. The massed hosts of East Anglia, the faithful remnant of Deira, were all halted on the battlefield, their faces turned to me, weapons lifted to the sky. A tremendous roar sent the echoes across the plain towards the distant Humber.

'Edwin, Aelle's son!' 'Long live the King!' 'Hail, Northumbria!'

Hundreds of spears clanged on their shields. This whole army was exulting, as though Woden himself had cast off his grey disguise and stood revealed before them. In the distance, Aethelfrith's most loyal Bernicians were fleeing north. But scores of his beaten Northumbrians were coming to throw down their weapons at my feet.

I was their king.

In front of me, the stone walls of York gleamed like pale gold. Somewhere, as in a dream, the crowd was roaring. I was aware of the close press of bodies jostling to greet my procession, the jolting of my horse on the cobbled road.

I was coming home.

A king has many homes. His court moves around his palaces and the manors of his thanes, blessing the whole country with his presence and sharing the burden of his keep. But in my dreams of a childhood that was snatched from me it was only York that stood up clear, out of the mists of forgetfulness. I had been too young even to name this place which I could picture. I had needed Wiglaf and Lilla to tell me it was York. Now I recognized the reality. My city of golden walls.

Wiglaf had not lived to see it again. Death had claimed the commander of my bodyguard, only hours after the battle that opened the way here.

There had been another loss. Raegenhere, Redwald's son, fallen honourably at the spearhead of our first assault. They would bury him in a long barrow, like a ship, with treasure heaped around him.

Yet today Redwald's red countenance was beaming bravely at my side. 'Are you well satisfied with what East Anglia has done for you? Can I go home and assure Witburg we've hammered out a lifelong alliance on the helmets of those dead Bernicians?'

I grinned too. This was not the day to parade our grief. Just for the moment, I felt like a boy again. 'The Bernician people are mine now too, remember. It's not just Deira you've given me back. You've delivered me a kingdom greater than my father ever had. All Northumbria!'

His eyes narrowed a little. We both had our helmets off, riding into York in peace. 'You'll rule beyond the Giants' Wall, all the way to the land of the Picts, who paint themselves blue for battle.'

'And the land of two-headed dogs and women who walk backwards with their heads tucked under their arms, for all I know,' I laughed.

'You'll need a sizeable army to keep such a kingdom safe, once we're gone.'

'I seem to have the makings of one.'

Every day, more of Aethelfrith's troops were returning to vow their loyalty to me. Lining the roadside, here in the heart of Deira, old warriors who had served under my father were waving their caps and sticks in the air, cheering his only surviving son. People who had never met me were shouting that they were willing to follow me, lay down their lives for me, just for my name and genealogy, and victory on the River Idle. I was their king, descended from Woden. I was the sacred guardian of their land.

I held my head up higher. Northumbria was not merely

Redwald's gift to me. This time I had led my own warband, smaller than Redwald's by far, but all loyal Deiran men, not East Anglians. This victory was mine as well as his.

The gates of York were open. I was riding through.

Hooves clattered on uneven paving blocks. Inside the walls, this city was not all stone. Close to, I could see more greenery around me than yellow masonry. Weeds grew through the old streets. Tiled floors were smothered by fireweed. The brick halls the Romans had built in ancient days were tumbling, felled by the push of trees shouldering up through their foundations towards the light. Their pride collapsed like the statues, as beams rotted and mortar flaked and ivy thrust its roots into every crevice.

'Your York looks more like a forest. Why do you want to make your capital here? Better to clear a space in the greenwood, good English fashion. Build yourself new timbered halls, fresh thatch. Or are you dreaming of making this another Canterbury, and you as great an English king as Aethelbert of Kent used to be?'

'It's you the kings hail as Bretwalda now.' I stole a sideways glance at him. Redwald was my friend, my ally. He was called Chief of Britain, as Aethelbert had been. I must not damage his honour. 'Was Canterbury a city like this, then?'

'The same stone walls. Old ruins from the giants' time.'

'Rome?'

'Aethelbert even had men from Rome there. They'd rebuilt some temples.'

Queen Bertha's Christian churches. We were on dangerous ground.

I was silenced. A frightening thought was pulsing in my chest. If such men had once built this city of York, then, like Canterbury, it could happen again here.

We were almost at the top of the street. The hall in front of me was magnificently English. Warm wood, not stone. Planked timbers made a rib cage for it, rich with life. The thick fur of thatch had mellowed, softly dark with recent rain. A riot of serpents, wolves, tendrils, fruit, studded the doorposts and the eaves with vibrant colour.

I held my breath, uncertain. Was this the same palace in which I had played as a boy? Was this the hall where my father had sat in his carved high seat giving out justice? Were those the queen's rooms, where I had sat held to my mother's breast, my face pressed against her flesh-scented tunic? Surely there should be something in these gaudy carvings I should remember? Could I have forgotten the long red tongue of that horned snake? The rough-worked fur of that bear with the small black eyes? I was not sure. Carvings like these were common to many halls. I had been very young.

There was a mass of people, smiles of welcome snatching for my attention, bodies shouldering forward to assert priority. A surf of more subdued colour washed around the platform in front of the main door. Servants' faces strained for a closer look at their new master. They were cheering a greeting to me. Was their warmth genuine, or merely prudent?

Last week, they had been the servants of Aethelfrith and his queen, my sister.

Where were Acha and all her children now?

At the head of the steps were those wearing the finest clothes. Noblemen too old or infirm to go to war. Women decked in their newest cloth and brightest jewelry. And one strange figure who needed no explanation. The feathered cloak trailing from his shoulders, the marks darkly tattooed on his face, most of all, the frenzied passion in his eyes, spoke what he was. I expected the others to bow before me. I had defeated Aethelfrith. I was their warleader, their king, now. But I was startled by the awe with which the priest of Woden flung himself on his face at my feet. Then he raised his arms high.

'Hail, Edwin, Aelle's son, descended from Woden! In the name of the gods your fathers honoured, hail! King of Deira, beloved of Lady Frigg and life-giving Thunor and death-dealing Tiw, hail!

Lord of the Bernicians, mighty wolf of battle, hail! Hail, King of all
the Northumbrians!'

He smelt powerfully, like the cave where a wild animal sleeps.
His voice was deep, harsh. The words rang from the walls, over the
heads of the suddenly silenced crowd. Only I and Redwald were
standing now. And even I was not sure whether I should have
bowed my knees at those names.

There was liquid from his rattle spattering my face, my hands. I
fought off the urge to dash it away. I did not want to think what
coloured it so darkly.

I must be the one to act. I nerved myself to take his hand and
raised him up. The priest's face was hollowed over long bones. His
nose jutted. The eyes were deep set. He looked, though his skull
was uncovered, like a man in a battle helmet, save that this shape
was bone, these cheeks stretched skin, the eyes guarded only by his
sharp brows.

'You must be the chief priest of Woden.'

'You don't recognize me? I offered you to the All-Wise Father
when you were born. Coifi, guardian of the English folk's gods,
and of the gods' king, at the great temple of Goodmanham.'

The name shook something in me. My guts turned, with a small
boy's terror. All these years, I had hardly heard or remembered that
name. Yet now, spoken from this man's lips, it brought a dark wave
of nightmare rearing to overwhelm me with memory.

'Your gods know this land was always mine. I come in peace.'

'The gods of war welcome the one who has given them drink.'
Blood sprinkled me.

'The gods of life welcome the one who makes life for them.'
Scented herbs fluttered around me.

'The gods of death demand obedience.' Ashes were smeared on
my forehead.

I must keep my nerve.

'I shall honour those who have given me victory.'

'Then a blessing on the King's house and the King's bed and

the King's fields. Edwin of Northumbria, in the name of Northumbria's gods, do not betray this land.'

Coifi was standing back. I had passed this first test. The palace door was open. Blue smoke clouded the shadows of its great hall. No torches were lit, mid-afternoon. I crossed the threshold. The daylight quickly faded behind me. My boots thudded on the boards through the whisper of rushes. The chair stood high on its dais, beyond the smoking hearth. Its carved back rose tall enough to dwarf me. I knew there was a crowd of people following me, but I walked forward alone.

A second chair, slightly lower, stood beside the king's. I must send to Mercia for my queen.

There were four steps.

Before I sat on that throne, I reached out my hand to its carving. Was this really the seat from which my father had ruled? Or was it some newer thing of Aethelfrith's? Giddy with the thought that this might be all a vision, nothing substantial, I gripped the hard edges of the raven-carved arms. The oak was solid, the shapes sharp under my curving palms. I drew a deep breath of realization, turned and sat.

The yell rocked the pillars that held up the roof.

The scene before me swam with coloured shadows, then steadied. The hall was full of my Northumbrian people, women and men. Smiles stretched, expectant, faces lifted, lighting the gloom with fair English heads. I drew a breath deeper still. My own voice rang in a triumphant shout.

'Welcome, people of Deira! Welcome, people of Bernicia! Welcome, all Northumbria! I, Edwin, son of the sons of Woden, swear my life before you, to be your just true king.'

A roar of assent greeted my oath. Even Coifi was grinning like a fox. There must be ceremonies at Goodmanham more awful than this to affirm these vows. I pushed that thought behind me.

They were coming forward to swear to me now, all those that had not surrendered their swords on the battlefield. In a little while, reality faded away into the rituals of kingship. I was like a god in my own temple, receiving sacrifice. All my boyhood, Wiglaf and Lilla and the rest had taught me the manners of an English chieftain, even when I was playing in the heather on Welsh Mon. I acted the part easily now, like the plays the mummers perform at Yule, remembered from one year's end to the next.

At last the long ceremonial of acclaim was over. The throng ebbed out of the hall. The shadows returned, deeper now. Servants – my servants now – piled logs on the embers of my hearth, began to fire the torches round my walls. Still I sat on, as though to leave this chair might be to step outside the spell and see my kingship vanish.

Chapter Thirteen

I trod soft-footed through the queen's chambers. My mother's rooms. She must have embroidered some of these hangings with her own hands. I felt my eyes stretch wide with wonder.

'Acha. My own sister! She slept here as Aethelfrith's queen. Did she never accuse him for what he did to Father? To me?'

'Acha was as much a victim as you were.' Redwald comforted me with his big hand on my shoulder. 'That pillow will have been wet with tears for both of you. Would you wish any woman Aethelfrith the Ferocious for a bedfellow? He married her to get Deira. She had no choice.'

Lilla came across the floor from the hearth. He held out a small wooden thing, half-hidden in the grip of his fingers.

'See this? Not all the wounds were on the battlefield.'

I bent to peer at it. A little head, crudely carved. Two pricked ears, one snapped short. Lilla unfolded his hand, so that the toy horse lay across his palm. One leg had been freshly broken.

A rush of tears filled my eyes. I groped blindly for the horse.

'After all these years? Here? I wept for that toy more than for my father. I was playing with it in Catterick, the day we heard Aethelfrith had killed him. I never imagined I'd. . . .'

'Aethelfrith had sons,' said Lilla. 'Seven by your sister, and a daughter Aebbe. They were too young to fight. They say there was an older half-brother Eanfrith. He took a wound at the Idle, but got away.'

I stroked the horse, my eyes downcast. 'Where are they now?'

'Running north. Don't worry. I'm sending off men on fast horses this very hour.'

'To bring them back?'

'Aethelfrith's sons? What do you think?'

He saw the look of horror on my face.

'Kill them? Is that what you're saying I must do?'

'Edwin, any live son of Aethelfrith is a danger to you.'

'Hound those children to death?'

'As their father hounded you. Half my life I've stood between you and murder.'

I twisted the broken horse between my fingers. I was learning how to be a king.

'If they catch my nephews still in Northumbria, let them do what they must. But tell them they are not to cross the border. I'm not strong enough yet to do battle with the Scots.'

I fondled the damaged ear of the wooden horse, its splintered leg. I showed it to Redwald. 'I have two sons of my own. When they come from Mercia, this is going to be my first present to them.'

'Sons are a joy and a grief.'

I looked up swiftly at the break in his voice. His round red cheeks could not help but look merry whatever his mood. They were glistening now with tears. I clasped his arms to beg his forgiveness.

'How can the house of Deira thank you enough? You've given it back to me, and more as well. And it's cost you your own son.'

'It was the Sky-Father's will to take him from the battlefield. Isn't that what the shamans would have us believe? At least I won't be the one now who has to break the news to his mother. Oh, you needn't be tactful, lad. I know what you're thinking. Every warrior in my army will be saying the same. Witburg will bear it more bravely than I do. Better her firstborn dead on the battlefield and the skalds praising his deeds in song, than to have him run for his life, like Aethelfrith's eldest.'

'I ran from Catterick.'

'You couldn't hold a sword then. And you've won it back gloriously.'

'You've done Northumbria a great favour. We shall be your loyal ally.'

'And redeemed my shaky honour?' He grinned lopsidedly, wiping the tears away.

'All Britain honours you. Give Witburg my thanks. Tell her I won't forget what she did for me, and what it's cost you both.'

Redwald took the broken toy I had forgotten I was still holding. I saw his full lips tremble. He would be remembering Raegenhere as a boy. He handed it back to me.

'Yes, keep it. Give it to Northumbria's rightful heir.'

'I still can't believe I'm a father, a husband, a king. All my life I've been running like a hunted deer, or hiding, afraid every moment of a knife or poison. My bodyguard have been all my family.'

'Didn't you grow up with Cadwallon of Mon?'

'Cadwallon? He despised me.'

'And now you're both kings. Will you be a better friend to Gwynedd than Aethelfrith was? Or do you mean to conquer the British too?'

Conquer Cadwallon? I hesitated before the enormity of the thought.

'I haven't had time to plan. There are going to be so many things to decide on my own.'

Redwald laughed genuinely then. 'Oh, kings are never alone! You'll soon learn that. They'll all bow themselves double before you and tell you you're all-powerful. But they'll still want their own way. You'll have the wise men of your Witan, each with an eye on his own manor. The priests will advise you what the gods want, which means what they want. And when you think you've shut the door on them, you'll come home to your queen. Is she a strong lady, your Coenburg?'

'I found her strong enough, but not as forceful as some.'

We shared a smile of complicity, like guilty boys.

'Shall I stay and see you crowned king at Goodmanham, with the proper ceremonies?'

I hugged him. 'My father's crown! I was brought so low, I hardly hoped to see that day.'

'You're a greater king already than your father. I'm relying on a powerful ally.'

He clasped my shoulders. Our thanes stood back respectfully. But now there was a disturbance. Lilla came almost running back through the ranks. He knelt, out of breath, before me, eager to serve.

'My lord. The men are leaving. I've put Tostig in charge. If Aethelfrith's brats are anywhere in Northumbria, they'll ride them down and finish them off for you. You can sleep safe.'

His brown eyes were bright. He was so eager to guard me, like a faithful hound.

I put my hand down on his shoulder. This was the friend who had protected my life for so many years, when I had nothing to reward him with but gratitude. I tried to shut out the picture of my sister's children.

'Lilla, Byrtferth's son, by my first gift as king, I appoint you Thane of Derwent and counsellor in my Witan.'

His soldier's face coloured dark under the tan and stubble. He must have expected this reward, surely? But his eyes swam with devotion, as though this was a gift more than he deserved. I felt smaller in the face of his selfless loyalty.

As I raised him to his feet, the queen's rooms thundered with male shouts. Comrades were crowding round to clap him on the back, exchange jests at his new nobility. Probably they were jostling for a little of his luck to advance their own fortunes.

Slowly I became aware of a patient stillness on the far side of the room. Through the hugging, laughing ring of warriors I saw a woman standing in the doorway with two small girls. Her dress was plain, her hair close-veiled. But she stood straight, and her face was not old, though there were lines furrowed between her brows. When the hubbub subsided and she saw she had claimed our attention, she made a reverence, more to me than to Redwald.

'My lords.'

'The lady Breguswith,' a steward announced, a little late.

There was a moment's blankness in my mind. Then knowledge lit my face into a huge smile. I almost ran towards her, my hands held out.

'By all the gods, Hereric's wife!'

'His widow, my lord.'

Her look was very straight. My hands halted one moment before they seized hers. Hereric, my eldest brother's son, older than me. The only other male of my father's line to escape. Aethelfrith had found him out, in the British kingdom of Elmet. Hereric had died of poison. I had survived.

'I heard that news. I've grieved for you.'

'When I heard the beast was dead, I set out from Leeds as fast as I could. I wanted to pledge my loyalty to the king who avenged his kinsman.'

'Frigg knows, I've little enough family for a king. Welcome to your home, Breguswith, that was once Hereric's.' I looked around for someone to address my orders to. I was still unused to the authority of a ruler. I must learn to command thousands, as Cadfan and Redwald did. 'This lady and her children shall be housed at my court as long as they choose. We've both been exiles long enough.'

There was another cheer at this. I bent my head to the two small girls. The elder stood beside her mother, straight and fair. She looked at me with grave, intelligent eyes, that had the grey in them of our English sea.

'My daughter, Hereswith.' Breguswith laid a hand on her tall six-year-old's head, with justified pride. The girl had dignity and grace.

The little sister was a toddler, chubby, square-chinned. She would never have the beauty that Hereswith promised. Where the taller one's braids hung shining like white gold, her mouse-coloured plaits stuck out from her neck, short and spiky. She was not the slightest in awe of the King of all Northumbria.

'I'm Hild,' she announced to me, not waiting for an introduction. 'It means "Battle". I'm very fierce.' And she roared like a bear cub.

There was a shout of laughter from my men. I scooped up this new-found great-niece in one arm, chuckling. 'You've come too late, Hild. The battle's won.'

My merriment was met with a belligerent scowl. I freed one hand to show her the toy I was still holding. 'Do you like horses? This used to be mine when I was a boy. You can play with it, until my sons arrive.'

Hild grabbed the carved animal and wriggled so that I had to set her down. She set the three-legged horse on the floor and examined its wounds. 'Poor horsey. Was it hurt in the fight? Can you make it better?'

Breguswith's eyes met mine over the children's heads. 'Thank you, Edwin. I and my daughters will be proud to call your court our home.'

I was the King. I was mending my broken family. One line, at least.

Tostig's band came back empty-handed from their pursuit. Acha and her small children had escaped over the border, with Aethelfrith's eldest son.

Weeks later, Lilla brought more news to me.

'We know where they are now.' His stiff face suppressed all emotion. 'The Christian Scots have given them sanctuary. Aethelfrith's boys are with the monks on the island of Iona.'

I had my own woman again.

It was no use to remember my Welsh Mairi, running with her sisters and brothers on the seashore of Ynys Mon, the lightness of her feet, the toss of her ringlets. Coenburg was a big-boned wholesome English queen. She knew what her duty was. I felt the strength of her through the fine woollen sleeves when I took hold of her arms. I strained her body to mine, and began to possess it. At first she laughed, then grew still, resigned, under me. I did not need the warmth of her heart. I had been alone too long with fighting men like Lilla, whose love was dearer to my soul than any wife. But this queen knew she was my brood mare. She was better than a slave-woman, whose brat, if she bore me one, would not be a prince.

Coenburg had brought me two princes from Mercia. Osfrith stared at me with troubled eyes, as if I was a stranger. Little Eadfrith looked at us all alike with the incuriosity of a chubby baby.

Coenburg was stirring in my arms. Her voice recalled me to duty. 'Isn't it time to take Eadfrith to the temple? You're the King. You have to dedicate your son to his ancestor Woden.'

I had no choice. I had toughened my soul as I had armoured my heart. I was an English king now, leading an English warhost. I took my son to Goodmanham to satisfy our English gods.

The drums quivered in my blood even before we came in sight of that high stockade. Banners tufted with feathers flew from the prow of the roof ridge. Smoke was already making a mystery in the air. The fear I always felt was tinged with a dangerous excitement. There was power here. A warrior king needs all the power he can get, for himself, for his sons.

I wore my parade armour, burnished rings and plates scrolled with gold. The bear-crested helmet was on my head. I had the standards of Deira and Bernicia, of the one Northumbria, carried before me.

Behind me walked Coenburg, carrying the jewelled basket in which she had laid the baby, like a young animal being brought to sacrifice.

Coifi was waiting for us. I saw the hungry gleam in his eyes, like a crouching polecat. He needed me. His own honour lay in the honour I gave his gods. If I should fail in the duty of an English king, Coifi would be struck down with me. The gods would desert us both. He knelt before me.

Why did I remember that little woman Nevyn, scolding kings in the name of her God?

The weight of English destiny, and the mass of Northumbrians at my back, carried me forward through the open gate, to the temple steps. I carried my head high. I had to look as though I led this folk. But they were pushing me on. What I believed had nothing to do with it. A king is not free. I and Northumbria were one. Its life depended on my manhood. I was its ruler, descended from its gods. I was its slave.

There was a thrill through my body, entering the dark temple. I smelt blood, fire. The burning aromatics dizzied my senses. Names welcomed me, beating through the pulse of the drums. '*Woden.*' '*Thunor.*' '*Tiw.*' '*Frigg.*' Behind the ranks of Coifi's priests were other women, hair braided with corn, faces smeared with earth, their dress darker. They smiled at me less openly. Their voices were a low thunder, like the tug of the undercurrent on shingle, '*Mother Erce.*' '*Mother Erce.*' '*Mother Erce.*'

I surrendered myself to their power. My breathing was not my own, ruled by rhythm of the drums. My blood was rising. I held my baby son. The knife was put in my hand. I was possessed.

I made the cut. I saw the pulse spurt life-blood. Coifi's dark-veined hands were holding the bowl that caught it. The smell of his unguent was rank in my nostrils.

Eadfrith began to cry.

The sound brought me back to my senses. I knew that, if the gods had ordered it, I would have killed my son. My will was not my own. In this sanctuary, as long as the drums beat, I would have done whatever they and my country demanded of me.

It was only a black kid I had killed. Its blood was coating my hands. The flayed skin was off now, wrapped over the rich dress of my child. His little face was smeared with its blood. He would be safe now. He was Woden's heir.

I had been carried into this temple and dedicated to Woden. So had my father. It had not saved him. He had not died honourably on the battlefield. Would I?

The chanting had stopped. I was shaking.

Afterwards, walking home beside the Derwent where no one could overhear us, I asked Lilla, 'Can any gods really protect us?'

He stared ahead. 'There's one who would walk alongside us and carry our cross.'

The regret in his voice made me look at him sharply. He would not meet my eye. It made me angry.

'Are you still harking back to the past? Well, think about Cadwallon, then! Won't he carry his son into a Christian church and pray to God the Father for the same help as I've asked Woden? Would you back him on the battlefield against me?'

Lilla spun round on me with a fury I had never before seen in his face.

'Edwin! When have I ever been disloyal to you? But you don't know what it's costing me.' Then his scowl softened, and he was looking at me as he did when I was a boy. 'Did you hear old Cadfan's dead? Cadwallon's King of Gwynedd now. He's sworn he'll take revenge on Northumbria for the slaughter at Chester.'

PART TWO

Chapter Fourteen

I marched on Gwynedd.

I had to do it. I had to stop Cadwallon.

I was Bretwalda now. Redwald of East Anglia was dead. All the English kings hailed me leader. Edwin, Chief of Britain. I rode with the winged globe carried before me. It went in front of me wherever I walked.

I could mass my own great warhost now. Their spears glittered behind me under the slatey Welsh sky. We crossed the Dee, where Aethelfrith once slaughtered the Britons. Now it was my turn. Cadwallon came to meet me. I threw my troops into the battle against Gwynedd. Cadwallon ran.

How could I stop then, with a victorious army behind me? I went after him.

We Northumbrians stood on the shore of the Menai Strait, facing Mon. There was a lump in my throat which I could not swallow, like unchewed meat. Surely this could not be real? It must be a fairy island hung across the narrow grey water, conjured up out of an enchanted sea to delude me. I could not have galloped on those smudged blue hills after Cadwallon. I could not have played with Cadfan's daughters on those sands. I must stop my ears against the sound of bells and singing which could not, must not, be carried to me on the breeze.

Rhun the priest had told me that when the Roman legions invaded, the British druids made their last stand on Ynys Mon.

Here was their most sacred stronghold. The legionaries had halted in fear and trembling. Across the water, priests in white robes cursed them. Black-clothed women danced and shrieked. When the soldiers summoned up courage to cross, they had to fight their way forward through spells and suicidal frenzy. Screaming druids ran through their ranks with blazing torches. Women tore at their own breasts. Those holy Britons died in hundreds on Roman swords.

The whole island shimmered in the unsteady air. Chants beat in my ears. The women danced.

Was Nevyn over there on the beach, cursing me? Was Queen Rorei tearing the black dress from her breast? I must not think of Mairi.

I heard my own voice give the order. We crossed. It was Welsh warriors who met us.

There are rarely more than a few hundreds in a battle. I knew the names of dead warriors I stumbled over. Sometimes I recognized the face of the man I was killing.

We harried Cadwallon's fleeing remnant across the island, through the low scrub of gorse and alder, past the sandy shore. He was running east.

I had him trapped on the last beach with his back to the sea. The exultation rose in my throat. There were only a few of the Welshmen, dismounted now. Cadwallon always looks less terrifying, separated from his horse. I picked him out easily, though he was not the tallest of men, the same arrogant head, the jut of his hips.

I have known this same terror, this same blazing hope of victory, cornering a wounded savage boar.

This was my time at last.

I wanted to speak the challenge myself, but I could not trust my voice. I made Lilla demand it in my name.

'Edwin of Northumbria, Bretwalda of all the kings in Britain, calls upon Cadwallon of Gwynedd to surrender his weapon. He may keep his life if he kneels at Edwin's feet and offers him homage. The Britons must acknowledge English sovereignty over them. Gwynedd will pay the tribute demanded to Northumbria. Cadwallon shall hand over his son to be raised as a hostage at Edwin's court.'

Now, now, I should be revenged. Now, justice would be done. I would make Cadwallon squirm as I had. I was Edwin, the King.

The little island of Glannauc shimmered behind the Welshmen. As the sun slipped clear of the cloud their limbs became skeletons, black against the golden air. I heard a shout on the wind, but it made no sense to me, as though the British tongue had been washed from my memory. Only the growl of the men around me told they understood it was defiance.

Then the growl turned to alarm. My troops were running forward, boots stumbling on the uncertain beach. The sea danced behind Cadwallon's men. I stood like one spell-struck. Then suddenly, with terrible clarity, I saw what was happening. The curragh came swooping in, oars flashing, green water swirling along her leather flanks. Spray shone like laughing teeth. The boat grounded. Cadwallon was already splashing out to board her. The air was thick with English curses as my soldiers rushed to close with the Welsh rearguard.

There came an inhuman scream. Then another. My men were breaking and running. Behind them, demented furies came pounding. Cadwallon's riderless horses, goaded into frenzy, were bearing down upon us. I saw yellow teeth bared, eyes rolling, their slashing hooves more relentless than any steel. There were human screams now. Blood spurted from men trampled to the ground before my eyes.

I stood my ground and killed the horse that came for me. I slashed its throat. As I watched it slump to the stones, I hoped it was Cadwallon's.

It did not take long. The horses were wild with terror, not with anger. When they had all died or bolted, we English were left alone on the beach in the sharp wind. There were no men left alive between us and the water's edge. The Welsh boat was a black speck, blown towards Glannauc like a cinder from a bonfire.

'Where are the nearest boats?' I raged at Lilla. 'Get after him.'

I stared wildly at the cliffs beyond him. I swung north and south. Cadwallon had lured me out to the last headland, far past habitation. I could only grind my boot against the stones.

He would not escape me. With all the speed I could, I raised a fleet of fishing boats along the coast. I set a ring of them around Glannauc. My heart hammered hard with the fear that he might already have slipped through my net. I had to see him kneel to me. Cadwallon must acknowledge me the victor with his own lips.

They told me warriors had been spotted on the cliffs. I gave orders to maintain the siege. We held him prisoner on that island for a month.

It was time to close the net.

My ship launched out into the great sweep of the Irish Sea. It was a laughing day on the water. The spume caught the sun in jewelled fans. I scooped up cold handfuls and tossed it to the sky.

The voyage was longer than I had calculated. Nothing to break the rolling lines of waves. We were in the middle of a vast plain. Somewhere beneath us there might be enchanted cities, drowned mountain ranges, the realms of merfolk. The wind blew colder.

Slowly, painfully, we closed on Glannauc.

He did not meet us on the beach. He knew he was beaten. He had less than twenty men now. I had brought scores.

For days, we stalked him over the cliffs, searched every damp cave, crouched under boulders in the heather listening for betraying sounds of flight. The bright air grew dark with the smoke of burning cottages where my men could get no news.

We came upon him suddenly, by a hovel under the lee of a hilltop, like the one where Nevyn had her hermitage. It was a holy man's this time. He had the same grubby white tunic. The same fanatical independence in his eyes. He held out a cross at us, as if it could bar the way to Edwin of Northumbria.

'Get back, sinner, in the holy name of Father, Saviour, Spirit. Cadwallon has sanctuary here. Do not take one step further on to this holy ground.'

He was a short man, with a bald freckled head. His waist was fatter than you might have expected from a diet of herbs and eggs. He seemed very sure of his authority.

As we closed in, Cadwallon leaped up on to the hillock above the hermit, looking taller himself now by comparison. There was only the sheer cliff behind him, but he was laughing. He had little to mock me for now. I had slaughtered the best of his warriors. I had conquered his kingdom. I had him caught at the ocean's edge. Only the past of our boyhood reared up between us to make me feel smaller.

And the memory of the day of my baptism.

I started forward. A bitter cry was torn from my lips. I do not know what words I shouted, or in what language.

The hermit swung his cross at me, two-handed. I saw dark wood against the brilliant sky, descending.

I do not remember what followed. I have a last vision of Cadwallon's face beyond that cross, black moustache lifting, mouth opening in astonished horror.

When I came to, the hermit had been executed horridly. There was little of his white wool tunic that was not steeped in red.

Cadwallon had vanished.

'He just ... went over the cliff,' Lilla protested. 'For that first moment, we only had eyes for you. And when we ran to catch him, there was no path down, no body on the rocks below. There's no beach under there, only wicked water.'

I walked past him. I was trembling with anger. The drop dizzied me. Lilla caught my arm.

The water was black in the shadow of the cliff, far beneath. The waves came sucking in, as if unwillingly. I heard them crash in the hollow of the cove, out of my sight. They swilled back out in a baffled tangle of seaweed and brown foam.

We stayed and searched the small island. We did not find Cadwallon's body.

But I was the victor. The greater island of Ynys Mon was in my hands now, not his.

Wipe out that memory of exile, of humiliation. When I sailed across the Menai Strait I left it with an English name. Anglesey.

Chapter Fifteen

She must be coming. There is a shout from my people far down the street of York, by the city gate. I can feel my tension mounting. A few more moments and I shall see her. What will she be like?

There's excitement on the palace steps too. On either side of me, Osfrith and Eadfrith are fidgeting in their wedding finery. I steal a glance at my sons. New tunics of blue and red, short mantles stiff with gold and silver embroidery, all hung about with glittering arm-rings and neck chains, like little warriors. They should be smart enough to impress Kentish folk, shouldn't they? In a few more years, these lads will really be warriors. Osfrith's frowning, trying to look like one already. I have a feeling young Eadfrith's holding back the tears. That's not good, for a Northumbrian warlord's son. He may need a strapping.

A king must marry again. It's a waste of a marriage bed to leave it empty when it could give me entry into an another man's kingdom. Since Coenburg died, Breguswith's been mother to my two lads as well as her daughters, Hereswith and Hild. But it needs more than that. A queen's a valuable piece on the board.

Aethelbert of Kent's daughter. That's a big step up. I was a prince on the run when I took my first bride in Mercia. I've come a mighty long way since then. Edwin of Northumbria. Mercia's never been big in English history. Not like Kent.

But Aethelbert of Kent is dead, and Redwald of East Anglia. I'm the one who is Bretwalda, Chief of the English kings, now.

127

How will I look to her? My own gown should be grand enough, embroidered blue, furred with ermine. Why does my face feel stiff as a dried fox-mask on a pelt?

The roar is growing louder, like the surge of waves over shingle. There they are. There's a shock as the bridal procession comes into view under the weed-grown arch of stone. What am I afraid of?

I have to keep the dignity of a king. The clatter of hooves is ringing sharp on the old paving stones of York. The street is full of the ranks of her own retinue and the escort of Northumbrian thanes I sent to fetch her, but beyond I begin to glimpse the swaying frame of a horse litter. It must have been a long bruising journey from Canterbury.

I'm not a green boy. I don't expect much in the way of romance. Still, I shall have to bed this woman. I feel expectation tightening my throat.

The curtained litter is approaching the steps. The horses halt. I must move down these steps and do my duty.

There's a sudden flutter of panic below, like butterflies disturbed in a summer meadow. The noblewomen of York are flanking the steps. Breguswith has made sure they're all crowned with flowers. There's Hereswith, with a wreath of honeysuckle set gracefully on her ash-blonde hair. But the commotion is little Hild, pushing her way out in front of the taller ones. Look at her. The imp's made herself a brilliant crown: poppies, cornflowers, buttercups. But it's slipping off at a tipsy angle, only hanging on to her hair by the spines of hawthorn she's woven dangerously into it.

The litter is waiting, the ranks of Kentish men drawn up on either side. A little movement snatches at my attention and wipes all other thoughts from my mind. From inside, fingers are parting the curtains. The leather is swinging open. A long white arm reaches out.

Sunshine is dazzling me. In that shadow I can't see my bride.

I have her hand in mine. It is cool, steady.

I must help her descend. Her head is bent over. I still can't see her face.

But I hear her voice. The first sound from Aethelberg is a little gasp as her neat shoe touches Northumbrian ground and she straightens her legs. Then a bubble of laughter as she almost falls against me on unsteady feet. I've caught her, a slighter body than Coenburg's.

I feel the shock, like a thunderflash. I have got a better bargain from Kent than I ever expected.

She is young, quite tall. Her hair is a deeper gold than Hereswith's, warmer than Hild's mouse-locks, the colour of beech leaves turning. It is escaping around her rosy face from under her veil, in waving wisps. She raises merry blue eyes to mine.

I had not expected to fall in love for the first time since I left Wales.

She is a princess. She knows the formalities. She bows her head to me, attempting another, steadier curtsey.

But I am the King. I can seize what I want. I catch her up in both my arms and plant a kiss on those lips. Behind me, my whole court is cheering. Aethelberg is rosier when I let her go.

Something bumps into my legs, like a badly-trained puppy.

I look down and find Hild. She couldn't be patient, lined up with all the waiting women who used to serve Coenburg. She's come tumbling out from between them, tripped down the steps and fallen on her knees at Aethelberg's feet. The lopsided coronet of flowers has parted its last thorn from her plaits and dropped on the cobbles. Our belligerent Hild is reddening with shame.

But now there's a peal of merriment, like a thrush's song. Aethelberg has slipped her arm from my grasp and is bending to help Hild scoop her flowers up. She's smiling directly at the little girl. And I can see the spell working that already has me by the heart.

'This is a pretty homage,' she laughs. 'The fine ladies of Northumbria lay their crowns at my feet to honour their new queen. I thank you, lady. What is is your name?'

'Hild,' my great-niece gulps.

'Lady Hild, I shall need more women to help me here. Will you be the first of my Northumbrian ladies-in-waiting?'

Hild gazes up at her in rapture. I can see she is going to be Aethelberg's adoring slave from this moment.

My bride links Hild's fingers in hers to help her up.

'My friends call me Tata.' And she lifts the warmth of her smile to include me in this invitation.

My body melts and then hardens agonizingly. I start to lead her up the steps.

I sense an alteration in the atmosphere, as if clouds have moved up to dim the sunshine. I'm startled to realize that not everyone in my court is so enchanted by this vision from Kent.

My Northumbrian warriors ought not to feel intimidated by anyone. We are the conquerors. The Scots, the Picts, the Welsh pay tribute out of fear of us. The other English kingdoms respect us. Yet I can see my men drawing themselves up taller, stiffening their moustached faces, strutting a bit too proudly. I feel they are putting on an act, boasting their manhood for the benefit of Tata's Kentish escort.

Why do we northerners always feel like this, as though what comes from the south must be more fashionable, more civilized? We are convinced they will laugh at us for barbarians.

It's affecting the women too. I thought my court ladies looked splendid enough in their holiday dresses. But they are looking down at their clothes now, casting sideways glances at the Kentish ladies. And what about the strangers? There's one with her hand over her mouth, trying to hide her smile from my Northumbrian women. Why? What's wrong?

It takes me a little while to see the difference. The women themselves will have spotted it immediately. My dead queen's waiting women are dressed in their best tunics. Tata's ladies are finely got up too, though dustier from travelling. But these southern women's clothes are not the same. In York, we've never seen such braided jackets fastened with golden clasps, over those striped skirts. It breaks my heart to see even our lovely Hereswith touching her loose blue tunic. I think she's suddenly doubting if it's suitable.

I feel a flash of rage.

I am not the only one. There's a stream of angry incantations on my right. Coifi, my chief priest, has also seen something not to his liking.

I follow his eyes. The grooms are leading Tata's litter away. I can see two men who must have been riding behind it. They do not look English. They are clearly not warriors. I think they never have been. One of them is a tall gaunt figure, dressed in a dark gown. He is looking at everything about him with a piercing gaze, as though he expects a dagger in his back rather than an invitation to a wedding feast. His companion is a rounder, red-faced figure, balding early, and smiling broadly enough. But my eyes are drawn inexorably back to the taller man. A cross of ivory and gold swings on his breast, gleaming against the black cloth. A pain grips my chest. It is like the one in the shadows of Redwald's temple.

Tata must have seen my stare. She's tugging my arm, coaxing me towards them.

'King Edwin, may I present to you my priest Paulinus and his deacon James? They come from Rome. You know you promised my brother I might bring my chaplains with me, as a condition of my marriage settlement.'

The pair of clergy bow to me. The deacon James seems humble and willing. It is the priest Paulinus who scares me. He is so tall that his stoop scarcely brings him low enough to honour me. My treacherous heart is thundering. There is something else I have had to swear to secure this marriage. That I, King Edwin, descendant of Woden, will listen while these men preach Christianity to me.

I have said nothing about my past. No one in Christian Kent, and only a few of my bodyguard here in Woden's Northumbria, know that I was once baptized on Ynys Mon by a British priest.

No, not Ynys Mon. Anglesey. The past is dead.

Age is starting to silver Paulinus's black hair. His face is bare of beard or moustache. He stands out in his very plainness among the bristling bejewelled English courtiers. Besides that cross, he has only a brooch to fasten his cloak and an emerald ring on his hand. His clothing is rich enough cloth, plain and dark, subtly but not extravagantly bordered. Yet he is not like any British priest. Instead of the mane of hair hanging down the back of the head from a high shaved forehead, this Roman wears his cropped in a ring around a small bare circle.

He has straightened up from his bow, but his neck is still stooped forward. His eyes are darkly bright, gazing at me with an odd intensity. He reminds me of a cormorant, staring down from a rock, poised to strike. I am the fish.

'Sire, I am to have the great honour of preaching in your court. You yourself shall hear the good news of Christ from my unworthy lips.'

'We're Northumbrians here. We have English gods,' I snap.

Preach all you like, Paulinus. You will not move me.

The light has faded in my bride's face. But I shall never confess to her, or her priest, or anyone else, that I was once a Christian but then reneged. Only Lilla and a handful of others must ever know that.

They are taking Paulinus's horse away to the stables, a fine black stallion. Woden's priests are allowed to ride only a mare or a gelding.

At least the plumper of those clergymen has a sense of humour. The deacon James has handed over his own broad-backed pony and is making for my young great-nieces. It's not Hereswith's grace that has brought out his ringing laugh. He's stooping to talk to little Hild, who is clutching a poppy fallen from her crown and still gazing up at my bride with adoring eyes.

Tata slips her hand through my arm. Those eyes catch my heart again, like the sweep of bluebells in a springtime wood. Her smile manages to convey both deference and confidence.

'My lord, I am grateful for such a warm welcome to Northumbria. Will you not show me into my new home?'

This wedding feast is more uneasy than I expected. Both parties are still sizing each other up. Their boasting is too loud, the groups too tightly knit. I feel each is laughing secretly at the other's strange ways. We are all English, except for Tata's Roman chaplains. Northumbria and Kent speak the same language, more or less. We should be able to understand each other better than this.

The two who are not English look weary now. They are a little bewildered and on their guard.

Romans. A strange thrill goes through me when I think that name. These two men of flesh and blood have come from that great city, whose empire raised these walls of York, but which is beyond my imagining.

I am not the only one who feels it. I am aware of a chill further down the table, like the draught from an unshuttered window. Someone else is watching that Roman pair, with more jealousy than curiosity. He is no warrior, either. Coifi's face is smudged with paint marks. The sleeves of his gown are sweeping the trestle table with tassels of tufted fur. His feet in their striped catskin slippers are shuffling the rushes restlessly. My chief priest is gnawing his meat without appetite tonight, his eyes malevolently on his rivals.

Lilla, too, looks uneasy. We have been strangers at many other kings' tables, he and I. Here in Northumbria we thought we were the masters at last. But he is eyeing the Kentish thanes who have come with Tata. They are more different from us than Coenburg's Mercians, in their speech, in their dress, in their ways. Kent is an old, proud English kingdom. These newcomers seem very sure of themselves.

But when at last Tata has left my side, and the women run in pink-checked and bright-eyed to announce she is ready, I let my male friends drag me laughing to her chamber. And everything is different.

This bed was once Coenburg's. The girls have been busy. They have swept away all the sad evidence of my first dead wife. Hangings glow in the lamplight, shaken free of dust and mended. The furniture has been waxed until it gleams. My feet walking towards the bed tread the scented rustle of fresh herbs. Over the pillows hang woven flower wreaths and plaited corn dollies. And my heart leaps into my throat to see Tata sitting up smiling under these tokens of fertility. She is wearing Hild's coronet of cornflowers and buttercups, and she is laughing as she holds out her arms to welcome me.

Coenburg was never as merry as this. I have made a good bargain, for my country and myself.

Chapter Sixteen

The singing haunts me.

York is not Canterbury. If there were churches here long ago, they have tumbled into nameless rubble. There is no one left to tell, since the Britons fled west. I am a fair man. I have allowed Tata to set aside a chamber of the Queen's hall for her chapel.

How was I to know I was giving voice to someone just as persuasive, in his own way, as Paulinus's passionate preaching?

James the Deacon, they call him. Not quite a priest. James does not look like a man who weaves magic. He seems a bluff, high-coloured character, much more like an Englishman than the gaunt, black-eyed Paulinus. But you should hear his magnificent bass lifted in song as he leads the chanting. You forget the ordinary man for the extraordinary music, deep as the thrum of drums to quicken the heart, thrilling enough to lift the spirit

His chanting reaches me across the Queen's empty hall. It is like the tramp of an enemy warhost advancing. It makes my blood pound.

No, the hall is not quite empty. Someone else is here, peering in through the half open door of the chapel, as if afraid to cross the threshold. Hild, doubtful, but curious as a shaky-legged kitten exploring beyond its mother's bed. Her head shoots round as she hears me coming, and her untidy plaits bounce.

'Oh, it's only you, Uncle.'

'Half of Britain fears the coming of King Edwin of Northumbria. But not you, Hild?'

She reddens. It catches my heart to see that she is at that awkward stage when she is ceasing to be a child and does not yet understand what a woman should do. A year since, she would have hugged me round the waist and teased me with her smile.

Their service is coming to an end. James's voice thrills with a great 'Amen'.

Before I know what is happening, Hild is tugging my hand and hustling me behind a shadowing pillar. I am the King in this palace. But we act like two guilty children who should not be caught peeping.

The Christians are streaming out now. Tata comes, smiling, as though the peace of spring sunshine is shining in her heart. Close beside her is Hereswith. I watch more of my Northumbrians crowding out of that small space after her. Lilla is there.

I feel betrayed.

Hereswith has fallen under the magic of Tata's smile. She would follow her new queen anywhere. Her eyes are down now, rapt, reverent. I hear Hild's sharp intake of breath, like a sob.

I know what stings. Her lovely, graceful elder sister, walking so readily now in Tata's shadow, almost indistinguishable from a Kentish woman. They are not alike, my young queen and her new friend. Hereswith's grave intelligent face will soften in a secret smile that curves so delicately, it seems meant for no one but herself or some inner companion. My beloved Tata has a running fountain of laughter. She makes the huge damp halls of this capital, shadowed by Roman ruins, dance with a merriment we never knew before she came. Yet these two young women are close companions now. Each finds some need fulfilled in the other.

Hild worships them both. But she is too brave, too honest, to put this love above loyalty to her country. As I am.

'You won't change will you?' she whispers to me fiercely.

'Is that what you're afraid of?'

'Hereswith is changing,' she scowls.

The Queen's party have gone. Like outdoor slaves, guiltily spying in on their master's feast, we tiptoe across and stare through the open door.

At the far end, beyond the light from a small side window, we see a table spread with a clean embroidered cloth. A golden cross, set with garnets, candles in silver sconces. A gospel book in a heavy jewelled cover.

'Don't be afraid, Hild. This can't hurt us.'

She rounds on me passionately.

'It will! We're Northumbrians. Won't Woden and Thunor and Tiw be angry with us if we forget them? Lady Frigg might stop the harvest. She could, couldn't she? What will happen if the Queen doesn't sacrifice to her?'

There are proud tears glittering in her eyes. I see adoration for Tata battling with her intense love for the country her father was driven from. Hild is no longer a child. She sees clearly the responsibility a king and queen have for their people. I have given Northumbria back to her. She will always be loyal to me.

'The Queen says her own prayers for Northumbria,' I comfort her. 'Don't you think it's a good idea to have all the gods on our side?'

'Hers aren't English.'

I take her stubby hands in mine and kiss them. 'Northumbria is all I ever lived for. Don't be afraid, Hild. I won't betray it.'

She grins up at me, blinking away her tears. Her smile is radiant now. 'Whatever anyone else does, we'll stay loyal. We will, won't we, Uncle Edwin? Even if it's just you and me.'

Tata has changed the weather of our Northumbrian court. I swear the sun shines warmer than it used to. But sometimes a keen, cold wind blows too and makes me shiver. I have paused before the door of Tata's day-room.

I feel I have heard this powerful voice before. It is low but intense, the inflection foreign. I cannot place it, but the sense that I ought to know disturbs me deeply.

I get control of myself and take the last pace to the doorway. The curtain hangs partly open. I can hover unseen.

Tata sits curled on a low chair, her eager face turned to Paulinus. He has a book open on his black-skirted knee. One long bony finger is tracing the words. They must be Latin. All books are written in the Romans' language. I learned that much at Cadfan's court. But the words have changed. This Roman is no longer reading directly from the book. His raven eyes go winging out over his rapt audience. He is re-weaving his tale for them in English. He speaks it haltingly, but well enough. I think the women of my court find an attraction in his Italian accent, which sometimes rests on unexpected syllables. They feel a motherly sympathy when he cannot find a word and all the power of his passion is piled up behind a dam. It is true he can make a simple sentence sing like music. His English words flow more liquidly than the thunderbursts of sound shot from between our own lips. He has his audience entranced now: the Kentish ladies Tata has brought with her, some noblemen I have allowed in her escort, and my Northumbrian nieces with the other women from Coenburg's household.

I listened to many Christian tales in Aberffraw. I do not know this one. Why are the noble Perpetua and Felicitas, her slave, being led out together to their deaths, singing hymns before a roaring crowd, gored by a mad cow, their throats cut? I can guess. This priest looks hungry as his gaze sweeps over his audience. It is almost as if he sees my shining-eyed Tata and all her women, walking out into the arena with the same courage, willing their flesh to the same martyr's death, confessing Christ. Paulinus is a compelling storyteller. Under his spell, some of them might do that.

But one of the upturned faces looks frightened. Hild is eleven. It comes to me with a shock that her face is no longer rounded with puppy fat. That chin will always be square, determined. Hild can never hope to compete with the slender grace of her sister. But she is less of a child than she was.

Yet it seems odd that Hild, of all these young women, should be alarmed by the violence of these martyrs' deaths. She, more than the others, I should expect to imagine herself facing it like a warrior. She still boasts as loud as a boy that her name means 'battle'.

Paulinus has lowered his eyes to read again, this time in Latin. And I see now that it is not his face Hild is staring at so fearfully. It is his book. She does not understand Latin. She cannot be attending to the story. Yet she is biting her lip to steady her trembling breathing. Watching her eyes, it dawns on me that what is scaring her is the writing itself. Those pages are covered with signs, as full of dangerous meaning as magic runes carved on stone.

The rain drums against the shutter, while Paulinus's voice shakes with passion, takes on the colour of drama and different voices, thunders with authority.

I cannot read. There were plenty of Christian scholars on Cadfan's island who would have taught me, had I wished. Even Cadwallon can read a little. I scorned the craft as unmanly, ignoble, and my bodyguard backed me. Why does an English king need to read? Does he bake his own bread, or shoe his own horse?

And yet, a smith also is no ordinary craftsman. You may meet the Hooded One, who should not be seen by mortals, at Weiland's Smithy. Words are a craft of the wise. Rhun told me the old druids of Britain never allowed their wisdom to be captured in writing. Yet these Christians are building themselves a store of power, book after book. Hild has realized what she is seeing.

Paulinus is switching to English again, for the benefit of my Northumbrians. Hild's chin has set in an obstinate line. I watch her bend her head and stab inexpertly at her embroidery. But Hereswith's needle stays still. Her grey eyes remain rapt on Paulinus. She joins with the Kentish women to breathe out a passionate 'Alleleuia!' as the story reaches its climax.

Tata has seen me watching. The intensity of her expression sparkles apart into that winning smile. She is jumping up to hold out her hand to me. Tata has the dignity, the breeding, to carry herself as Queen Aethelberg before the people. But at home she is as merry as the youngest of these girls who fill my palaces now with their laughter.

'Edwin! My lord, it is not right for you to be standing outside my door like a sentry. Come in and share this story-feast with us. Paulinus can enchant us out of this cold rain into the sun of Jerusalem, Bethlehem, Rome.'

'I was kept out of Northumbria half my life. This land is all I need.'

'That's what I said!' Hild's yap of loyalty makes us all laugh. She sticks out her lower lip and glowers at us under her escaping hair. 'I'm always going to stay English,' she mutters. 'Like Uncle Edwin.'

The child is shrewd. I do not feel part of this gathering. Tata still has me by the hand as I try to turn. Lilla is standing close behind me.

Paulinus's voice stays me. It is always low and courteous, but curiously authoritative for a foreigner speaking to a king in his own palace. 'Sire, it was part of your contract that you would listen to the teaching I bring.'

It seemed an easy thing to promise then. As if I did not know his gospel stories from childhood, as well as the English sagas of Thunor and the sea serpent, of Woden losing an eye, of the giants who lusted for blessed Frigg. What harm can they do me now?

I had not reckoned how those stories would turn against me, how I would feel myself to be the traitor Adam, shut out of the garden of Eden by the angel's flaming sword.

I am Edwin, greatest of the English kings. I should not run from what I fear, any more than Hild can drop her embroidery on the floor and bolt from the sight of that writing which it is not safe for her to understand. So I take the cushioned seat Tata leads me to.

140

She nestles at my feet, leaning warm against my knee. I fondle her hair, while she looks up at me and not Paulinus. He is thundering now about Judas, hanging himself in horror for betraying his Lord. I keep my face steady.

Lilla is squatting on the floor behind Tata's women. I watch his wind-tanned face turn up to listen. Catching his expression, I know what I have robbed him of.

Chapter Seventeen

Things seem to fall right for Tata as easily as laughter flows from her. In her company I feel we could walk on the clouds of the sky, she and I. I am the greatest king in the land, and she . . . she looks merrier than ever this morning, walking towards me through the meadowsweet on the banks of the Ouse. Her hands are full of flowers. She clasps them round me, so I cannot see their scented lace, only the blue of her eyes. And they are laughing.

'Edwin. What would you wish me to tell you more than anything else?'

My spirit gives a great leap. I know certainly what she must mean.

'A child! You're sure?'

I struggle to free my arms to hug her, but she imprisons them. Her face below mine is honeysuckle and roses, her smile is perfect. All this for me, and now a son from her.

'I didn't dare to believe it at first, so soon. But yes, the women I brought, who served my mother when I was born, say it is true.'

Her eyes are cast down now in modesty. This is women's wisdom. I break my arms free of her hold, but I do not hug her yet.

I let my hands slide below the clasps of her jacket, over her belly. Tata is young. She is still firm, flat, between the mounds of her hips. I feel her body stir towards mine. I fear I shall suffocate with love for her. I have roused both of us, but this is more than desire. I crush her in my arms.

When I release her lips, she laughs breathlessly. 'It is not such a great thing, surely? You have two sons already, my lord.'

'But neither of them is your child.'

'I pray God I shall bear it safely for you.'

And with that word, I feel terror. Childbirth is both holy and dangerous, for the woman, for the baby. Men have no place in it. The greatest warrior cannot defend his wife in her childbed. Both lives are in the hands of the gods and the goddesses.

'We'll go to Goodmanham tomorrow. We must make sacrifices for the unborn. To Frigg, to Mother Erce.'

She pulls away from me. I can see distress in her eyes. There is always this between us.

'You promised I should take no part in heathen worship.'

I place my finger on her lips. 'Nor shall you. But someone must. This land expects its rituals. I've been lucky in war. But if a battle should ever go against Northumbria, the people would blame me. If . . . if you should be . . . unlucky too, they might say that when my sister was queen here, she kept the English ways.'

Tata smiles now, victoriously. 'And where is Acha now? Fled away from Northumbria with her children to the monks of Iona.'

'Still, I must do the duty for my family. An English king is also a priest.'

I do not tell her what I know in my heart, that the gods of this land expect more from me than I am giving them. It is not often that I go to the great temple at Goodmanham now. I listen obediently in Paulinus's chapel. I allow him to terrify Lilla and Hereswith with his sermons. Coifi scowls at me because I sit through Christian services when I should be sacrificing to Woden. Yet I cannot ever become Christ's man now. Once, long ago, I took a step I wish I could forget. I broke that vow. I cannot confess my dishonour and I cannot make the vow twice.

I have nowhere left. The dragon gable of Woden's temple looms more menacingly over me after each absence. I still feel the dread of it. But I do not believe in the rituals I perform there any more.

I see the abyss at my feet. Nothing can save me now.

And yet, aren't I Edwin of Northumbria, victorious in every battle? I drove Cadwallon into the sea. My land is at peace.

I am a good king. *I am a good king.*

I have done what had to be done in the sanctuary of my father's gods, in the Queen's name and my own. Tata is quiet, a little pale. I am not surprised that she's standing up from the table and bowing to me, withdrawing with her women to bed early.

I shall not sleep with her tonight. She thinks I have fouled myself. I dare not tell her I have committed a worse betrayal.

It's a new morning. Yet there's a quietness between me and Tata as we walk by the stream. The air is oppressive too. It ought to be a bright autumn day. The sky is clear enough, and the sun is shining on yellow leaves.

I reach for Tata's hand. It lies in my mine, cool, unresponsive.

'What is the matter, Tata?' I say, though I know.

'I feel so strange and heavy. As though something terrible is about to happen.'

'What I did yesterday was for the baby's safety, and yours. And for Northumbria.'

'Look.' She is crinkling her eyes, though not with her usual laughter, staring up through the parted branches. 'The moon and the sun are riding the sky together this morning. Yet I can hardly see the Lady Moon now. Can you?'

'The sun's too bright for her. He's king.'

It sounds harsher than I meant. She is silent. We walk on, through the soft strewing of last year's leaves.

The morning is growing darker. I look up, expecting to see a thundercloud creeping up on the sun. The sky is still blue, but dimming with every step. Branches screen us from the sun, but that does not explain why a twilight gloom is thickening under the trees.

I halt, look round. Lilla has been strolling some way behind, with Hild skipping on one side and Hereswith sedate on the other. He has stiffened too. I see his hand move to his knife for reassurance. I do not think any weapon can help us.

'What's happening?' whispers Tata. 'Edwin, is the sun dying?'

The songbirds have fallen quiet. A fearful silence hushes all of us. Only the stream at our feet still hurries on, loud, cold. Moments ago, this was a cloudless morning. Now with every heartbeat night is falling.

'Look! I can see the stars!' Hild squeaks.

Tata suddenly clings to me and I to her. Our awestruck eyes turn up. A dark mouth is gnawing the sun away.

I cannot look any longer. I am blinded twice over as the sun goes out. And now there are voices in plenty yelling in this dreadful dark, cries of terror, shouts of alarm. Men are cursing, women sobbing.

Then, out of this night, the voice of James the Deacon, deep and beautiful enough to make me weep.

'Out of the depths we cry to you, Lord, have mercy on us.'

'Amen!' That plea was torn from me. .

I open my eyes and it is still night. The stars burn, garnet, crystal, amethyst. But flames are leaping round the blackened sun. I stand in awe. The brook rushes over boulders, loud as the echo of my breathing.

The moments drag like hours. Slowly the blackness lifts. The sun creeps back until it is brilliant, whole. Day is restored.

But the thrill and terror of this morning will always haunt me.

Tata and I release each other, smiling uncertainly out of shocked faces. Tata gives a hiccuping laugh.

'It's a sign, isn't it? For the baby? Bright sunshine after danger.'

Now that my eyes have steadied, there's a silhouette on the path in front of us, Coifi, in his shaman's regalia, is screaming to

Thunor like a madman, his fists shaking the air. The Thunderer controls the skies.

'What do you say, Coifi?' I challenge him. 'Isn't it a portent of victory for this child the Queen is carrying?' I hear myself gabbling too breathlessly, too fast.

He spits to either side of me. Now he is down on his knees on the rutted path, shaking out his otterskin pouch. He starts frantically casting bone counters, blackened with runes. The muscles of my stomach tighten as his tattooed fingers knot themselves into criss-crossed signs.

'I see the shadow of tragedy,' he snarls. 'Black treachery is coming to you from a strange land.' His eyes shoot venom over my shoulder.

Paulinus is striding down the path towards us. I have one glimpse of his gaunt face as his dark gown sweeps past me. He kicks Coifi's rune bones flying into the fallen leaves. Latin prayers rain down like hail.

Always, when I hear his foreign accent, I shiver. It is as though I have almost caught the cloak-tail of a dream I do not want to remember.

Coifi is scrabbling in the undergrowth for his counters, cursing horribly. I should be angry on his behalf. This is Northumbria's chief priest Paulinus is insulting.

Tata pulls me round to face the Roman.

'Your majesties, the meaning of the eclipse is plain. In baptism, there is a moment of darkness when we go under the water. Then we are raised up into glorious light by the power of Christ's resurrection. We stand in the splendour of eternal life. This sign was for you, sire. Christ requires your soul.'

I have commanded warhosts. But I find authority desert me now. I cannot look at this pale intense priest stooping towards me. I cannot meet his eyes.

I am trembling on the brink of the stream. Tata must feel me shuddering. She squeezes my arm, her confidence restored. She gives me a little shake, willing me to answer.

'Edwin. What's the matter with you? In your heart, you really want this. I can feel it.'

A king is never alone. There is a circle round me now, watching, waiting. Hereswith, Lilla, Coifi, Hild. With an angry gesture, Woden's priest sweeps the scattered counters back into his pouch. Their rattle releases my tongue.

'When the King decides, it is for all Northumbria. I am not a common man, free to speak for himself.'

In a burst of anger, I pull myself away from Tata, walk past Paulinus fast along the riverbank. My breath is shaking.

When I think I am alone, I subside on a fallen tree-trunk, elbows on knees, head down, staring at the hurrying river. The thrushes are singing again.

My nerves prickle. I look up and find Lilla is watching. His eyes haunt me.

'Can you never leave me alone!'

His face sets into obstinate lines. He has reproached me only that once. 'There is news I think you should know. Cadwallon was not drowned. He's in exile in Ireland. Word is that he hates you even more than Aethelfrith.'

Daffodils are springing golden between the hazel trees. My boys Osfrith and Eadfrith are swinging from the branches, imitating the red squirrels clowning among the catkins. We have moved to my palace on the banks of the Derwent for the spring festival of the goddess Eostre.

The mornings are brightening earlier, yet I know I am treading down fear, as dark things that died in the winter are smothered by the spring's new growth. This is Tata's first child. The first-born is the hardest, isn't it? She came to me last summer so vital, so laughing. Not even her women can tell me how she may be in childbirth. We all know that ahead of her soon lie pain, the possibility of one death, or two.

Lying beside her, I caress her body and feel the child quicken.

'You're too thin.' I stroke her face. As her belly is swelling towards its time, her face has grown gaunt. The skin is stretched over her cheekbones, her eyes are hollow. 'You shouldn't be fasting. You need to eat for two.'

'It's Lent.' She says it simply, as though that answers everything. 'Forty days our Saviour fasted in the wilderness. Shall I not watch with him, who died for me?'

I have allowed her this. I grew up at Cadfan's court, a guest at his table. I know what it is for Christians to refuse all flesh and fowl, all eggs and cheese, all honey sweets. I have to pretend this fast is strange to me.

It is new to Hild. Tata doesn't compel the Northumbrians of her court to follow this Kentish discipline. But the girls love her too much. Christians or not, they try to do as she does, simply for fellowship.

I caught Hild yesterday at the kitchen door. She was staring in at the fat hunks of cheese, a roast goose set in jelly like amber, cakes of oatmeal drenched in honey. Her eyes were huge with the hunger pangs that must have been howling in her belly like wolves.

The cooks were laughing. A fasting queen is an insult to their pride. One of the women held out a lump of bacon, streaked with thick white lard. Hild grabbed it and stuffed it into mouth. I watched her broad cheeks bulge.

She didn't see me.

I am awake at the dead of night. The room is utterly dark, but Tata is moving, sliding heavily out of bed.

I am suddenly very afraid.

'Is it the baby? Shall I call your women?' My whisper sounds hoarse.

'No. Go back to sleep.' She kisses my forehead. 'This is only for us.'

And into my fuddled brain there comes the knowledge of what this night is. Easter Eve.

There are candles in the room beyond the door, where her women sleep. Figures are stirring there too, dressing silently. I've caught the gleam of Hereswith's silvery hair crossing the light.

Then Hild's fierce possessive whisper. '*You're* not a Christian.' As though a mooring rope is slipping from her hands.

I cannot hear what Hereswith answers as she bends over her younger sister. Tata has joined them now. One of the Kentish women is wrapping a cloak warmly round her. They are going out of the door. The open rectangle lets in the faintest greying of starlight. They have put their candles out. The pale blur of Hereswith vanishes with the rest into the darkness.

The bed is still warm beside me, where Tata was lying. I feel a cold bereavement in my heart. I know that Hereswith's place will be the same beside Hild.

I start to lie down. But there is another unexpected movement in the gloom. A small dark figure is stumbling out after them. It must be Hild. She has halted in the clouded grey of the doorway. I can make out that she is still fumbling with her clothes, clumsy hands mistaking openings, making nonsense of strings and buckles. I hear her swear like a soldier. Then she is gone.

Sleep has deserted me. But I do not know what makes me get up out of the warm blankets and follow Hild.

The night is not winter-cold, yet it strikes fresh and clean on the skin. I did not stop for my boots. I feel like a boy again, treading soft-footed over the beaten earth and on to dew-cool grass. I know where they are going. I let the sound of the river guide me.

The Queen's hall at Derwent is smaller than in our palace at York. I have allowed Paulinus and James to build her a separate chapel, only a little thing of wattle hurdles under a straw thatch. No light shows from it.

The rush of water is close now, but without a single lamp showing, it is hard to find the place under the leaning branches of clustering oaks.

A skein of singing is thrown out to me like a rope, that one rich bass leading the lighter voices. I would know that voice anywhere: James the cantor, the cheerful clergyman who prepares their chapel for each celebration, rising to glory only when he lifts his voice, leading them all in a mighty chant.

Somewhere in the darkness under these oaks, Hild must be listening too. I cannot see her. Does she feel, as I do, this music thrill her body?

I wish I could be like Hild, coming to this Easter for the first time. Hild does not share my weight of memories: the royal chapel at Aberffraw, British priests like Rhun, celebrating in a glory of vestments and lamps, though their life outside the church is so plain and simple, Cadfan's family pouring out into the sunshine after the Eucharist, Mairi. . . .

No!

I conquered Ynys Mon.

But Hild is innocent.

Suddenly the singing has ceased. Paulinus's voice cries out a fervent shout, '*Christ is risen!*'. And all the voices in the chapel give back to him in joy, '*Alleleuia!*'

Then glory breaks, dazzling my senses. Lights fire from the chapel: one star of flame, another, two more, then dozens. There is a fragrance of incense on the night air. James's bass note booms out the most triumphant hymn of all.

Goose-pimples are prickling my flesh. I am dazed, desolate that I am no longer part of this, and never can be now.

Almost too late, I realize people are starting to come out of the chapel. The greater mystery of the Eucharist is about to begin. The unbaptized Northumbrians are leaving.

I duck back under the oak boughs. That taller shape must be Hereswith. Hild is running towards her. In the light from the windows I think I see tears on the older girl's face.

'Oh, Hild! I wanted to be part of it. It's so beautiful. The life that comes from his death. But I haven't made the vows. I haven't been sealed with Christ's sign. I haven't received the gift of the Holy Spirit.' Her voice aches with adolescent longing.

I hear Hild's voice rough with strained loyalties. 'We're English. Uncle Edwin gave us a home. He's saved Northumbria for us.'

'But, Hild, if only Edwin himself would change!'

'He never will. And nor shall I.' Hild turns away.

A handbell rings. They have come to the holiest act.

I have no right to listen.

Chapter Eighteen

Pussy willows are breaking out in silver fur, violets are carpet-ing the woodland banks and every blackbird in my kingdom is shouting for joy. I have got her back with me. This is her feast day. Easter.

Today, I can indulge my queen. Hild can stuff herself as openly as she pleases. My board is loaded with geese, salmon, venison, boar. There is a tide of ale.

They are taking the trestles away at last, leaving Tata and me enthroned on the dais, while the court moves back to the edges of the hall. I signal for the entertainers to resume. There have been praise-songs while we ate, but now there is room for dancing. The lads are nimble. They take our breath away as their slippers dart between the sword blades.

Lilla is guarding the gold hoard beside me. At my command he tosses them down a fine chain. That pleases them. They can scarcely wait to bow to me before their hands are tugging at it, pris-ing the links apart to grab a share each.

There's a mumming play next, with a comic horse and a fool got up as a woman. They have a king in a tipsy crown. I'm supposed to applaud him. This is a festival.

I think I'm drunk. I want to slip the anchor of my mind and send it headlong down this current of merrymaking. I want to crush Tata's laughing face to my breast, so that I do not have to meet her eyes. I know what she is hoping.

Most of all, it is Lilla's eyes I try to avoid. We have had our chance. We cannot take their baptism twice and not confess the first one. And if Lilla tells Paulinus what happened in that pool at Aberffraw, he will betray me too. All Northumbria will know I am Edwin the apostate, Edwin the coward, Edwin whose Captain went to the cross like a hero, Edwin who deserted him. Tata will know.

I cannot bear to imagine the look in her eyes.

Lilla is loyal to death. He will not betray me.

A horn startles me. Heads are turning towards the door. There's a rustle of excitement. We have visitors.

These are not men that I know.

The steward's voice vibrates with self-importance. 'The Lord Eumer, envoy from King Cwichelm of Wessex.'

His escort have left their weapons outside the door, but they look like experienced soldiers. Is Wessex coming to pay homage to Northumbria? They're a jealous lot. Cwichelm thinks he should have been hailed Bretwalda when Redwald of East Anglia died. You could see it in his eyes. Who was I, Edwin, so long an exile on the run, to lord it over all the English kingdoms?

I'll tell you why, Cwichelm. I had the victorious warhost to prove my right. You didn't have the nerve to stamp your boot on the Britons as I did.

This Eumer is thickset and his grey hair hangs squarely round his face. His mouth looks grim. He does not seem to be sharing our holiday mood. Still, he is carrying a rich-wrapped bundle in both hands.

The ale is thickening my tongue. As I lean forward it is not easy to keep my balance. The year is early yet and the fire is heaped high this afternoon. I peer at him across the smoky hall.

'Is our brother Cwichelm sending a gift for my queen's feast? Come nearer, then.'

He is starting to walk towards me and I want to laugh as I notice how his legs are bowed. My court is curious, craning their faces to

153

watch him pass. Hild, of course, has wriggled to the front just below this dais.

I have been ten years Northumbria's king, but I can still enjoy the sight of a Wessex thane coming respectfully to the foot of my throne. I do not know what is going through his mind, but he is acting the perfect ambassador. He has stopped just below me. Platitudes of greeting from Cwichelm roll past me. None of this is sincere.

But his gift looks real. I am intrigued to know what one king sends to a rival. Will it be something mean enough to insult me?

He's unwrapping the tapestry. Pinpoints of light dance on the thing he is holding balanced across his palms. I see what it is now and, in spite of myself, I am impressed. A splendid Saxon knife, fully half as big as a sword. As he holds it up, the filigree scabbard sparkles with the firelight. The hilt is gold, set with many coloured stones.

This is the long-bladed knife, the *sceax*, for which the Saxons are named. Is Cwichelm admitting at last that I am fit to be lord of both Saxons and Angles?

I have been looking at the gift, and not at the man, Eumer, kneeling on the step below me. Now he raises his face to mine.

'Edwin, King of Northumbria, King Cwichelm of the West Saxons sends you this homage. Wessex was one the few kingdoms you did not honour with your presence when you were an exile, running in fear of your life. Now you are hailed a greater king than all the rest. Take this knife, then, as a measure of his esteem.'

He draws the weapon slowly from its scabbard. It is truly magnificent. He swivels it, turning its point to me, displaying the runes chased on the blade. I lean forward. This is fine craftsmanship.

A nerve of fear quivers inside me. A Wessex smith has forged magic into these signs.

There is a shimmer of something like oil along the honed edge.

The scabbard slips from Eumer's hands, making a little clatter down the wooden steps.

Faster than a harper's fingers, the thane's hand twists the bright hilt. Light flashes from blue steel. Stupefied with ale and meat, I can only stare as the blade thrusts up towards my belly.

Tata screams as her chair screeches back. I sit incredulous for one more precious heartbeat. Then muscles spring to duty and I twist backwards.

I cannot escape. The carved arms of my throne are imprisoning me. The warrior instinct still makes me fight for my life. I shoot out one booted foot, struggling to kick the man's arm sideways. It skids on his leather wristband, jars against tensed bone and sinew. We are wrestling for my life.

For a crucial moment, Eumer's back has hidden the truth from my court. Now a roar of rage shudders the roof pillars. The hall erupts as a confused mass of Northumbrian men and women comes rushing forward to save me. What hope have I got that any of them can reach Eumer before his blade drives home?

My foot is slipping. A snake of light streaks towards me as the blade rushes up. I'll have to risk slicing my hands to grab at it. There's only the smallest space left between that gleaming point and my body.

Across that fatally narrowing gap, a man hurls himself. I'm knocked sideways. I had only a soft gown, but now I'm wearing a human body for a breastplate. I've lost sight of Eumer. My head is thundering with yells I cannot stop. Somewhere Tata is still screaming, a high cry like a wounded animal.

A sharp pain strikes below my heart.

The body shielding me has slumped, heavy, crushing me into the carved wood. It lies suddenly still. There sounds to be fierce fighting going on somewhere else. I cannot see.

To free my head I must push away the man who saved my life. I can feel a warm tide flowing down my thighs, trickling under my skirt down my shins. I do not want to think which of us may be bleeding to death.

I must not name the man I am cradling on my lap, now that I have unmasked my face from his smothering tunic. My fingers play with the cloth: fine moss-green wool, embroidered on the hem with madder rose.

Lilla was wearing a tunic like that.

For this Easter feast, my friend wore no armour, no leather jerkin. Warm, living flesh was all he could offer me for a shield.

All my life, Lilla has waited to protect me from this moment.

I am burning. There is the roar of flames in my ears. I have died. I am roasting in Hell.

The Devil leers over to torment me. He has Cadwallon's face.

'Was that a groan?'

'His eyelids moved. He's coming round.'

These are not Welsh taunts. They sound like English voices. Yet there is still smoke clouding my eyes. Through it figures loom, stooping over me. If I am not in Hell, why am I red-hot?

'How are you, my lord?'

There is something odd about this voice. It's not that I don't know it well, of course. Gyrth, the youngest of the bodyguard who snatched me away from Catterick, has grown middle-aged in my service, deep-voiced now. But this is not the voice I expect to hear first, the friend who has been closest at my side through every crisis of my life. Who is it I wanted to hear? I struggle through this fog for a name.

Lilla.

Pain enters, like the point of a knife beneath my ribs. What else is it I must not remember?

And now I do. The warmth of his willing body, flinging itself across my own to block the assassin's blade, the gush of blood that tells me there is no hope, the heaviness of him across my lap, the face stiffening as they lift him off me, his eyes seeing everything and nothing.

'The pain's bad. Look at his face.'

'It's not a deep wound, and it missed the heart.'

'It would have been much worse than this if. . . .'

'The gods will hail Lilla a hero in Valhalla.'

'No!' That is not what Lilla wanted. I creak the word out. Even to whisper is pain in my lungs. How could such a small knife-wound do this?

An older man is speaking, more self-important than Gyrth. 'Lie still, sire. It's best you don't try to speak. The wound itself is small and it shouldn't have caused you a fever. The knife barely reached you. I fear there was poison on the blade.'

It's my physician. I can't remember his name. Nothing else matters, except for this one piercing truth. I have lost Lilla.

And I may have cost him eternal life.

I lie helpless as a baby, while they dress the wound again, hold drink to my lips, wipe my sweat away.

There was something else. Gradually pieces of the pattern, like coloured flecks of millefiore glass, are catching the returning light.

'Tata? She was crying out. Women were running to her. Tell me he didn't strike her too!'

I try to rise on one elbow. I can see them all looking at each other. I'm gripped by a terrible fear.

Gyrth lays me back again. 'It was the baby, my lord. She was near her time.'

'Is it. . . ? Is she. . . ?'

I can hear anguish in my voice. The physician is reproving me. Sigulf, that's his name. The murk is clearing from my brain. A learned man, very careful for his dignity.

'There is no news from the Queen's hall yet, sire. A first child is often slow. I offered my own wife's services, but she was not admitted. She was told no other wise woman was required.'

'The Queen's Kentish midwife doesn't want your heathen charms, is that it?' My lips twist in a bitter grin.

We are taking enormous risks, Tata and I, committing our safety to different hands.

I feel myself tumbling into a deep dark pit, exhausted.

I have woken, still exhausted. The pain is bad. In Wessex, Cwichelm's shamans must have chanted powerful spells over this poison. But they were not powerful enough. I'm alive. The King of Wessex will tremble when he hears that.

But there is still Tata.

This room is stifling. I throw the blankets off and feel the air on my uncovered legs. But my sight is clouded.

'Sire! Lie still.'

Coifi is in the room. This is real smoke I am breathing. I can hear rhythmic incantations, an insistent drumming. How much of what is curing me is Sigulf's medicine, how much Coifi's spells? Is there any such boundary?

Coifi is nimble for his age. His crooked legs uncurl from where he was squatting and propel him to my bedside. He looms above me with an air of ownership over my body.

'The Queen?'

'There's no news yet, sire. Her women will let no one else in. Even that Roman has to jabber his spells outside. So we shall all know where to point the finger if anything goes wrong ... which Frigg forbid.'

I have a sudden picture of Hild scrambling on to the dais, where Eumer was fighting my thanes to his bloody death. Her ususaly bold face was shocked, her eyes terrified. Was it for my wound, or Tata's?

Hild is a child still. They wouldn't let her in either. But have they let Hereswith stay with Tata?

'How is she?'

Coifi's lips narrow. 'They say the Queen has not much pain.'

'If I could only see her.' Somone must comfort me. I need Tata.

'You're too ill, my lord. The women will tell us as soon as there's news.' Gyrth looks haggard. He must have been watching at my bedside since they carried me here.

Lilla would have stayed beside me. It feels like losing my shield in the thick of battle. I shall never see my friend again.

I am seized by terror. 'Have they buried Lilla yet?'

'Tomorrow.'

'Never fear, sire. I promise you he'll have a splendid funeral.' There is a glitter of triumph in Coifi's eyes. This will be his day.

I must see Paulinus. There is something terrible I have to ask him.

'Give me my gown.'

'You can't see the Queen, my lord.' Gyrth moves swiftly to support me. I'm as weak as a baby myself.

Sigulf the physician is pushing his way past Coifi and arguing as vehemently as he dares to urge me back to bed.

'Get out of my way,' I gasp. 'You've done your job. I'm not going to die.'

None of them can forbid me. I am the King. Yet I'm staggering, leaning on Gyrth's shoulder. I can't tell any of them what really terrifies me.

It is only a short distance from my hall across to Tata's smaller one. Yesterday, I would have skimmed this courtyard lightly, going to my wife. Now I'm dragging my weary body, as though across a battlefield after days of fighting.

At my painful approach the doorkeeper snaps to attention. I can see his eyes asking rapid fearful questions of Gyrth. The wolfskin robe Gyrth wrapped around me is darkening with the seep of blood through my bandages. I understand the dread in all their minds.

There are three lives still in danger.

I must make an effort to draw myself upright. I'm still Edwin, master of North Britain. Never mind that my face feels grey with grief and pain.

The door is swinging open. The hall seems full of women, turning their faces in alarm as their king is announced. Hild comes running across.

'Uncle Edwin! What are you doing out of bed? Is it true the knife was poisoned?'

Her plain face is alive with anxiety, but I peer past her. I have to find Paulinus. The edges of the hall are wavering uncertainly. I start to limp forward, past the fireplace.

Suddenly, all their heads have turned away from me, hushed, listening. I have become irrelevant.

Tata is behind that curtain, in the thick of a battle I shall never experience. There was a woman's cry, not quite a scream, almost joyful. I do not understand it.

Hereswith comes stumbling out. For once the grace of her walk has deserted her. She looks shocked. Her hair has escaped the golden fillet and there is blood on her pale cheek. Only her eyes are shining.

'Praise God, it's here.'

Through the heavy brown curtain I can hear it now, the high, thin wail of a baby.

'It's alive!' And all the women are cheering, like warriors when the fighting is over.

Hild's voice leaps out urgently. 'But is Tata safe?'

The curtains part again. The midwife is standing before me, a broad, dark-faced woman, confronting me with the authority of her craft. She is holding out a bundle to show me.

The thing is tiny, swaddled tightly in linen and lambswool. Gyrth steers me forward. A little flower face peeps out, showing milky, dreaming eyes that find no relevance in a father's face. Can it be mine, this miracle?

The midwife has lowered her eyes, bowing herself and the baby she is holding.

'You have a daughter, sire, thanks be to God.'

'Ah!'

They will think this drop in my voice is disappointment. A king needs sons, but I already have Coenburg's pair growing towards manhood. I had not expected to be so moved, so touched with wonder, to see a girl child.

160

This is Tata's daughter.

I cannot stop my eyes piercing back at the midwife. I am desperate with the need for knowledge. 'Will the Queen live?'

A little cry comes from the other side of the curtain.

'Edwin?'

Gyrth cannot hold me back, nor the women prevent me. We two are survivors of a shipwreck, groping to find each other through the storm. I stagger through, into the animal-smelling muddle of the birth chamber.

A silvery daylight is falling from the window, on to the confusion round the bed. The edge of its shaft touches the pillows where Tata is lying. She is pale, exhausted, but she is reaching out long arms of delight to me. Hereswith is back, kneeling by her side, a smiling angel. Seeing me come, she rises, bows and escapes.

There is too much for words to tell.

'My dearest.'

'My own love.'

'How much you must have suffered.'

'You too.'

We are lost in holding, comforting each other.

'What happened to Lilla? No one will tell me.'

I stroke her hair. 'He has done his last service for me.'

'Oh! If I could see his poor body, I would bathe his feet with my tears and wipe them with the hairs of my head.'

I bow my face over her breast. The pain is very bad now.

'I have lost one precious life, but you've given me another.' And the tears break through the dam.

There is a disturbance behind me. Paulinus comes sweeping in, though Hereswith is trying to keep him back.

'Your majesty! The heavenly Trinity has delivered you, your wife and your child from death this glorious Easter Day. This baby. . . .'

My shoulders slump. Gyrth springs to help me back to bed.

I cannot ask him about Lilla now.

Chapter Nineteen

I will sit in this chair, though the pain is bitter. Shivers are racking my body, rushes of heat. But I will not have them say that King Edwin is dying, that he is weak and wounded, that he must not go out.

Lilla is being buried today.

The wind is cold. The heavy wolf-cloak cannot keep it out. Sigulf is angry that I've left my sickbed to sit on this hill above the Derwent.

I must be here. They have laid him out like the great warrior he is, his spear ready at his side, his shield glinting at the sky. Where were these weapons when he needed them?

They have banked firewood under him, so he is lifted above us, as he deserves to be. We shall raise a barrow over his remains.

I must do Lilla this honour, though my heart is sick that Coifi is sending him into the grey silence after death with all the rites of Woden's warriors, when he would have chosen to lie in a simple Christian grave. Look at him now. Too late they have dressed him in his gold-flecked armour. They have washed the blood from his poor pale limbs.

I can never wash away the feel of his blood clothing my knees, his unarmoured body thrown across me as my breastplate.

Lilla is dead. I should be dead, but I am not. If Paulinus's God is the true one, what will Lilla say at the gates where Saint

Peter stands sentinel? '*I betrayed Christ my King for loyalty to Edwin.*'?

I have made Lilla a traitor. Will he burn for me?

I am burning now.

The heat is scorching my face. There's a torch in my hand. Gyrth has to support me as I lean forward. The flames catch on the kindling and roar up. Gyrth pulls me back from them. They are leaping across the burnished steel and bronze of the weapons. Lilla's body twists in the fierce heat, as though he were still alive. The air is dancing with devils of sparks and ash. I shut my ears to the howling incantations of Coifi and his priests.

I have done what I could. I ordered the Romans to pray for my friend's soul.

The austere face of Paulinus haunts me. 'Your friend was not baptized. He had his chance for eternal life. It is too late for him, my son. But not for you.'

Those words are nails in the coffin of my heart. I am filled with despair.

'*Greater love has no man than this, that a man lays down his life for his friend,*' I told him.

Paulinus looked startled. 'You know the scriptures, sire?'

I have nearly betrayed myself for Lilla.

The smoke is thinning. The breeze whirls it sideways and leaves a high clear blue.

Out of a heaven like this skylarks used to sing. Nevyn once sat in the heather and threw back her head in a peal of laughter. 'Boys! Do you think the arms of God aren't wider than that? Of course we need the grace of the Church. It's a hard road we walk together. But before everything else he looks for the will of the heart. The love of Christ begins there.'

Nevyn and Rhun have a different idea of God from Paulinus.

I look down towards the chapel, through the twisting flakes of ember carried on the wind. I listen, but I cannot hear the deep voice of James singing a mass for the dead. Is Paulinus praying?

The pyre collapses. There is a last burst of flame. I can see the body no more.

Lilla is dead. Lilla is dead.

Paulinus is scornful. 'Is this gratitude, sire? Before I came to Northumbria, I heard that King Edwin was the greatest of men, a generous gold-giver. But God has delivered to you three priceless lives: your own, your queen's and your child's. Will you still give him nothing in return?'

I will make a deal with him. 'My daughter Eanfled shall be baptized. And she may take a royal escort with her, twelve Northumbrian men and women. Will that satisfy you?'

I see the flame in his eyes. He has won the first of my Northumbrian English, and a princess.

If Lilla had lived, could he have been one of those twelve, and kept his British past silent?

It is not enough. 'But you, sire? You lead this whole country. The people look to you.'

I stave him off.

It is cool by the riverbank. There are not enough leaves yet on the trees to screen the breeze. Slowly, my strength is returning. Paulinus will baptize my little daughter at Pentecost. Before then, he and James must instruct the catechumens who will accompany her.

There is someone already at the river's edge. Hild. She will never be tall like Hereswith, but today she looks more of a square-set, stocky child than the twelve-year-old young lady she should be. She is hurling stones into the stream with a furious concentration.

'What's wrong, Hild?'

She turns her honest face. Her wide grey eyes are bright with tears. 'She's going to be a Christian.'

'Baby Eanfled? I've promised Tata. A king must honour his debts, mustn't he? It was on the feast day of Christ's rising I escaped the assassin and she bore the baby safely.'

'I don't care about the baby. It's Hereswith.'

'Oh. I see.'

She throws another stone, her mouth set to stop it trembling. We watch it plop, the water sucking it under, the ripples spreading. I put my arm around my niece's shoulders, and feel the muscles taut to stop them drooping.

'Hild,' I say, 'the "battler". Still fighting?'

'Tata gathered us together and named the twelve Northumbrians to go with the princess Eanfled to her baptism. Six women, six men. She chose Hereswith first. You should have seen her face.' And now Hild's voice does shake.

I hold her closer. I know the bond between these sisters. I picture the birch-white grace of Hereswith, her face tilted so passionately to the Queen they both adore, her eyes shining like starlight. Hereswith has longed for this as much as Lilla. It is only my own silence which has kept her back.

'Not you, Hild?'

'I was terrified she'd ask me. She looked straight at me and I was certain she was going to call my name. But then she laughed. Tata's got such a bubbly kind of laugh, hasn't she? She makes you want to do anything for her. But she only said, "Don't look so frightened, Hild. I shan't force any of you under the waters of baptism. You have to want Christ with your whole heart." And then she wasn't laughing any more; she looked so sad. I think it was you she really meant, not me. But Hereswith was smiling, sort of pale and brilliant at the same time, like the moon rising. You know the way she does.'

'And you didn't want to follow them, not though you love them both so much?'

'*You* love Tata. And you're not a Christian.' She says it defiantly. She is as loyal as Lilla. What have I done to you, Hild? Where am I leading Northumbria?

'Were you really terrified? Would you do it, if it wasn't for me?'

Hild wriggles free of my grasp. She picks up another stone, but does not throw it. She stands, juggling it in her hand, considering. Hild has a mind as sharp as any of my counsellors. She weighs both sides before she speaks.

'I try to imagine what it must have been like when our great-great-grandparents came in the longships. Mustn't it have been exciting, sailing across the sea and sighting an unknown land? I'd want to be the first one to jump ashore. When Paulinus reads to us out of one of his books, that's just as strange. I go all funny inside just hearing the Latin, even before he puts it into English. There's power in those books, isn't there?' Hild's eyes turn up to search my face. 'Do you think I could ever learn to read?'

'If you want to. Tata can, a little.'

She flings the stone away, a bad throw that rattles off a rock. 'But it's not Northumbrian, is it?' she scowls. 'It's all very well for those soft folk down in Kent. We're not like them, are we? We're Woden's folk, and Tiw's and Frigg's. We fight for what we want. Our power's in the spear, not a book. Only . . . you were there. I saw you in the starlight, that Easter midnight. You were listening outside the chapel, Uncle Edwin, weren't you? What did you feel when Paulinus gave that great shout, "Christ is risen!" and all the lights burst into flower and everybody yelled back "Alleleuia!"?'

We both stand silent.

Pentecost. Wind and flame. I, Edwin, King of Northumbria, descended from Woden, have come to Tata's chapel to witness my daughter's Christian baptism.

Eanfled is a pale baby, small and delicate as a windflower. I try to imagine that one day she may be a tall, free-striding woman like her mother.

Now, unwrapped from her swansdown and lambswool, naked in Paulinus's long arms, she looks even more vulnerable. A little snowflake of a baby.

He demands oaths from her sponsors, turns his black sleeves back, goes down the steps into the small baptistry, only a tank beaten from lead scavenged from the Roman ruins. My queen's oratory is a modest place compared with the temple of Woden at Goodmanham.

I find Paulinus more alarming than Woden's priests. He dips my child under the water and I fear she will drown. The threefold signing, in the name of the Trinity of Father, Son and Spirit. Each time I shudder. The words are nails in my flesh. It does not matter that this chapel is a hundred and fifty miles from Aberffraw, that there are four walls around us, thatch over our heads, not a rushing waterfall and a sky where buzzards wheel, that Paulinus's face is dark and stern where Rhun had laughing eyes. I have been here before. Never mind that the words are not quite the same and Paulinus says the British Church is wrong.

When he lifts the child out of the basin, she begins to scream. She is laid in her mother's arms, wrapped fresh in white. I see Hild's face. Her eyes are huge. It is not the baby or Tata she is looking at. She is staring down into that troubled water, as though searching for her own broken reflection there.

Hild cannot feel what I do: the roar of that waterfall, scattering spray over us, as I lead my Northumbrians into its cold death, Rhun's strong arms raising me up to where the blue heaven blazes over me and all the blackbirds are singing psalms to their Creator, the sun too brilliant to look at, the rushing water carrying my past away.

I cannot have that moment back again.

Cadwallon's dark eyes mocking me, even as he welcomes me into his Church.

It was your fault, Cadwallon! You cheated me. You drove me out.

Now Eanfled's Northumbrian escort are coming to the baptistry. They are all grave, conscious of the importance of this moment, for themselves, for Northumbria. Tata is looking at me, still nursing the baby in her arms. I know she is willing me to make the same declaration. I must not look back at her, in case my eyes betray me.

Let me watch Hereswith, with the same intensity Hild is giving her sister. The taller girl looks like an angel. her hands crossed on her breast, her grey eyes lifted. Her face is rapt, almost as if she sees heaven. The old dress slips from her shoulders. Paulinus deluges her with water. She is visibly shocked by the cold, humiliated, lost. Paulinus holds her steady for a moment before he lifts her, drenched, blind, gasping like another baby. The fatherly hands of James the Deacon, the Kentish ladies who are now her sisters, are helping Hereswith up into a new life, clothing her in Whitsun white.

I look across the pool and see Hild biting her lip. She has lost her sister to the Christians and her own chance to be the first Northumbrian woman to take this challenge.

Paulinus has not done yet. He stoops over me like a hawk. 'Sire, what more sign do you need? Our human lives are short and dangerous. Why will you not decide yourself before it's too late?'

Even sparrows turn and mob the hawk that torments them. 'Can't you at least let me alone till I've paid Lilla's honour-price? Let me have vengeance on Cwichelm of Wessex first.'

Chapter Twenty

I am not a coward. *I am not a coward.* What man dares say that to my face?

I can bind on a sword again, though the scar from the knife-point that struck through Lilla still makes me wince. I'm not finished yet.

We are riding down on Wessex. The warhost of Northumbria is marching behind me. The winged orb of my standard struts in front of me. I can rival any Roman general who conquered Britain.

I have buried the past, the long shame of exile. Now I'm going to slaughter Cwichelm for the treachery of trying to take my life.

Gyrth has edged his mount closer to mine. 'Does your wound still pain you, my lord?' He is very conscious of his responsibility, with Lilla dead. Too conscientious. He lacks Lilla's sensitivity. Gyrth doesn't allow the tactful space of the lifelong friend who understood my need of privacy.

'It's nothing to the wound Cwichelm's going to get when I meet him face to face.'

Gyrth grins. This is what my men want to hear. This is why they follow me to death.

'Is it over?'

I'm staggering over rutted ground. Out of a hot sky the crows are spiralling down like a plague of flies over a corpse. There are many corpses. I must have killed some of them.

I do not remember clearly.

'You were magnificent, my lord. You fought like Thunor hurling thunderbolts in a raging storm. I don't know what magic they put on that knife Eumer tried to kill you with, but you've turned their death-curse back on Wessex.'

'Did I kill Cwichelm?' I weave uncertainly off my course. I am not sure where I'm going.

'No.' Gyrth catches my arm. It hurts where he holds it, but I think I'm more bruised than cut. 'But Wessex won't be troubling Northumbria again for a very long while.'

He has found me my horse, held under the edge of the trees. It seems an impossibly long way up to the saddle, but a king always has help. I am not a warleader who sits on horseback, directing my warriors from a safe distance. I was in the thick of it, Gyrth and the others making a shield wall round me, but my path through the enemy clear in front. We slaughtered them.

They're cheering me to the stars tonight. It's not only cowardly Britons and Picts my warhost can thrash. The West Saxon warriors were as English as we are. Northumbrians are the best. And I'm their king.

The ale cups are sparkling with starlight. The flames leap up on shaggy pelts and bearded faces. Teeth flash and praise songs roar. The men are drunk with power as well as ale. One of Coifi's priests is dancing before the gods, live snakes on his staff making grown warriors leap for safety. We have won. I'm alive.

I'm still alive. If I had died in this battle, men would have honoured me, women would have wept over me. The skalds would have sung how the Valkyries swooped down from the sky to bear off Woden's hero.

Only Tata would have broken her heart over such a death.

We march into York in triumph. I fix a grin on my face, turning from side to side as the Northumbrians cheer me. I have avenged Lilla's honour. No one can call me a coward.

We've reached the palace already. Tata comes almost running to meet me. The golden disc of ale is swinging in the cup she is carrying with both hands. Her intelligent face is alight as a girl's, as she turns it up to kiss me. I hug her fiercely.

'God kept you safe. I knew he would. And there's even a present waiting for you indoors. All the way from Rome!'

I swing down from my horse. Her fingers lace warmly through mine and she tugs my hand. I let her lead me out of the milling crowd into the privacy of my own quarters.

Someone else has followed, deferentially catching my eye by his very stillness. Paulinus's head stoops slightly forward on his long neck, like a cormorant's. His desire reaches ahead of his eyes. The spirit burns in his bloodless face.

He is only my queen's chaplain. He has no authority over me.

Yet I feel the power of his presence. He moves smoothly into my line of vision now, obeying Tata's insistence to show me a leather case. She cannot wait for me to open it, like a small child with a Yuletide present.

'It's from the Pope himself.'

My stomach tightens. They will not let me rest, these two. They mean to harry me until I surrender. I motion Paulinus to undo the fastenings.

In spite of myself, I gasp with pleasure. Pope Boniface means to flatter me. Tata is holding up a tunic which is unlike anything I have in my chests. White, with a pattern of gold ornament, like a Roman toga. The apostles wore robes like this in the paintings in Cadfan's church.

The thought confuses me. To hide my flushed face I bend to examine what lies underneath. My hands lift out a gorgeous cloak, lined with soft black bearskin, but brilliant outside in scarlet wool and silver embroidery.

'There's a letter,' cries Tata. 'He sent me one too.'

The marks on the parchment she is showing me dance with a knowledge I do not have. I swore as a boy I did not want it.

Could Cadwallon read this?

'Don't you want to know what it says?'

'Read it.'

'*To the illustrious Edwin, King of the English: Boniface, Bishop, servant of the servants of God. Christ is offering you the medicine. . . .*'

I do not have to listen to this. It is not the first such letter. They mean to trap me.

My hands fondle the scarlet wool, the gold-edged toga.

I am Edwin the King, Lord of all Northumbria, conqueror of Britain north and west, hammer of Wessex. Even the Pope in Rome knows of and honours me. I am not that boy running for his life, an exile on a Welsh hillside.

Paulinus helps me settle the cloak around my shoulders. I wish I could see myself. I can tell how magnificent I look in Tata's eyes. This is how an emperor should appear. The warmth that clothes me comes not from the old vanished Rome of the Britons, whose boast is falling into ruin in Chester and Caernarvon. Pope Boniface's gift is a tribute to me from the new and living empire.

Do you see me now, Cadwallon? Did you think when you taunted me that I would be the great king and you the exile?

The festival of Yule. This time should be the wild joy of the winter's turning. Stars are blazing in a frosty sky, the flames leap and the wassail bowl goes slopping round, wetting our eager hands with golden juice. The drums thump out for the dance and feet stamp as men fling their women round the circle.

My ears are haunted by the eerie notes of the pipes the Britons play and the flashing feet of their dancers, pointing their toes as sharp as sword blades. It is a long while since I have let myself remember dancing a reel with Mairi in Cadfan's hall at Aberffraw. How will Mairi remember me, now that I have conquered the country of our childhood?

I feel like a man living in an elegy. I have lost one life. I despair of winning another. The thickest fur-lined robe cannot keep me warm this winter. I, Edwin, the undisputed ruler of north Britain, still feel a nobody, while everybody else is rejoicing round me.

No, not everyone. A shadow slides over the floor towards my chair, a figure deliberate, silent, in catskin slippers. The shadow creeps across my knees, darkens my face. Coifi, Chief Priest of Woden.

'You have betrayed your ancestors, sire.'

'I have made no decision yet.'

'Then what are you doing here? Three days of Yule have gone, and you have not offered a single sacrifice. Is great Woden dead? Am I doing nothing but keep a memory of our All-Father? Are you waiting for the temples at Goodmanham to crumble, as the worms eat at the wood and the rooks carry the thatch away for their nests? Do you want the World Tree to fall while you sit here? Does the Day of Doom begin now, when the whole human race is consumed in fire or cold ocean, and the Wolf and the Serpent rend the world, and the gods themselves die?'

I shudder inside the bearskin. His insistent voice tells me what I know. Yule is the pivot of midwinter, when fire and sacrifice must bring the sun to life again. I have done nothing this year to make it happen. In the temple, the gods are waiting in vain for me to bathe their feet in blood.

We have another festival. The Christians are singing their carols in the winter lamplight around my wife's chair. Hereswith, like a silver-haired angel, with bliss in her face, kneeling at Tata's side, bending over our own royal baby who kicks against her swaddling bands and croons her own tunes.

Paulinus looks up and sees me. I can see desire to have my soul leap naked in his eyes.

They stalk the palace like game cocks eyeing each other, these two priests. I have done what I promised. Paulinus thunders his sermons before me. I sit with arms folded, my face set. Not even

Tata herself, pleading so sweetly, knows what is going on in my heart.

Paulinus is terrifyingly eloquent. He paints the fires of hell, the archangel Michael with his flaming sword, Christ the Reaper heaping the treacherous weeds on the bonfire and welcoming the good wheat into his barns. One thing moves me more than all his sermons. The bluff deacon James has no such power of preaching, but he makes the little oratory throb with his bass chanting, as if his voice holds a love too big to be contained by four walls. Even in my own halls his spell pursues me.

I have escaped to the Roman walls. Walking here, I can look out over the leafless forests of the plain of York, the bare brown fields. Yet still his chant thunders in my head.

'Holy, holy, holy, is the Lord God Almighty, who was and is and is to come.'

'Are we being very wrong, Uncle Edwin?'

I know the voice, but when I turn I see a stranger. Hild has passed her thirteenth year. For the first time I catch a trace of Hereswith in her square-jawed face. Longings, too large to put a name to, are beginning to film her sensible grey-blue eyes with dreams. But Hild is too honest not to see our danger.

Her short-fingered hand slips into mine, cold without mittens. 'You can feel it too. Goodmanham.'

'I promised Paulinus. I have not sacrificed to . . . idols.'

I feel the tightening of her hand.

'But if we don't? Can they keep Northumbria safe? Tata's God and Christ and the angels?'

'They call him the Creator of the whole world, God of gods and King of kings.'

'But what if he isn't?'

We both turn east, looking to where the sanctuary across the Derwent has always drawn us with powerful cords.

'Can't you feel it?' she whispers. 'The way we used to go.'

Even up here, in the bright clear air on the walls, we can both feel the forest dark, thickly shadowing the climbing valley with its awe of massive trees. Hild's fingers clench on mine.

'We'd never have dared to go there cold and sober, would we? We had to be light-headed with fasting and spells, before we set out. At Yuletide, we'd be wrapped up in fur, our boots pounding on the hard ground, and we'd be clapping our cold hands as we danced our way to the gods. I'd have a chaplet of ivy and holly, only I could never keep it straight on my hair, could I? We took whatever leaves and berries were bright with winter life. Remember how our breath used to steam, and the drums and rattles and horns used to beat in our blood?

'And suddenly we'd come out from under the trees and we'd be in the sharp light of the clearing. I'd feel the old power in the trees they'd felled, crying out for the hurt that had been done to them. Only those trees had had to fall to make room for something more powerful still. We'd be looking up at that high fence round the enclosure, and creatures with masks waiting at the gates. And I'd know that what was inside was even more awful.'

She shudders.

'You should be a storyteller, Hild. You have the gift.'

She blushes darkly. 'But now it was your turn. You were the one who had to ask admittance for the Northumbrian people. Coifi would summon us in. All the priests would be chanting incantations to keep us safe. And there, inside the temple, we'd come face to face with it: that carved pillar, freshly painted, but dark at the roots with the drink he always demands. You'd pour out the blood.'

'But all the time, I was thinking how Aethelfrith the Ferocious must have stood on that very spot, making sacrifices to this same god, to ask him for my blood.'

'I was always too frightened to look up at it,' Hild mutters.

I'm still holding her small hand. I know the terror she means, that threw us prostrate on the floor, making his Tree rear over us, taller, more terrifying. This midwinter too, I should have been there. I should have held the knife, the bowl, done the things Coifi told me.

I have done nothing.

We should all be there, King, Queen, thanes, warriors, all the Northumbrian nobles, priests and common folk. No fire has been lit to Thunor. No blood has been poured for Mother Erce. No prayers have been chanted to Lady Frigg for the spring to follow.

'Will it still be all right?' breathes Hild. 'Can the sun come back, if we don't ask them? Are the flowers going to open? Will the cows drop their calves? Will the fields stand full come harvest-time?'

I shoot a look at this niece of mine, who is still half a child. Her eyes are gazing out towards Goodmanham, intense as though she is issuing a challenge to Woden himself. Hild already understands power and suffering. Aethelfrith murdered her father, as well as mine.

She turns to me doubtfully. 'Paulinus says Christ made a sacrifice of his own body. We don't need any other sacrifice, ever again. And yet. . . they eat his flesh and blood.' Her eyes grow huge. 'That's their great mystery. Until you're baptized, you're not allowed to see that.'

'It's not what you think. It starts as ordinary bread and wine,' I reassure her. 'The priest blesses them, and they become Christ's body and blood for us. That's the moment when they ring the bell.'

Too late, I see the truth flash in her honest eyes, like lightning over the grey North Sea.

'But they never tell you that, not unless you're going to be baptized! You know, Uncle! You've been there. At their Eucharist. You never told me you were a Christian.'

I drop her hand, which is suddenly hot with indignation.

'It was a long time ago. You forget, I was brought up in a Christian country. The whole of Cadfan's court. . . .'

The steady grey-blue eyes fix me with their spear-straight gaze. 'And I thought I was being loyal, waiting for you to lead Northumbria to Christ.'

Chapter Twenty-one

I feel like a stranger, sitting in my wife's chambers. Hers is a smaller hall than mine and the fire leaps warmly. Her women are spread around her like a meadow of flowers, fair braided heads bent over their sewing.

Hild looks uncomfortable, too. Her short legs never seem to bend with the same ease as Hereswith's longer limbs. Poor girl, she's almost swamped by that thick crimson curtain she's stitching. I feel my lips twitch in sympathy. Too delicate for Hild the intricate embroidery that will grace Tata's bodice for a festival, or the gold and silver thread for the altar hangings of the Queen's chapels. But she stabs away doggedly, loyal to whatever service Tata asks of her.

While the women sew, the Roman reads to us. His voice comes deep with passion out of his narrow, stooped chest, a note of harshness almost to breaking. At times his eyes fly up to his audience, dark with intensity. He fixes his eyes now on one of his hearers with a single-mindedness that makes her shudder. Hild is visibly startled when his gaze lights on her. Yet she will not look away. More often than not, her eyes are on him and not on the curtain, where her needle is straying. Then she glances down and gasps with dismay, catches back the straggling stitches with impatient fingers and struggles to thread the wool through the needle again.

I have been watching her. Each time she flexes her bent legs, she wriggles a little closer to the priest's knee. I think terror and curiosity are warring in the girl. She is afraid that if she slips the rope that still holds her, the current will sweep her away.

Will Hild betray me to him?

Paulinus is reading from the Acts of the Apostles. Suddenly his eyes seek out mine, accusingly. I feel a recoil of guilt. Why? The Roman is paraphrasing the written Latin into the bolder poetry of our English tongue. I am to be left no excuse for not understanding.

'When Peter laid his hands on the new Christians, the miracle of the Holy Spirit possessed them. A false magician, Simon Magus, saw this and offered great wealth to buy this power. But Peter cursed him, and all his gold and silver.

'So it will be with all the heathen who dedicate their treasure to idols. But, worse than that, Britain too has false holy men, who shave their heads with the same tonsure Simon used. Simon Magus was a baptized Christian. When Augustine brought the gospel to the English, the bishops of the British Church refused to accept his authority. They baptize their people with a different rite from Rome's. They celebrate Easter on a different day. God cursed them at Chester when Aethelfrith slew their monks.'

His eyes hold mine. He is like a cauldron seething towards the boil. My mind flies to my own baptism by Rhun. He cannot know, can he?

And then my heart bounds. For the first time, I seem to see a small gap in the spear ring which surrounds me, through which I may yet dash to safety. If the baptism of Rhun's church was false. . . .

I stride from the room, tearing myself away from the eyes that pursue me: Tata's, brimming with love and alarm, the embroidery hovering over her lap so that I have to tell her curtly to stay where she is – I need no help; Hild's, suddenly more adult than her thirteen years, the flash in her eyes like that in my bodyguards' when they realize we are going into a decisive battle; Paulinus's, dark with the thrill of belief that his words are finding their mark.

I come out of our wooden palace to walk on the old stone walls which ring York round. This is my favourite refuge. Here, at least, Gyrth allows me space, though he has come out of the hall behind me. Let him see my silhouette against the pale winter sky, the black, lonely shape of his king, in keeping with my heart.

I start to pace the massive Roman stones, in boots too soft for this freezing weather. I can feel the hard cold of the walkway, uneven now where the wall is slipping, settling back into the landscape from which it was wrenched. The wind is biting through my gown, though it's lined with good beaver fur. I'm holding myself too tense to shiver.

I lift my face to the wind. Let me look on this land, my land, for which my father gave his life. Northumbria: the rolling billows of trees, grey without leaves; the flash of the flooded Ouse, a sash of silk round the city walls; my people at work, ploughing the bare brown soil, driving donkeys along slippery roads, staggering under the weight of laden buckets. York at peace, where blood has flowed. My land, my peace. A greater realm than my father ruled. So many people, looking to me.

Can the British Church really be false? Into my heart comes a memory of Nevyn, on a heather-clad hillside of Ynys Mon, where there was only a whisper of difference between the skylarks' song and the chorus of angels.

The truth hits me. Could I face Nevyn now? She was never soft with princes, though she wore a slave's tunic. I invaded Ynys Mon. My soldiers scoured the land and turned it into Anglesey. I do not know what happened to Nevyn.

On the road below a young woman is coming, side-saddle on a mule, with her baby tied in a shawl. She glances up idly, starts when she sees the richness of my dress. I cannot hide who I am. She stammers confused respect, which the wind almost blows away.

She must know I have not been to Goodmanham this Midwinter

to do what the English gods demand. All my people are waiting. It is the king's duty to keep this land whole. The destiny of the English rests on me.

The air is too bitter, my soul too cold to be bared. I seek refuge in a little turret built where the wall angles, to shelter a Roman sentry, a retreat now for an English king. There is a stone ledge to serve as a bench, a flight of steps up from the court.

I sit here hunched, with my back to the cold wall and the roofs of my palace rearing beyond it. Before my eyes instead is a square of grey sky, just a little of that huge heaven over the plain of York. I must concentrate on this. No skylarks here; no hawk swinging its threat high over the ground; no Thunor's thunderbolt; no angels' highway. I am alone. I, King Edwin, feeling Rhun's sign of the cross on my forehead burn like a brand.

Paulinus says the rites of the British Church are invalid.

I see Rhun's lean face, his laughing eyes, feel the strength of his hands lifting me from the water. Can I deny that?

If it were true, I should never need to tell Paulinus, or Tata.

Is this desertion, or my salvation?

I do not know how long my face has been sunk in my hands, knuckles clenched against the impossibility of any decision I can still make with honour.

'*Christ, help me.*' I dare not say these words aloud.

Somewhere along the wall a birch tree clinging to the cracks scrapes its boughs over the stones with a sound too like an iron knife forced between ribs. I screw my eyes tighter shut within the darkness of my hands.

The warmth of the touch shocks me. I've heard no footsteps on the stone stair. I sensed no warning of a human approaching. I'm shuddering violently, like a tree about to fall. He holds me still. The firm pressure of his two hands enfolds my bared head.

My body remembers this, long before my conscious thoughts. I know I must not uncover my eyes, leap up, reach for my weapon. I crouch beneath his touch, tensed for the gap to be bridged, for light to shine on the knowledge which is lying in ambush for me. And yet I find I am yearning for the wound which is coming.

'You remember this sign, Edwin.'

It is not a question. The double recognition which springs to my mind confuses me utterly. All these months, and I have failed to make the connection. All this time I have listened to the thunder of his sermons, the persuasion of his stories, the righteous anger of his argument. Only now, with the clasp of his fingers on my head, I feel the truth.

I am a young man again, at the end of my hope. In Redwald's court at Ipswich I sit waiting for the verdict that will deliver me into Aethelfrith's malice. All the escape that is left is the goblin-haunted fens and the cold sea that carries slain warriors away.

Then these hands fall on my head. This voice speaks. This is the stranger who promised me my kingdom. And I promised I would serve his King.

I feel the flood-surge rising, threatening to tear away the last tree-trunk damming the river and sweep me headlong down the current. I throw myself on my knees, so that I might not have to look up and know that it is Paulinus.

The Roman restrains me. 'It is not to me you kneel, my son. I am not your King. But Christ who is, promised you two kingdoms, here and in eternity. You have taken hold of one. What of the other?'

I am aware of the chill in the stones, striking up through my knees to the pit of my stomach. I have known an enemy on the battlefield defeated even before his sword engages with mine, as soon as he realizes whom he is fighting. This man has such power over me. I scrabble for time, like a man who has dropped coins in the mud.

'The King of Northumbria is not a private man. Whatever I decide, the nation will follow me. They chose me for their warleader, but in matters of wisdom, I don't decide alone. There's the Witan of Northumbria: earls and thanes, priests and skalds, the wise women. It will take time to call them together.'

'Summon them now.'

I start to rise. I'm almost eager now. I'm the hero dashing through this gap between the spears to victory.

His hand stays me. 'You, Edwin, are their king. What will *you* say to your Witan?'

I spring to my feet, pushing his words away with his hands. There is action to be done. It is too late now for thought. As a warrior charging towards the spears knows that the outcome is already past changing, I find a wild rejoicing that there can be no turning back. I have dropped all doubt and dishonour behind these battlelines. Rhun's baptism was false.

'I believe . . . the Christ of Rome has power to save me.'

I need never see the contempt in Tata's eyes.

I am the King. I'm sitting alone on the dais before my Witan, but the tide of destiny has lapped to its high water-mark and reaches up to me, even here. Below me, the wise and noble and brave of Northumbria are gathered in a horseshoe. Their familiar faces are turned up to mine, but they're altered today, as mine must be, by the sense that we have reached our historic moment. There's Coifi, with the reptile tattoos of his priesthood seeming to writhe as his cheeks twitch; Earl Wighard, too crippled to lead the spears into battle now, his face blotched and crusted with age, like lichen on a boulder. I have always thought of Gyrth as younger than most of these counsellors, but the years are overtaking him too. It is the distant past now, when he and Lilla and the rest snatched me away from Catterick to safety at Aberffraw. They're fallen now, most of that bodyguard, but Gyrth remains. His face is stolid, carved. He would no more betray a change of emotion than the frowning beasts that guard my doorposts. Gyrth would not betray me.

They are all loyal to me, yet I have to sit above them in a loneliness beyond words.

The slightest movement of my finger and Gyrth marches

forward, up the steps, to set my standard in the socket beside my chair. I steal a sideways glance at the winged globe. I am the master of this world. It's far more than Northumbria; all north Britain enjoys the peace of a strong king.

The old wound of the assassin's knife-point grips me in the chest.

I am a good king. *I am a good king.*

I grasp the rough-feathered ravens carved on the arms of my chair. I am willing myself to believe in my own honour.

I must speak first. My voice sounds harsh. 'I have summoned this Witan to counsel the King on the future of Northumbria. You all know that when I married Queen Aethelberg, it was written into the contract that she and her people should be free to practise their Christian faith and I too should listen to her priest. It was Kent's hope that the King of Northumbria would accept their Christ. This is no light matter for the royal family of Woden.

'But you have witnessed the favours given to me by Christ: my life saved from treachery, my daughter safely born, my enemies defeated. Do you say victory for Northumbria lies that way? Shall I call Paulinus into this hall to preach this new religion to you?'

Their eyes shift uneasily away from me. On the left-hand end of their horseshoe Coifi, Chief Priest of Woden, sits in his full regalia, feathers, furs, rattles, pouches. His eyes stare out through the ritual contortions of beasts netting his face, like a warrior's through the holes of an iron helmet. He is no less fearsome.

I am afraid of this man. He can prevent this decision. But what will happen to Northumbria if he delivers us back into Woden's power?

Earl Wighard comes straight to the point. 'What's the King's own mind?' He was a canny fighter, when he could still carry sword and shield. I may need to parry him now.

'It's my wish to keep silent until the wise of Northumbria have given me their voice.'

'I say I'll follow my king, to death or Rome.'

'Aye.'

The rumble of assent which follows Wighard's declaration is uncertain. They see the possibility of change drawing closer. On the faces of some at least dread is evident. They would have shown no fear if I had told them Cadwallon was marching on us for vengeance at the head of a massive British warhost. Warrior, poets, wise women alike, they know well what is happening. I am setting an axe to the roots of the World Tree in the temple at Goodmanham. If I do topple Woden, will Northumbria itself collapse? Their eyes stray back to Coifi.

I must seize the moment. 'Well, Chief Priest? You, more than any of us, are the voice of those we have called our gods till now. What do they command you? Will Red-Handed Tiw and Thunor the Hammerer run away from this challenge from the one they call the Prince of Peace? Or shall I let Paulinus preach conversion to the Witan?'

Coifi hauls himself slowly upright, hampered by his robes. He is not an old man, but both his hair and face are greyed, as if by long immersion in the smoke of sacrifice. From the magpie feathers braided in his hair to the striped catskin slippers on his feet, he bears the marks which set him apart from ordinary men. A priest of Woden may not bear weapons or ride a stallion, but the knees of the hardiest warrior weaken before his power, cowed by the presence of a different strength.

My chief priest raises himself upright now in silence. This is a man whose every action has the drama of ritual. His human figure is lost under the fur-tailed cape, his features veiled behind those tattoos. Only his eyes gleam free. I tense, like all the others, waiting for the wrath of his condemnation. For loyal conservatives, this is the champion who can rescue them from the terror of change. To those who already fear Paulinus's hell-fire more, Coifi is the opponent most to be dreaded.

He gives me a slow, twisted smile. I feel physically sick, waiting for his onslaught.

'Your majesty. . . .' His fingers are working at the bronze and amber clasp at his throat. He twists his neck within the confining collar as if struggling to escape it. His voice is strained. 'My parents gave me to the gods when I was an infant too young to talk. All my life I have served as acolyte, priest, now chief priest, to King Aethelfrith and to you. For Northumbria, I've fasted, prayed, sacrificed, before All-Father Woden and every god and goddess. And what have my masters and mistresses done to reward my devotion? Consider it well, all of you.' He swings to include the whole hall in his contempt. He even laughs, a little. 'When was the last time your king led you to the temple of his father's gods? Does he make the royal sacrifices for the wholeness of Northumbria? Does he heap his priests with gold? No, not for many months now. When his Kentish queen bore him a child, did he dedicate his daughter to Frigg?'

Fear is moaning from some of them.

'No. The King of Northumbria has found himself another priest, a different counsellor.' His attention swings back to me and I stiffen against the brilliance of these eyes. 'And what about me? I've been waiting for One-Eyed Woden the Wise to vindicate me with blood. Why hasn't Eostre withheld her spring from this land? I expected Thunor to hurl his hammer at you. Tiw should have heaped your battlefields with Northumbrian corpses.

'But no. Northumbria is peaceful and prosperous. You have cowed all your enemies. Your people love you. I hear them say that a young woman with a newborn baby in her arms could walk your land from the eastern shore to the west and no one would dare lift a hand to molest them. Oh yes, you're a great king now. If there are living gods in temples like Goodmanham or in the castles of the sky, then they have bitterly betrayed their chief priest. Or else I have been sacrificing to blocks of wood. You ask me what I think. Well then, I should like to know if there is real power somewhere else.'

His fingers have clawed the clasp open. The enormous cloak of variegated pelts slides to the floor with a silent rush. There's a hiss of astonishment all round the Witan. That robe used to invest his spare figure with a larger dignity. We find ourselves staring at a stranger. Coifi, too, is looking down at his cast-off garb as if in surprise. Then he shrugs his narrow shoulders. His smile splits freer now.

He takes his seat in an awed hush. None of us knows what this means. He's starting to disentangle the feathers from his hair, strewing the floor around him. If it were not for the tattoos darkening his skin, he would look like a plucked chicken.

I cannot find the breath to speak. The hall is hollow with our silence. The wind moans, and a gust of hail spatters the far window-frame.

Then, in through that unshuttered hole shoots a tiny brown flicker of a life. A bird goes darting from rafter to rafter, too frightened to perch for long. Rescued from the enormity of Coifi's defection, we stare at this minute drama over our heads. Now it comes flying into the brightness over the central fire and sharpens into definition as a common sparrow. I will it to alight overhead, safe, warm. It sweeps another circuit and settles on a beam. I watch it gratefully. My royal hospitality will keep it secure.

In the silence, a log falls, releasing a rush of warmth. The crash sends the sparrow into flight again. It goes speeding over my head, out of the fire's reach, flinging itself through the smoking torchlight behind me. Even as I twist to watch, I catch my breath in dismay. I have a last glimpse of its tiny body dashing out through the western window into the storm. It is gone for ever, lost in that howling gloom.

I feel I am that sparrow.

I force myself to turn back to our business. Their faces are still lifted to where they saw the bird vanish. I incline my head courteously towards Earl Wighard. He's a veteran of my warhost. His skin shows seamed with scars, even wrapped as he is against cold and age. Uncovered, he could boast far more to prove how often he's looked death in the face, to defend Northumbria.

'Well, Earl Wighard? It seems that Woden's champion doesn't wish to fight his cause. What does the most famed spearman of Northumbria say?'

He looks over my head for a long while to the gale-lashed window hole, then lowers his eyes to meet mine. 'Did you see that sparrow, sire? It found its way out of the storm and hail into the light of our feast hall. For a few moments there was a fire blazing and a stout door against the draught. But that poor bird couldn't stop. Just a few more beats of its wings, a few flutters of its little heart, and it was out through another hole into winter darkness. We shan't see it again. Are our lives more than that?

'Look at me. If I'd died on the battlefield, I might have been taken up to glory in Valhalla. But what have I got to hope for now, old as I am?'

Doubt stalks the floor, with death behind it. What can any of the English hope for, without a hero's death? Coifi leans forward, like a slanting staff, to listen. Wighard faces his gaze.

'Coifi is right, sire. Even our greatest gods fear the coming of the dark. At the end of the world, the jaws of the Death-Wolf will swallow them as well as us. What do our English gods offer us, for all we give them? Does this Paulinus say there's a land of light beyond that window? If he knows a Father whose sky-feast will never end, if his Christ has really slain the Wolf, I say we should listen to the Roman.'

'Is there anyone here who would speak against that?'

I can feel some minds struggling against assent, as the sparrow beat its wings against the roof that could have kept it safe. Still no one speaks. One little bird has silenced all argument.

The doors of the hall are flung open. But it is not Paulinus. I am facing Tata.

Her face is eager. Her blue eyes fly to mine, her hope transparent. I sense how intensely she has been praying while we were debating. She walks towards me. I still do not know how a woman

188

can look so much like a queen, taller than common, her straight spine lifting her proud head high so that the light catches the rippling strands of her hair looped in many knots of gold, and yet, even after childbirth, still a merry girl herself. I dare not disappoint her.

Hereswith glides like a silver shadow at her shoulder, her guardian angel now. And Hild. . . . I meet my niece's eyes, round with curiosity. It comes to me like a knife-thrust. Hild knows my past. Before those keen grey eyes, I feel myself on trial.

Tata and her retinue sweep towards the dais, like reinforcements at the crisis of a battle. I force the muscles of my cheeks into a smile for her, and hold out my hand. She seats herself in the chair beside mine, with a perfumed whisper of her skirts. and I feel a rush of warmth towards her. I wish everyone else would go away. My body is longing for her, so joyful, so sure, so single-hearted. Nothing must happen to separate me from her.

But she's standing again. The throng round the hall has swelled to the whole court now. For a moment I'm confused. Then the voice of James chanting a deep litany signals the truth to me. He is bearing the cross forward. I rise. In that uncertain movement, I seem already to have made my decision.

Paulinus follows. I feel my throat tighten with apprehension. He has put off his plain black tunic. Today he comes dressed in the most gorgeous panoply of the office of bishop: cloth of gold, finest white linen, lace that has taken months to work, a tall ecclesiastical crown, the crook in his hand banded with silver, studded with amber and amethyst. They make a magnificent casket of clothes to hold the man himself. Tall, burning, stooped forward, he sweeps towards me, as if his eager head is hastening to this encounter faster than his more disciplined body will allow him. I know a tremor of doubt. Can this really be the man who spoke so quietly to me in the darkness of that East Anglian night? Were these indeed the hands which rested on my head, giving me courage and confidence, when I was at the end of my hope? Or was that an angel?

James has stopped singing and his bluff features flush a deeper shade of red as he concentrates on setting up his cross opposite my royal globe. The emblems of Rome flank me now on either side, Church and State.

Paulinus represents the Roman empires of heaven and earth.

Tata flashes a smile at James to reward him. I seat myself again and sign to those whose rank entitles them to do the same.

Paulinus stands before me, more imposing than ever. He signs himself at three points. His eyes appeal to Heaven. I feel the strength of the weapons and armour he is girding on. Now his keen gaze moves slowly round the hall. He lets it dwell on every face, commanding attention. Then he turns, and at last his eyes find mine.

He is a sorcerer. I feel myself falling under his spell even before he speaks. I already feared his influence. I have watched him move the women in Tata's rooms to cries of pity and ecstasy. I have heard her chapel walls ring with his eloquence. I underestimated his power. Paulinus is one of those orators whose authority swells with the size of his audience. Before a crowd like this he is awesome.

His voice is resonating somewhere in my guts. I am hardly paying attention to what he is saying. From the moans and the gasps of longing I know the same emotion is sweeping all of them. We are a flock of lambs dominated by an eagle; we are children terrified by his thunder. Now his voice sinks, sweetens. He is pleading with us. He holds out strong arms of love to rescue us. I begin to see a dawn of light. High God becomes an infant in a stable, while angels stoop in wonder. I watch amazed the lepers cleansed, the mourners dance for joy. Then the horror of Christ's crucifixion stuns us all into appalled silence. In the hush of early morning we hold our breath in the garden where Peter and John kneel at the empty tomb. And now light dazzles from the rafters as we follow Paulinus's ecstatic gaze and see Christ ascend into the realms of glory with hosts of angels casting down crowns before him.

I hear the Great Father bend from his throne to welcome his Son, 'Well done.'

The bishop's eyes are on me now. All that is required is the letting go of my past, washing with water, sealing with the mark of the King of glory, the gift of the Spirit. How could I ever have thought that what was done in a cold pool on a Welsh hillside could compare with royal majesty like this?

Tata's hand is clasped over mine. Her face is warm with longing. How can I refuse either of them?

Paulinus's back is turned on the passion-swayed crowd. It rests, as I know it must, on me. I am their warleader, their king. I must go first.

My eyes shift from his. All Northumbria waits for me to answer. Earl Wighard is tightening his lips, summoning his courage for this last great charge. Coifi, his curling smile accusing me, is willing me to take vengeance on the gods who failed him. James's lips quiver eagerly; I think he is already rehearsing some great psalm of praise under his breath.

I come to Hild. She is staring at me. What do those steady grey eyes want? Then her look flickers sideways to Hereswith, and an expression of silent longing consumes her face. I see the truth. I am too late to deliver Lilla. But I can free Hild.

If I deny Rhun's baptism.

The unavoidable moment is here. Another breath to draw. A few short words to speak. My kingdom's destiny hangs on this choice.

So, for the good of Northumbria, I say again before my people those few, rash, dangerous words, whose memory has haunted me so long.

'I accept Christ. May God have mercy on me, a sinner.'

And Cadwallon is not my godfather.

Tata is throwing her arms around me, kissing me ecstatically. Her tears are wet on my cheeks.

Paulinus, black eyes brilliant with joy, turns back to my court. 'Will you follow your King?'

A roar of desire meets him, drowning out his question even as he voices it. He has roused a ravenous hunger in them.

'*Aye!*'

'We are for Christ!'

'We will die for him!'

They thunder like cattle stampeding.

Over Tata's shoulder, I see that Hild is yelling with all the rest. Tears are streaking her face too. She reminds me of an obstinate pony that has backed away from the saddle for so long, but now bends, trembling, before her rider, only to find his hands and seat and knees know and love her, and the two of them are galloping madly on the road to glory.

I feel a pang of regret, for the loss of that intelligent, questioning look in her grey eyes.

But the pain eases a little. I have denied Rhun, betrayed Nevyn. I have slammed a shutter over my cowardice. I may have damned my own soul. Yet I have changed a kingdom. The gate is wide open now, and I see the English of Deira and Bernicia rushing to freedom through it.

It is not over yet. Coifi is advancing on me, his face fired like the rest of them. His eyes glitter now like a madman's. He comes kicking off his catskin slippers, spitting on his arms to scrub the paint away. He flings the otterskin pouch of his old calling at my feet. All the closely guarded secrets of Woden's magic tumble out before our appalled gaze. Withered berries, tiny shrivelled carcases, nameless pebbles. Is that all they were? One sweep of a maid's broom would banish them. Coifi himself grinds them under his calloused heel.

The air is cleansed by the booming joy of James's psalm and all the Christians of Kent and Northumbria take up the song. My own throat aches with this remembered music. Once, I stood beside Mairi and Cadwallon and we sang such praise.

Coifi has still not done. He is rushing back the length of the hall, scattering the excited crowd. The great door stands unguarded. The sentries have abandoned their watch to cheer with all the rest. From the stack of weapons left against the wall my former shaman seizes a spear and brandishes it in vengeance over his head. Again, that dislocating jar. It is not lawful for a priest of Woden to bear a weapon. He whirls defiant, silhouetted against the winter daylight. Coifi is unfamiliar now, stripped of all regalia, as frightening a figure as ever he was in his shaman's dress.

He does not wait for my permission to address me. All taboos are gone now. He is yelling at me like a man too drunk to hold.

'Sire! Give me the right to be the first to profane the temple of Woden, who betrayed me, throw down the pillar where I sacrificed for nothing! Who rides with me to Goodmanham?'

'*I!*'

A hundred warriors, inflamed with their new religion, roar their willingness. I cannot hold them. I know how they feel, the terror of what are they are now denying. The need to smother that fear with precipitate action. I long to go myself, to crush thought under the pounding of galloping hooves. Already I am seizing my sword, still laid on the table before me, hilt facing the hall in token of a peaceful council.

Tata grasps my arm. 'No, Edwin! Pope Gregory counselled the English Church to respect the sacred places of the heathens. You don't need to destroy Woden's temple. Only remove the altars and those dreadful idols. Let Paulinus re-consecrate it to Christ.'

I shake her off. I feel as wild as all the rest. I need this violence as much as Coifi does, to wipe out an old hurt with a new. But perhaps it should not be my hands that do it.

'Come here.' I buckle my sword round Coifi's bony hips. 'Leave your priest's mare in her stable. If you can bear a weapon now, you can ride a stallion too. Take mine.' The words come slurred. I am as deep drunk with this as he is.

He screams hatred, shakes the spear over his head.

My warriors are already mounting, armed for the gallop across the plain of York. James's chant has come to a faltering close. Paulinus stands, paler than ever now, as if shocked by what he has done.

'No, my children!' he cries, but no one hears him now.

Neither of us can stop this. I do not think I want to. Let us make an end.

I watch the dust of their speeding horses settle between the trees. Then I pull my hand from Tata's and turn away, saying unnecessarily loud in the half-empty hall, 'May we never see such evil again.'

Chapter Twenty-two

I ride to Goodmanham this new morning, soberly, with my court. I must see for myself.

We slow our mounts as we emerge from the forest where the dale climbs up into the Wolds, as my warband must have done yesterday. I lift my eyes. I cannot believe I will not see the massive, spiked stockade of Woden's sanctuary, the dragons rearing from the high gables of its thatch. The fear of this place has dominated my soul back into the shadows of my infancy.

I focus slowly on an iron-grey sky, empty of everything but more rain. There are no dragons. No roof but a few jutting, charred timbers. The breeze brings a reek of sodden embers. In a scared silence, I dismount with Tata and we walk forward.

Heat still steams from the awesome mounds of ash, that the night's rain has not quenched. Baulks of wood, blackened and pitted, lurk under the grey coating that clings to our boots. Are these beams from the roof, or the remnant of things more terrible? I am shaken to my core. I have done this. A word from me has made a total ruin of the English gods.

There is a line of men and women I do not recognize, murmuring fearfully. Their clothes and skin are filthy, streaked with soot. Only as I drew closer I realize that yesterday these were the gods' acolytes, wise women, shamans. Catching the madness in their eyes, I imagine them running into the open as Coifi screams his challenge to the sanctuary from my stallion. I see their horror as the holy man charges through the gate, girded with my sword, brandishing the spear no priest may carry. I see the faces of women who speered the future but never foresaw this blasphemy. I hear the panic of shamans dedicated to cursing Woden's enemies, suddenly bereft of words of power.

At the guts of my being I feel the shudder as his spear hurtles through the air, ripping apart the veneration of centuries. Here, where I am standing, it flew in through the door to the dark heart of the temple, where a sacrificial knife was the only blade ever bared. My heart shakes with the thud as its wounding flight embeds itself in Woden's Tree.

And then his scream, 'Fire it!'

How many scared moments before even the bravest of my warband grabbed up a brand from the fire of the gods' smithy and flung it at the towering thatch? My eyes go up through the sky-filled ruin. That torch crouching on the roof, its red jaws smoking like a wolf's on a winter morning. Then little wings of golden flame beginning to dance. The wind catching them and sweeping them into a sea of flame. Crashing breakers sending a spray of sparks cascading on to lesser buildings. Among the mass of men and women below screams of anguish and cheers of triumph impossible to distinguish through the roar of the fires. Sacred pillars blackening, swaying, crashing; altars going up in smoke. Coifi's authority preventing any rescue, silencing every spell.

The ruin is almost total. Only those sullen wisps of smoke, the faceless form of charred carvings. I stand shaken. My past has been destroyed.

And then realization begins to rise, the flames of joy. It is all over. It is not only Woden's worship that lies in charred embers this morning. I have beaten Cadwallon at last. I have avenged the long, long bitterness of that day when he welcomed me into the Church of Christ and then laughed in my face as he denied me Mairi.

I can start anew.

The sunlight breaks through the sodden clouds as we leave the sanctuary, and suddenly we can breathe freely. Perfume washes from wet wood. Light is transforming the beaded heads of every grass blade into gold and crystal. The blackbirds have never shouted so joyfully.

Tata squeezes my hand. She would hug me, here in front of the attending court, if she did not think it inconsistent with my dignity.

'Oh, Edwin, I feared this day would never come. I have longed so much for you to take this step. To save your soul, of course; nothing is more important than that.' She turns her face to mine, almost my equal in height. 'But also, I want you to love what I love, as I love you.' And now the laughter is coming back into her eyes. 'And there is something else.' She murmurs it low, but almost singing with joy. 'I think I am carrying your child again.'

I am shaken to my core with love and gratitude. How could I have hesitated so long? How could I ever have risked losing Tata's faith in me, her joy?

As soon as we are home I snatch her close. I think I am hurting her, but she suffers it bravely.

'There must be a royal church built for your baptism, sire,' Paulinus demands. 'It's not fitting that the King and his whole court should be baptized in one of the Queen's chambers. It should be a stone basilica, to rival Canterbury's, but we have little enough time for that between now and Easter.'

'It shall be the best that Northumbrian builders can do in forty days.'

'The great temple at Jerusalem took forty years. The finest dressed stone, cedars from Lebanon, carvings from master sculptors fit for the King of Heaven. All the English know is timber and thatch.'

'There's stone enough in York. If you can find masons to show us the use of it, you shall have a stone church later. Will that please you, Bishop Paulinus of York?'

197

I am in a good humour. This kingdom needs a chief priest to replace Coifi.

He stoops his head, to hide the eager flash of black eyes. Except when he preaches, Paulinus is deferential to kings, but he has ambition. 'Sire, when Pope Gregory sent Augustine to Canterbury he had a dream for Britain. The pattern of imperial government in Christ's Church. One archbishop for the south, in Canterbury, with twelve bishops under him. And another, equal to him in the north, also pastor to twelve dioceses.'

I cannot help but laugh. It seems my offer is not enough. 'I'm King of Northumbria, Bishop, not Pope. I can give you a headquarters in York, and permission to campaign wherever you want. I have no authority to create you archbishop.'

'With respect, sire, I have already sent word to Rome to tell Pope Boniface the news he has longed so much to hear. I think the Holy Father will know what is needed.'

We inspect the cleared space under the open sky, surrounded by the giant masonry of Roman York. The old grandeur is tumbling. A smaller thing is rising hastily. The workmen are hammering planks towards the high arched outline of the roof beams. As I step under their barred shadow, men move respectfully aside. Paulinus shadows me. The littered space is larger than the Queen's chapel, but narrow enough. We are hampering their work.

'There will not be room even now for the whole court,' I judge.

'You will come first, of course, with the two princes. Your noblemen will accompany you. Since the Queen and the princess Eanfled are already baptized, the other ladies can wait outside until the men have finished.'

Poor Hild. She could have claimed the honour of being in that first cohort last year, with my daughter. It was gentle Hereswith who marched in the front line then, not Hild, the battler. Now she must wait her turn with the other women.

I walk forward, to where two men are digging the baptistry into which we must all descend. Rain has been falling steadily through Lent. Groundwater is rising here, ankle deep even before the little tank can be lined with clay and faced with marble plundered from Roman temples.

Paulinus draws up his hood. 'The sooner your men can thatch the roof the better. Your Britain has a sorry climate, and Northumbria strikes colder than Kent.'

'The Britons. . . .' I catch the words back. I must not remember the beauty of Welsh voices weaving harmonies in the open air around a standing cross, the monks pausing in the act of hoeing a field, uniting across the abbey in one ringing psalm of praise, straight up to heaven. There was no roof to shut out the sky when Rhun reached out his strong hand and led me down over the rocks into a rushing stream bound for the Irish Sea. The shock of a peat-dark pool, the waterfall thundering above me. I seem to remember there were daisies in little Rhiainmelt's red hair, and a merlin hovering.

I am King of Northumbria now.

'Britons! Renegades. The Church of Rome moves forward like one great army under Christ's banner. You've seen the British monks' tonsure. It is not like ours, with our heads shaved in a circle, sign of our Lord's crown of thorns. Where did they get that barbaric habit of shaving the crown in front and letting their filthy tangles hang long behind? From the tonsure of magicians and druids.'

Yes, Cadwallon! I have enlisted on the winning side.

The rain has ended. This Easter morning we form our procession to claim new life from this resurrection. All we catechumens coming for baptism have put off our jewellery, our furs and embroideries. I feel the strangeness of simplicity, walking through my own capital, watched by crowds of my astonished people. Two Kentish earls attend me as my sponsors, the noblest Christians from Tata's retinue.

I know that Ostrith and Eadfrith are walking behind me, unnaturally solemn for teenage boys. I do not know what they believe in their hearts. We have not discussed it. It is unthinkable that my sons should not go where I lead.

James is carrying the cross in front of us. He lowers it carefully under the lintel of the door. We follow into the lamplit shadows.

This sanctuary, named for St Peter, is hallowed with a different sort of blood. It is no less awesome. Paulinus has sealed under the altar relics of the Great Fisherman himself, Christ's martyred apostle, to whom he has given the keys of his kingdom. Paulinus was right. This Roman Church has the stamp of authority. It recognizes dignity. Surely this is more suitable for a king than one where a bold hermit woman can berate a prince and a footloose priest appear on a beach as the Spirit moves him.

I was a military man and a king. So I move now with the discipline of the battlefield towards the baptistry where Paulinus stands.

We have rehearsed this. I renounce my sin. I swear my faith. I accept the salvation of Christ's death. Here, within the the walls of this wooden church, the sound falls dully. I close my ears to the distant echo of almost identical words in a far different place.

My sponsors lift my garments from me. Paulinus is ready. The water of the marble baptistry looks faintly muddied, though I am the first to enter it. The level hardly comes to Paulinus's knees. He stands like a long-legged heron, neck stooped to seize its prey.

I am that prize. He lifts a golden bowl and the water cascades over my head, smothering my eyes, shocking my body. Again and again.

'In the name of the Father.

'And the Son.

'And the Holy Spirit.'

I cannot breathe. The water is still pouring from my head. Then I take the first gasp. I have done it. I shall live.

The warm hands of James help me up the steps. Towels surround me to wipe my blinded eyes, mop my soaking hair. Tata comes forward to kiss me, radiant with happiness. There is a clean white tunic. Tata has embroidered this herself, white upon white. Silk threads of crosses upon costly bleached linen, simple but kingly. I shut out a vision of Rhiainmelt, childishly proud, dragging another baptismal tunic over mossy rocks, trailing through brambles.

After Tata, Earl Jaenberht clasps me as my sponsor.

I will not remember Cadwallon's embrace.

'You're shivering.' Tata exclaims. 'Put this on too. You must show yourself to your people.'

She is holding something else, besides the glistening white tunic which is flattening itself against my damp body. A magnificent cloak of gold. Her hands fasten its clasp of filigree gold, wild boars and running stags, on my shoulder. The weight and splendour of it makes me square my shoulders. The plain white tunic is a formality only. I am still Edwin, the King. My queen sets the gold circle on my head.

Paulinus on one side, Earl Jaenberht on the other, escort me out to the narrow door and the steps of the church. A river of faces swims before me down the street. A breaking roar of acclaim rolls forward. 'The King! The King! Edwin of the Northumbrians!'

I have delivered my people. I have made the way safe for them.

I return to the church and witness the long ceremonial as the noblemen are baptized. The sons of my Mercian wife are first to follow me. Strange that I hardly remember Coenburg now, though the brown eyes of Mairi haunt me still.

At last it is the women's turn. Paulinus and James will be busy for hours yet. As I head the procession out to make room for them, I see that a drizzle has begun to fall. Waiting outside, the court ladies are already wetted. I glance along the line of catechumens, and almost miss her.

Hild is holding herself resolutely grave and dignified. This is not easy for her. She is losing a little of her puppy-fat, but her lack of height makes it difficult for her not to appear a stocky child, flanked by so many tall noblewomen. Today she has pulled a modest veil round her chin, from which her face peers out like a bright moon. I miss the haphazard braids from which her hair is always escaping. But the hem of her too-long skirt is trailing in a muddy puddle. She flashes a rueful grin as she rescues it.

Then she catches my eye and the old Hild shines out for a moment. There is a steely eagerness about Hild which makes her gleam like light on a bared blade. But her gaze sweeps on past me immediately, for all my majesty of crown and stiff gold cape. Her lips are parted, breathing quickly, between terror and desire. All the intensity of her soul is now fixed on what lies ahead.

Hild is going honestly to her baptism. She has stayed loyal to me longer than she should, but now she is making her surrender to a High King greater than either of us. She is like a boy going into his first battle. For her, this is a day which will never come again.

I envy her.

Chapter Twenty-three

A mass of soldiers, peasants, invalids, beggars, children are coming scrambling for salvation now from every manor and hovel in Deira. Our little royal church can't contain them. At Catterick, James and Paulinus have baptized swarms of them in the River Swale. You would think a great flash flood up on the moors had carried all the logs in the kingdom down to jam the stream at this one pool.

'Sire,' Paulinus says to me after thirty days of work, 'we must go north now.' The fire is burning in his dark eyes like a fever.

Bernicia. I still feel I am stepping into a stranger's territory. This was Aethelfrith the Ferocious's land before it fell to me. I have never quite lost the tightening of my stomach when I see the rugged moors above Hexham, the black teeth of the Farne Islands, the crag of Bamburgh's fort.

'He's dead,' Tata reassures me, winding her strong, long arms around me. 'Bamburgh is yours now, as well as York.'

The baby is rounding her belly. I am the one who should be strong and comforting.

The North Sea is too rough for a baptismal font. Paulinus will take his stand inland, at my palace of Yeavering above the River Glen. We have turned away from the sea, the breakers on the half-submerged ledges of rock. the pale gold sands, the far-off island of Lindisfarne, lost in the mist.

Yeavering greets us royally. The heather is bursting into purple and the gorse is already shouting its gold. The royal halls stand on a terrace at the foot of Yeavering Bell. Always in our ears is the rush of the river, half-hidden in the oaks that fill this dale.

Again, that lump choking my throat when I see the temple of Woden and his like. I could wish there was another Coifi here in Bernicia to hurl his sacrilegious spear and fire it. Let them all burn. Let my past lie in ashes. From the scowl on Paulinus's face I believe he would damn it into oblivion too. But he is a disciplined man, for all his fanatic faith. He will obey the Pope's orders. We must destroy the idols, cleanse this temple, re-consecrate it.

'It is more important to fire the darkness in your people's hearts.'

'You have my permission to preach to them. I have summoned them to listen to you in my presence.'

So now they have gathered, in the great stand of Yeavering. This amphitheatre is my pride. The timbered benches soar in front of me, fanning ever wider as the tiers rise. The owners of lesser manors take the highest, most distant seats, in a long curve. Those somewhat more significant occupy shorter rows below them. Gradually the ranks narrow downwards as nobility rises, bringing the favoured thanes ever closer to me. A handful of chosen earls and the haughtiest ladies occupy the short front-line. All the leadership, wealth, honour of Bernicia funnels down to a narrow dais, this one chair, where I sit alone in front of them. There is no room here for anyone else. I, Edwin, King of all Northumbria, am the supreme ruler. No word needs to be said, but everyone here knows precisely their relationship to me and my authority.

Light glints on the winged standard placed before me. Earl Wighard lifts his hand, and the whole amphitheatre booms the loyal yell.

'Edwin! Edwin of Northumbria! Hail, the King!'

A great flood of warmth rushes over my heart. Yes! The past is dead. Aethelfrith the Ferocious is no more. I, I am King. Deira was always mine, through my father. Now, Bernicia in the north acknowledges me. I am all Northumbria.

These people will follow me through the river of baptism, as they would follow me into battle against the most blood-thirsty enemy.

The sun shines on the silver cross James is holding ready. Paulinus waits, like a raven hovering on the edge of a battlefield.

There is room on the dais only for one. The king of Northumbria is not meant to share power. But I motion the bishop forward.

I have heard Paulinus preach many times. Yet still his voice, harsh with emotion, straining to shape the English words with his Roman tongue, has the power to thrill me and make me tremble. When he thunders of Adam and Eve banished from Paradise, I feel again the compulsion to throw myself on my knees before almighty God.

That decision is done. I led that charge. I have won the victory.

Instead I let my eyes travel up across the ever-lengthening lines of those who listen for the first time. It is a stirring sight. All the wealth and pride of Northumbrian nobility, the sun-dancing jewelled chains of the men, the warm dyes of the women's tunics with brooches flashing on their shoulders, colour to vie with the brilliance of summer flowers on Yeavering Bell. And spread far around, over the rising grass banks where the young gorse shoots are pricking through, the common people of Bernicia, dimming the meadow with their duller garments. Hundreds upon hundreds have come in to hear this, drawn by obedience or curiosity. I let my eyes wander over their faces. Old folk who remember Aethelfrith's father, to whom I am still the newcomer. Children born under my rule. Farming women, craftsmen, who have done well from my peace. All my loyal Northumbrian subjects now.

They have never heard Paulinus speak before. The ranks rising before me against the sky are bowing their heads at the confrontation of their own sin. They groan, like thunder rolling along the horizon. A woman in the front rank cries out in distress. Many are weeping.

Paulinus's harsh shout drops dramatically. He is wooing them now with milk and honey, playing the strings of their hearts. From Eve comes a mother, whose son will save them. The waters of the Red Sea are piled back to let a whole nation escape. 'Comfort, comfort, my people,' sings the prophet under the willows of Babylon. 'You shall return.' The risen Lord holds out his wounded hands to his astonished disciples.

No one can stop them now. I, the King, have done this. But even I watch in awe as my Bernicians, once Aethelfrith's people who tried to kill me, stream forward for salvation in thousands.

Paulinus is trembling. He looks exhausted. Has he ever doubted himself, as I have doubted?

James's face, on the other hand, is one beam of happiness. James is a humble deacon, who does not know how great a power he wields in the singing he loves. James doubts himself often. He never doubts his God.

Paulinus's energy is inhuman. There is so much teaching to do to prepare so vast a crowd for baptism. They are pouring down to the River Glen, hundreds upon hundreds. James is weary but cheerful. He loves them with a fatherly care, shepherding this huge flock down for their dipping, lifting them up out of the water and setting them on the bank again. And still these men must teach yet more classes of catechumens who come pouring in.

I think Paulinus would never stop preaching if God himself did not pull the shutters of night. He is a fire sweeping these hills. He is an earthquake, changing the face of Northumbria. He and I are altering the nature of power in Britain.

Hild is happy. I come across her sitting on the grass. All around her are some forty children, grubby faces turned up to listen to this young woman, hardly bigger than a child herself. The wind is taking her words away. I shall have to come closer to hear. Too close. There is a commotion as the children spot me. They start scrambling to their feet to show their scared respect.

'Go on, sit down again.' I try to reassure them, to ease their confusion. I look around and there's a felled log, so I seat myself to watch them.

But I have broken the magic. I cannot be anything but Edwin the King. The children of servants and countryfolk cannot sit in my presence.

'What was the story?' I ask one boy, who is hanging his dark head and shuffling his feet.

'Jonah, my lord,' he mutters. His eyes are hidden under a falling lock of hair.

Then, 'The whale ate him,' pipes up one voice. It is a bright little apple of a girl, too young yet to understand the difference between herself and a king. 'He was in his belly for three days because he wouldn't do what God wanted him to. He ran away.'

'Lady Hild has taught you well!'

My eyes go over the child's head to my blushing niece. She has risen to her feet too, but Hild will never grow tall enough to draw herself up with the dignity of Tata or Hereswith.

'You seem to be at home with these children.'

'I just tell them stories.'

'You were enchanting them. You should have been born a skald. Even the smallest one can remember your tale.'

'It's like being given a treasure. When I've discovered something like this, I want to share it with everybody else.'

'A good noblewoman gives gold to everyone who follows her.'

'James is teaching me to read. Paulinus has a whole chest full of books.'

Her face is alight, like the expressions of the children when they were listening to her. There is a tightening in my chest. I could have learned those letters. There were scholar priests at Cadfan's court who would have taught me. But I and my bodyguard did not think it fitting for a warrior prince to read and write. I have a fierce memory of Cadwallon taunting me for an English barbarian.

I must not think of Cadwallon. The past is gone.

'Tata can read. I see no harm in it for women and priests.' I smile at Hild.

Hild's chin tilts defiantly. She forces the next words from her chest, as though they cost her great courage to say them. 'You know that Tata's mother was a Christian princess from France. She says they have houses there where women go. They give their lives to Christ in prayer and study.' The straight look in her grey eyes issues a challenge to me.

'Tata is your queen. She needs you here. Little Eanfled loves nobody as well as you. And there is the new baby coming.'

I do not know why it matters suddenly that I should not lose Hild. She is no beauty, and she has hardly grown to womanhood yet. But she stands before me with her unruly plaits like a solid piece of my Northumbria. Hild is loyal. I still remember her as a four-year-old tumbling into my hall, the very day I took my throne in York. We have both known exile, in fear of Aethelfrith. Now we are back, and no one must ever take our land from us again.

I wish my pale, timid daughter was more like Hild. There is nothing of my free-striding Tata in her either, except for the length of her gangling limbs. Was I like that in Aberffraw? Did I huddle in corners near the fire, big-eyed with anxiety? Did I stammer when I talked in front of Cadfan and Cadwallon?

The dreaming brightness fades in Hild's eyes, as if she had been shaken awake. She stiffens her shoulders and grins up at me, the old small, sensible Hild.

'Don't worry, Uncle. Even if all the rest of them run, I'll still be here.'

Her eyes circle the dale of Yeavering, up to the high peaks against the white-flecked sky where the buzzards scream. The River Glen chants incessantly under the leaf-laden oaks. The grass beyond my halls is brilliant with daisies and buttercups. Hild's home is Deira, as mine is. Yet her hands reach out and seize this wilder northern land, hold it to her heart as hers, as much as the rich plain of York and the broad slow tributaries of the Humber.

I rest my hand on her shoulder. 'This is ours now, Hild, all of it. There isn't a warleader left in the English kingdoms who would dare fight me for it.'

She turns her serious eyes up. Hild is never in awe of me. She can say things that no one else would put to Edwin, King of Northumbria.

'And what about the Britons? This was their land once, wasn't it?'

'The British are finished. I drove Cadwallon off Anglesey.'

The nails drive into the palm of my right hand. My left is gripping Hild's shoulder. I have had my revenge for a quarter of a century of a young man's humiliation under my foster-brother. But it still hurts.

Hild eases herself free of my stiffened fingers. She talks to me more frankly than my own sons dare. 'What about this new warlord of Mercia then? Penda? Have you heard Osfrith and Eadfrith? They're furious that he's grabbed their grandfather's kingdom. They're saying you should lead a raid across the Humber against him.'

'Isn't Northumbria big enough for my sons? With the Britons and the Scots and the Picts paying tribute to me? What's Mercia, anyway? Just the bits of Britain in the middle that the rest of us couldn't agree to carve up.'

She slips her arm through mine. 'If Tata's next baby is a boy, will he be king of all this after you? Or must it be Osfrith or Eadfrith?'

Hild talks of my death. She has gone too far this time, even for a favourite niece. 'The King of the Northumbrians is very much alive. I don't have to listen to treason from a spotty girl. Get back to the Queen's hall. You're supposed to be her waiting woman, aren't you?'

'Yes, sire.' She bends her knee, but before her head bows there is a flash in her eyes.

I stride away through the gaping children. There are larger crowds around Paulinus and James. I have done this. I have saved a whole people. I am Edwin the King.

Why should I fear to die, after all? Now, with the shame behind me, now at the height of my power? To fall like an English hero on the battlefield at the head of my warhost, with my reputation splendid and my honour untouched.

So small, my infant son. My son and Tata's. We bury his tiny body, still in the fine white linen gown of his baptism. Paulinus assures me he has died redeemed, washed clean of his original sin. Is it true really that babies, who look so innocent, come into the world clogged down with the foulness of Adam and Eve's disobedience? Does God condemn children who gasp their last before the priest comes?

I am speared by a sudden memory. Queen Rorei on Ynys Mon, one afternoon when the grey wind lashed bitter spray from the Irish Sea against our walls. There were tears on her cheeks too, and the fort howled with grief. Her baby was born dead. But Nevyn came down from the hills to comfort her, as she rocked herself before the fire.

'Be at peace. That little one was held in the palm of the Father's hand before you ever saw him. Didn't you feel him kick and dance for joy? He was alive inside the womb, wasn't he? And there is not the smallest sparrow tumbling out of its nest in the thatch but the good God sees it. He has made us to love him, and no one escapes his love, except by their own choice. Did this little one run away from God? He did not. He lives safe in that love forever.'

Paulinus has a sterner faith. But though Tata's face is red and spoiled with weeping, her baby was baptized in time. It is not for his soul she weeps. She weeps for the child she cannot nurse at her breast. She weeps for the son she longed to give me. I can't tell her I don't need her son, though I should have loved him greatly. I have Osfrith and Eadfrith, from my first queen. Osfrith is ready to join the warhost now. Eadfrith will follow next year. And they may see real war soon. Hild was shrewd. Mercia's new warlord is an ambitious neighbour.

'He was my son, not yours, Bishop. You needn't take it personally.'

Paulinus has a face that drops like an iron latch into its socket. He locks it now into stern lines of rectitude. 'The bible tells us King David wept before the Almighty, pleading for his newborn son. But God took him. It was a merited punishment for the sin of stealing another man's wife. Ever since I set foot in Northumbria, heaven has favoured you. Why now? Why should a righteous God take the child away from you?'

'You think I've got some beautiful Bathsheba tucked away somewhere? Good God, what man would look elsewhere with a wife like Tata?'

'Men are often tempted when their wives are with child. But I exempt you from that. I should have known. There are few sins it is possible for a king to commit in secret. And you would have confessed it to me.'

'You know my deeds better than anyone else.'

My present sins, Paulinus, but not my past.

'The sins of the flesh may be easily confessed, sire. But what of some other secret sin of the heart?' Paulinus is insistent as we walk away from the church. His stride grows longer. I am the King, but he is in danger of going ahead of me.

There is a dizziness like flies before my eyes. What if, after all, I have done wrong? It cannot have been a sin to accept Paulinus's Christ, can it? Look what good has come of it for a whole kingdom, the rapture on Hild's face. But my silence has denied the Christ of Nevyn and Rhun. Is that why my son is dead?

The crowd of York's people is thick on every side. But they are not smiling and cheering their king today. They are not pressing forward into the road for a touch of my clothes to bring them luck. They must feel it. The King's luck is running out.

Paulinus's head darts in sharp, swift stares. He has sensed it too. The heads of the crowd are turning. But not to us.

'Look there.'

'He's coming back.'

'From the left hand.'

I have spotted it myself now, in the blue, blowing sky, coming up from the River Ouse. It hovers mockingly over the golden stones of York. A black raven.

No one shouts the name, but a low grinding rumbles through the hundreds of English men and women, some recently baptized, others still unconvinced.

'Woden.' 'Woden.' 'Woden.'

I want to cover my ears. The skalds cannot unsay my genealogy. My father's father's father's blood, going back to Woden. I have been unfaithful to my English ancestry. My people know it.

'You.' Paulinus swings round to a soldier of my bodyguard, decisive as any warlord. 'Shoot it.'

Ricsige looks startled. He has served six years in my personal guard. No longer a boy, he has a leathered face older than his years. This is a man I have come to trust. He saved my life from a Pictish spear last summer.

'Bishop, even I can't hit a crow with a spear.'

'Then get yourself a bow. Don't tell me there are no fowlers in York this morning. Quick, man. I want that thing dead.'

Ricsige breaks from the ranks and runs. He is a practical man. I catch my breath as he stands now with a borrowed bow and a quiver full of arrows and draws back his elbow. Still the raven swings on the breeze and utters its harsh croak. It is taunting me. I would have hurried on, taken shelter back in my palace, let the painted walls shut out its cry of doom.

But Paulinus knows this warning is not for me alone. The common crowd must stay outside the palace. The raven scorns my royal refuge, declaims my treachery to the world.

The bowstring twangs. I do not want to look, and yet I must. Why should Ricsige, trained in the noble weapons of spear and sword, have any skill in the commoner's craft of archery? A bird is a small target in this wide sky.

The rise and drop of hundreds of voices follow the flight of Ricsige's arrow. 'A . . . a . . . ah. . . ! O . . . o . . . oh.' I hear a woman wail.

'Yes!' Paulinus's shout punches the air.

The black corpse is tumbling helplessly, feathers scattering. Still scared, the crowd is fighting now to get out of its way.

Ricsige strides through, picks up his bloody trophy, brings it back to Paulinus.

'There you are, Bishop. No harm will come to the King now.'

His eyes meet mine. He is tactful. He has not inflicted Woden's bird on Woden's descendant. I mark him out for promotion.

Paulinus turns. He goes marching back to the church, furiously fast, with the black bird of the enemy swinging from his hand. I stand and watch him reach St Peter's. The thatch of the church where I and my court were baptized has weathered already. The bold colours of the painted door-frame have softened. A trench outlines a new corner, far outside the footing of this first hastily built oratory. I am building the grandest church in the North of Britain since the Romans left. It will be in stone, as Paulinus wants, fit for a king and an archbishop.

I'm still near enough to see that rain has filled the bottom of the foundation trench. In its shadows, the blue sky cannot reach down to find a mirror of itself. There is no telling how much deeper it goes. Paulinus tosses the raven towards it. For a fearful moment the bird seems to take flight again. Then it drops for a second time. It hits the muddy wall of the trench, plunges in, is sucked under. One curled black feather floats still on the surface, seeming too frail and ordinary now to be the provenance of such fears. Paulinus wipes the dirt from his hands.

The fickle crowd cheers him.

You have speared a wolf. You think he has limped deep into the wood to die. Then a twig cracks. Through the gloom between the tree-trunks you see his yellow eyes. Blood flecks the foam that dribbles from his gums. Your wound torments him. His hate fastens on you. You are to be his victim now. This will not be finished until one of you lies dead.

Cadwallon is back in Gwynedd.

'I should have collared every fishing boat, swept the Irish Sea until I found him, stabbed him through the neck before I let him get away from Ynys Mon.' I pound the pillow.

Tata's arms come round me, stroking the hair back from my hot brow. 'It was his father's land. He's got it back, that's all.'

'He's King of all Gwynedd, and claiming to be a greater ruler than his father was.'

'As you are greater than yours. And you're his overlord. You defeated Gwynedd. They pay you tribute. Ynys Mon is Anglesey now.'

'It's hard to lose the tongue of my childhood. Cadwallon and I were boys on that island.'

She will never know. I am the greatest of the English kings to her. She does not understand that I shall never lose the feeling of smallness, of inferiority, which always swept over me whenever Cadwallon strode on to the scene, flicking the long brown waves of his hair, curling his young moustache, shooting contempt at me like a whip suddenly cracked, taunting my hopeless love for his sister. I shall always remain the younger foster-brother, the English exile, the heathen beggar at his father's court, until Cadwallon is dead.

'You changed that history. You are Edwin, King of all the Northumbrians, Bretwalda of Britain. Cadwallon is nothing compared to you now.'

'I have to smash him.'

I am holding Tata so hard I must be bruising her. She kisses me strongly on the lips. 'Gently, my love. What can be wrong?' She wraps the comfort of her arms around me again and I slide my hands under her shift to her warm bare back. She wriggles with pleasure and smiles. 'Take what you want. And there is something else to hope for. This time I will bear you a living son.'

I crush her more fiercely than ever. I am speechless with longing. Tata's love is pure gold, right through to the core. I want her son to rule Northumbria, be as great a king as I am. But for that, I must stay alive until he is grown. Osfrith and Eadfrith are warriors now. But I shall find more joy in Tata's son than in the children of my Mercian wife.

Tata would not have let me go when danger threatened. Tata will be loyal. Whatever happens to me, Tata will be loyal.

'You're hurting me.' She laughs, my queen, my lover. But it is not like her to protest, even in so small a way. I persuade my muscles to relax their grip.

'I thought I'd settled the old scores between Cadwallon and me, when I drove him off Anglesey. But now he's flown back like an owl in the night to haunt me.'

'Then take your warhost and finish him.'

'I shan't let him cross the Severn. This is our land now. Not one Welshman is going to set foot back on English soil and live. The English themselves are trouble enough on our border.'

'You're really worried about Penda of Mercia?' She wriggles away from me to rest on her back and look up at me in the half-light.

'He's ambitious. He kicked Coenburg's family out of the way to get the kingdom. Even his skalds don't claim Penda's descended from Woden.'

I feel the stiffening of her muscles, swiftly controlled.

'What do you expect me to do?' I growl. 'Garotte the skalds? Smash all their harps? I can't cancel my family's genealogy, just because I've renounced Woden.'

She kisses me again, sweet and lingering, apologizing. 'Love, love. What's wrong? Ever since they told you Cadwallon was back, you've been like a bear attacked by a swarm of bees.'

My turn to fling myself away and lie on my back, leaving a

narrow emptiness of space between us, which her stroking hand tries in vain to bridge.

How can I tell her? I keen aloud at my memories. Tata wraps me round with her body, arms and legs, kisses me passionately.

Tata is the greatest gift to me. She will bear me a son. And I will leave him the great, peaceful kingdom of Northumbria.

Chapter Twenty-four

The Severn is running red. If there were sandstone here, I should think we had ground it with our heels and dyed the river rich with mud. I rub my eyes, bleary with weariness. I was exaggerating. Thin, pink trails snake through the clear water, from the corpses slumped like rocks. The meaning is the same. Their accusation coils round the sodden leather at my ankles. Gyrth catches my elbow as I stumble.

'Is he dead?' I groan, a sob of longing.

'Did you take a wound somewhere, my lord? I didn't think you'd got worse than a buffeting from Welsh shields.'

'Cadwallon, man. Is he still alive? Has he got away from me again?'

Gyrth is silent, steering me across the uneven slabs underwater. He helps me up the bank. We are back on English soil.

'They can't have found him on the battlefield. The horns would have brayed that news to high heaven. There was a rabble of ponies galloping away when their infantry broke.'

It could not be that simple. I turn and stare. The bards are lying when they sing of the Welsh land as a red dragon. The spikes of its mountains hump blue across the horizon. They look unchanged. I think if Cadwallon had fallen, those hills would have tumbled too and the whole landscape of my memory be re-aligned. Behind me, English oak woods sprawl. Penda will not be pleased that I have marched through Mercian territory to beat my enemy.

I have failed. I have won this battle, but I have failed in the only thing that matters to me. Cadwallon is not yet dead. So this must go on, until it is finished.

My warhost is massing for my inspection. Tired though they are, they are trying to wag their beards and hold their heads proudly so that the sunlight gleams on their helmets and Thor can salute them from the sky.

No, I'm confused. It must have been Saint Michael and the archangel host who fought for Northumbria today. And for Cadwallon? Were there monks of Bangor chanting psalms for his side, like the hundreds of holy men Aethelfrith slaughtered at Chester? If so, the prayers of Rome's priests have proved stronger than the prayers of the British Church. I made the right choice, didn't I?

. . . Rhun. The British priest. Was he there? He may be dead by now. He wasn't a young man when. . . . Don't think of that! I wonder what became of that dancing flame of a little girl, Rhiainmelt. Think of the child, not the priest. She had green eyes, vivid as wet moss under the edge of a pool.

It is not the wolf's yellow eyes this time, staring between the tree-trunks. These eyes are wide and wondering. Her bright green stare accuses me by its astonished incomprehension.

I throw my hands over my own eyes.

'My lord?'

No, it was long ago. Rhiainmelt won't be innocent now. She must be nearly twenty, married for sure. Fat with childbearing, wise about men and pain and death. And treachery.

Rhun must always have known, and Rhiainmelt. The King of Northumbria cannot change a whole kingdom to Christianity and the British not get to hear of it.

Cadwallon knows. I stagger under the scorn as I imagine his incredulous laugh.

'You'd better sit down, my lord. It's been a hard fight. Gwynedd is no mean warhost, and it was their own homeland they were defending. All the more glory to you that you led us to victory.'

I fling him off. 'We're none of us as young as we were. But I'm not so decrepit yet I can't stand to thank my own warhost.'

When they've finished cheering me and shaking their spears till they shimmer like slanting rods of rain, I hold up my fist. 'Men,' I yell, 'Northumbria's the greatest. We can smash the Welsh on their own soil. We can stride across Mercia and stand here on Penda's border. No one can stop us. We march where we like, beat whom we want. I make the rules for Britain, east to west.'

That's what they like to hear. And a fragment of it is even true. This wasn't a great victory. We lost more men than I like. But we won. Cadwallon ran.

Not far enough.

And we have all the dales of Mercia to march back across before we ford the Ouse and touch the soil of Northumbria. We should set out now, fast, before Penda gets to hear of what I've done and moves his own warhost to intercept us.

The men are tired, but I'm their king. When I mount my horse, they follow.

There are too many trees in Mercia. We are far from the sea. There is not the crash of the waves against the cliffs at Bamburgh or the long bright sands of Morecambe. We have lost sight of the high hills until we reach the Pennines, to haul us like a rope north.

Trees hide wolves. The men march in surprising silence for a victorious warhost. Have they sniffed my mood? Eadfrith has taken a wound, a slash across the inner arm that came dangerously near to severing the tendon. He looks pale and unsteady on his black horse. His bodyguard are grim. It's shame for them that the king's younger son came near to spilling his life away in Welsh mud. They are grouped round him now, in case he falls. But Eadfrith's proud. He'll ride home to York like a warrior prince.

I glance around, into the trees. I shouldn't do that. It signals to my troops that I'm uneasy. This is a Mercian road. These are

Mercian trees. We startle Mercian villages as we tramp through them, going home.

Ricsige has sensed my tension. 'Penda's still a new chieftain here. Those were Britons peering at us out of the hovels. He's got their land now, but he's not king of their hearts yet.'

'I'm English too. I've taken British land.'

'They've no reason to betray your passage to Penda.'

Would these Britons bite us, if Cadwallon roused them?

We come upon English settlers. They watch us more calculatingly as we pass. They must know who I am, but it doesn't raise a cheer. Coenburg's father was their king, before Penda rose. Does that woman, leaning her cracked hands on the hoe and wiping the sweat from her forehead, remember I was once the fugitive prince who married her king's daughter? Would she care any more for me if she did?

Their indifference is worse than the hate of the Britons. I'm King of all the Northumbrians. I need their love, the swelling roar of my people as they see me coming up the road, the desperate hope of the sick, the struggle to touch my clothes. I'm Edwin, their king, their health, their wealth. I am the luck of the land.

My eyes focus on my standard, the globe like the sun with flaming wings.

'That's the Peak ahead.' Ricsige lifts his head. 'We're getting close to home. And no sign of Penda.'

The sun blazes on my standard again, the globe more brilliant than the golden stones of York. My procession dazzles with pomp and pageantry. I am the victor. Every step I take on the highway, over the old slabs of Roman empire, crushes the memory of Cadwallon like the weeds under my boots.

Tata has borne me a healthy son. There are panic prayers in my heart that Wuscfrea will live. Such a tiny infant he looks in Tata's arms, his face grave, awake, grey-blue eyes thoughtful. He is wrapped magnificently, like the rest of us. Cloth of gold surrounds the lambswool and linen of his white bindings. He went to his baptism in St Peter's, innocent of everything but the sin of old Adam.

Osfrith is walking beside me, blushing with pride. He's a father too. My first grandson, and not from Tata's line. Little Yffi's grandmother was a Mercian princess. I can feel ambition rise, like saliva at the crackling of pork. Through Coenburg's blood, Mercia could yet be mine as well, and my son and grandson king of the English midlands. History will write my royal family the greatest there ever was in Britain.

The cloak has gone back to its chest. I can pace again on my favourite walk, along the top of the Roman wall outside my palace. I avoid the turret room where Paulinus found me. The earth is fertile, the River Ouse swelling with rain, silver in the sun. The corn shows young and green where the oaks have been cleared. I spread out my hands, feel myself blessing this land. Northumbria, rich Deira, rugged Bernicia. Mine, both. I am Edwin its king.

There are steps on the rampart. I turn to find Ricsige and I am surprised by the warmth of the smile that comes to my face.

'Don't mind me, my lord.' He leans on the parapet, letting me understand that I can keep my privacy. He is respectful, but not afraid of me. I am reminded of Hild, though there is nothing childish about the lines scored on his face which make him look older than he is. 'It's a grand day.' His eyes love the land, as mine do.

I hesitate. I came here for solitude, as I do so often. But I have not found the peace in quietness I wanted. I stop and stare over the rolling forest with him. The early rain is drying and the trees smoke in the warm air. The plain stretches into the mists of distance, to where the Ouse winds its way into our great Humber, our southern border.

As if he knows, Ricsige says, 'Mercia's calling together its warhosts, from Middle England and Lindsey and the Peak. Penda didn't like our expedition to the Severn.'

'What Penda of Mercia, or any other king, likes is of no account to Northumbria. We are the greatest. We march where we want.'

He is silent for a while, biting the corner of his mouth. 'The word is, he's made a deal with the Welsh.'

A stab of fear. 'I can't believe that. You know what they say of him. Penda's sworn to be the champion of Woden, though every other English kingdom falls to Christ. And the Britons hate the English. He'd never make an alliance with Christian Britons, or they with him.'

'To damage Northumbria, he might. Penda has ambitions. He dreams of being a greater warlord even than you, my lord.'

He gives me a sideways look and a little laugh, to show the absurdity of Mercian pretensions. But I have not spent half my life in exile, dodging the vengeance of a jealous enemy, not to take such warnings seriously. I trust Ricsige's knowledge.

'If it were true, which side would they attack from?'

'He won't want Cadwallon to get the chief glory.'

'So, from the south.'

We both stare at the paleness on the horizon which hides the Humber.

'When?'

'Even Penda must fear the Northumbrian warhost. He'll have to gather a force big enough to rival it before harvest.'

'Three months?'

Ricsige's face gleams a golden-brown, darker than the silky fringe of his moustache and the corn-gold hair.

'You're not a married man, Ricsige.'

'I'm your bodyguard. That's honour enough. A guard's like a lover to his lord. The two of us shouldn't be parted.' He laughs again, short, military. I like this man.

'I had a thane once who gave his life for me, not on the battle-field but in my own hall.'

'Lilla? I know his story. I'd like to die like that for my king and have the skalds sing honour for me.'

'It grieves me that I never honoured him as I should have done while he lived, though he loved me dearer than his own life.'

'You gave him the title of thane, land, gold.'

'I would give you all that, for your loyalty. And something more.'

'My lord?'

'Would you like a wife?'

He looks at me oddly, uncertain what to say.

'Well, man? Couldn't you find time to love a woman too?'

'Who?'

'The lady Hild.'

He colours, like a boy. 'You honour me, my lord, more than I deserve. The King's great-niece?'

'I may be offering you more than you bargain for. Hild can be an uncomfortable young woman. She's a treasure, but more of a sword than a necklace.'

'I've heard them joke that her name means "battle".'

'It's as well to have Hild on your side.'

He takes my hand and kisses it, kneeling on one knee. 'I shall cherish the King's blood in my wife and in the son she will bear me.'

But he is not a man for emotion. He stands with a straighter back, looking south to Mercia.

'I think you should summon the other half of your warhost from Bernicia, my lord. The Scots are quiet enough for the moment. If Cadwallon joins Penda, we shall need all the warriors we can muster.'

Hild and Ricsige are handfast. I have tied their wrists together and laughed as they steered the loving-cup to each other's lips. They will be married this summer.

Hild stood very still and straight when I told her. Light flashed for a moment out of her grey eyes, brilliant as sun on an icicle. I could not tell whether it was gladness or anger. It unsettled me. I

223

am used to the honesty and openness of my niece's face. Hild does not have secrets from me. She is more of a friend to me even than Tata.

Will her marriage change that? Will being a wife make her flatter and dissemble, hide her own thoughts and say what her man wants to hear?

'Does this man please you? I won't force any woman of my family to marry where she doesn't want.'

'I'm not important, only the great-granddaughter of your father. No one would imagine a son of mine could be king. At least it's a weight off my mind that you're not going to marry me off to some southern prince for the good of Northumbria. I'd find that a hard request to say no to, but it would be a bitter sentence of exile.'

'You love Northumbria so much?'

'I was born in exile. I remember coming home, though I was only four.'

'The very day I entered York. You were the first to return, with your mother and Hereswith.'

'And you picked me up in your arms and gave me a wooden horse, only when Osfrith and Eadfrith got here from Mercia, you took it back and gave it to them. I was furious at that.'

'And we all laughed at you. We should have known better than to brave your anger. Are you angry now? Have I given you your freedom, only to take it away?'

'You must have given me to a man you think highly of.'

'I have. I trust Ricsige with my life.'

'A bodyguard lives to stand between death and his king.'

'Many brave men have fallen doing that.'

'When Ricsige risks his life for you, he does it for Northumbria. If he will take that risk, so will I.'

'Can you love him?'

Her mouth squares in that open honest smile at last. 'It seems we love the same things, he and I. That's a good enough beginning.'

We walk a little way along the wall. Then she turns to me. 'Why me, and not Hereswith?'

'Ah, your mother hasn't told you? There are other negotiations.'

'Am I allowed to know?'

'East Anglia. The king's son, Aethelhere, is interested in Hereswith.'

Hild's pale eyebrows rise. 'So we may be valuable pieces on the board, after all?'

'Aethelhere is not the king's eldest son.'

'But heirs have fallen on the battlefield before now.'

There is both calculation and sympathy in Hild's voice. She has no children of her own yet, yet she is an inspired teacher. I see the youngsters flocking round her when she gives them catechism lessons. She tells them tales of prophets and martyrs as stirring as any hero-tales the skalds sing in hall. Many of the boys she is teaching will die young too. Osfrith and Eadfrith will ride to battle with me when Penda comes to attack us.

And Cadwallon.

'So Hereswith could be a queen? But for me, the captain of your bodyguard. No.' Her laughter shouts, genuine, with no bitterness. 'Don't tell me. Hereswith is far more beautiful than I am. The fame of that long silky hair and the pools of her crystal eyes will have reached the fen country. Aethelhere can marry into Edwin of Northumbria's family and gets a treasure as well. I'm not such a good bargain, am I?'

I seize her hands. I must make her know I mean it. 'Who gets you, Hild, gets a warmer and truer heart than the most faithful hound who ever lay at her master's feet. I listen to my Witan, but often they tell me what they think I want to hear. I have one wise woman with the courage to tell me what I need to know. Believe me, Hild. I wouldn't want to marry you away from Northumbria if the Emperor of Rome himself asked for you. Stay here, Hild. Look after my children. Look after Northumbria.'

There is something oddly familiar about this short, determined woman, whom I love for the strength of her mind and not her beauty. Then the reason flashes upon me. I see that Hild is becoming gut-wrenchingly like another wise woman, in a hut among the heather above Aberffraw.

It is madness. Look at her. Hild is an English noblewoman, in the gaily striped skirt and the swinging beads and rock crystals Tata likes her ladies to wear. She is nothing like a hermit woman in a plain grubby tunic.

Cadwallon is coming for me. I want this battle. Either I must kill him or he will kill me. We cannot both exist on this earth together.

We are hunting from Catterick, up the Sour Beck. It's a brisk flying day, with white scuds of cloud racing us overhead. All my life, I've been a cautious man. That's how I've stayed alive. But I'm reckless now. I can see Ricsige galloping not far away. He turns his head to look at me as often as at the ground ahead. He trusts his horse. I trust Ricsige. Hild is behind us. She lets out a skirl of exhilaration. Osfrith's white-blond mane streams like his horse's tail. Eadfrith is more cautious. He makes it seem he is escorting Hild, but I know his eyes are keen for rabbit holes and hidden rocks in the heather. He will stay alive longer than Osfrith.

If Ricsige's choice were between guarding me and helping Hild, there would be no question for him. I am his reason for living. I am Northumbria. Hild does not question that.

The wolf streaks out, as if a giant had flung a spar of grey limestone over the hill. We pummel our mounts with our heels to drive them faster before we lose sight of him over the skyline. The breath of horses and riders snorts and strains. We are on the summit.

The ground falls away before us, lifting again beyond the Swale, to where the road runs down over the moors from Corbridge on the Wall. That catch of the heart. I am looking across the Tees into Bernicia. It has been fourteen years now, since I took this from Aethelfrith the Ferocious. It never ceases to thrill me. All one Northumbria, mine.

As if she read my heart, Hild nudges her pony alongside mine.

As a rider, she has a brave heart but a sensible head. She is growing into a wise young woman. She knows the wolf must be kept from the farms, from lambs and children, but she is not going to break her neck for a morning's sport. She is less of a boy than I used to think when she was younger.

She says now, like a voice speaking inside my soul, 'Do you ever hear anything of Aethelfrith's children?'

Her question startles me. It chimes so closely with my own recollection of Aethelfrith, yet I had not thought of his family.

'They fled to the Scots in Dalriada. They say there's a holy island off the coast where Christian monks sheltered them. Iona. The elder boys must be grown now. They'll have pledged their swords to King Domnall the Freckled.'

'You don't think they'll ever try to come back?'

'How? The Scots pay me tribute. Do you think they'd lend them an army?'

'When you were a young prince in exile, you found allies.'

I shake my head, laughing. 'I have feared much, all my life. I do now. Seeing danger before it comes has made me the great king I am. But not that brood. My Northumbrians love me too well. This country's rich, secure, peaceful. They won't want Aethelfrith's sons back.'

The north is safe. The edge of the shadow is creeping up from the south and the west.

'Wasn't there a daughter? I suppose they've married her off, just as you're disposing of me and Hereswith.'

Her laugh teases me. Hild is in a good humour with me and this morning. It is not to be expected she should love Ricsige, but she approves of him. She will do what I need her to, and what a wife should. And she will do it, not because I say so, though I am her king, but because it is right for Northumbria. She loves her country through Ricsige.

I scratch my brain for an itch of information I cannot quite locate. Then I find the spot. 'The gossip is that Freckled Domnall wanted to marry Aebbe himself, but she turned him down. She lives with her mother on the Island of Women, close to the men's abbey on Iona. They call such women nuns.'

Hild's eyes are catching fire. There is a hunger there. When Osfrith was a boy, he looked like that when we men told tales of war. 'Like those women in France, who work the abbey land with their own hands and pray and study?'

'Never mind what Frankish and Scots women do. This is Northumbria. We have no abbeys. Just you make a brave wife for Ricsige.' I smack her belly. 'And fill that up with English warriors for me.'

She laughs. I do not think it is mere obedience. Hild is sensible. She is not one to pine for what she cannot have: her murdered father, Hereswith's beauty, a nun's vocation. Hild will work with good humour and courage with what she is given. I feel her strength, young though she is, like a rock rooted in this hill.

'What's that?' she says. 'Coming over the hill beyond the Swale?'

My fist clashes on the horse's withers, making the harness jump and jingle. 'By thunder, they're here at last.'

'Our warhost from Bernicia?' There is excitement in her voice. She has something of Osfrith in her too, though she is a woman.

'Let Penda of Mercia look at this, and think whether he still wants to challenge Northumbria. That warhost has beaten the Picts and cowed the Scots and stamped my law on the Isle of Man. Let that devil Cadwallon remember how I humiliated him last time.'

She turns her head to look at me, very straight, very searching. She has reined in her own first heady excitement. 'Uncle, does this war have to happen? You're King of all this. Northumbria's flourishing like the garden of Eden. Why risk it? Can't you talk peace with Penda and Cadwallon?'

'Girl, you don't know what you're talking about? Did I start it? Mercia was our ally when Coenburg's father was king. But Penda wants to be chief warlord in Britain. There can't be two of us.'

'But Cadwallon? He was your foster-brother.'

My grin feels crooked, strained. 'You spend enough time with children. Since when did brothers not fight?'

Hild reaches out a hand briefly to me, before she gathers up her reins. The hounds have picked up the scent of the vanished wolf again. But we are no longer interested in that quarry. War is our hunt now. I start to trot down the northern flank towards the river crossing. I need not look directly at Hild since I am leading the way. But she dogs my heels and I cannot shake off her insistence.

'You're grown men now, both Christian kings.'

Hild is not twenty yet. She is not afraid of my anger.

'Come on. Let's race them to the ford!' I yell.

We gallop to meet the warhost who have come to double our shield-wall. They have seen us and the weary tramp from Yeavering springs into military briskness. They do not know it is the king himself yet, but the officers' horses pick up their hooves, the helmets are held higher, the standards nod and flutter. The infantry spearmen swing their aching legs as though the humpbacked miles of the straight stone road are only just beginning. We are Northumbrians, all of us. These are my brothers. Not all the Mercians and Britons who ever mustered can take this land from me. I won it. I have united it. This is mine.

Chapter Twenty-five

The Mercian and the Welsh warhosts are on the move. In the palace yard at York, my warriors are leaping to make ready, while the common soldiery are mustering in the fields outside. They are all straighter-backed, brighter-eyed than for many a month. These men want war. They love me because I will lead them to glory.

Tata watches us under the soaring gable-end that dwarfs even her tall figure. Eanfled is grasping her skirt from behind and sucking her thumb. Her small face is pale and hollow with anxiety. Of course I love this daughter of mine. She was the precious child born on that day when Lilla threw himself under the assassin's knife. But I wish she would hold herself straighter, look more boldly on the world. She is an English princess, descended from Northumbrian and Kentish kings. She has Queen Aethelberg for her mother and Hild for her teacher. That should be example enough for any girl.

The weapon-stone sings as iron and steel blades sharpen their teeth to bite. Men strut about in armour while there is yet no need. Even the horses have caught the excitement and are whinnying from the stables. The dogs are getting under everyone's feet.

Tata is clasping her arms tight against the wind. It's a cold summer. Occasionally she fondles Eanfled's head, but not as though her thoughts were on the child. Can my merry, high-hearted queen be afraid for me?

I find myself drawn across the yard towards her. Seven years, and I have still not got over my amazement that I married this Kentish princess for politics and fell helpless into the arms of love.

I feel a throb of terror. Could anything happen to harm Tata and my children? Neither of us can speak to the other of this. It is officially unthinkable that Northumbria could lose this war. In these matters, a warrior may be closer than a wife. Ricsige and all my bodyguard know what must be done should I fall. Tata's escort too are aware of their duty.

I cannot die. I will not give Cadwallon that victory.

Say something else to her, since the heaviest weight on our hearts cannot be comforted by a word from either of us.

'You haven't brought young Wuscfrea out to see his father's warhost gearing up for glory?'

'The wind's cold.' She glances at the sky. 'He's inside with his nurse.'

'He's our son. He'll lead this host one day.'

She glances sharply round the yard, where men go busily between the storehouses and stables seeing that everything is trim and ready for a marching army. There is nothing nervous in Tata's movements, but she is wary.

'Osfrith is your eldest son. And there's Eadfrith. Just because you love Wuscfrea it doesn't mean the Witan would hail him king. Still, God will grant you many long years before they have to decide.'

I seize the excuse to grasp her arms in the close-fitting jacket she wears in the Kentish fashion. She has a fine figure still. I hug her warmly. I can tease Tata as I would few other women, except young Hild.

'You'd do me out of my warlord's glory? If I must die, I'm supposed to fall on the battlefield, with my bodyguard heroically slaughtered around me. An English king isn't celebrated for dying in his bed.'

I have said at last what she dreads, in the laughter of a shared joke. I feel her hug me suddenly tight and I know she feels it, even while her laughter rings with mine.

'You're more likely to die at the feasting table when you see what I'm planning to celebrate your victory.'

I can imagine it now: the hall leaping with torchlight, the trestles bowed under the weight of boar and venison, salmon and geese. The skalds shouting praise-songs. Tata, loved for herself by all who know her, resplendent at my side as Queen Aethelberg. My mind's eye sees her carrying the foaming ale-cup to honour every warrior who fought. She honours me daily by her courage, by her grace, by her beauty, by her love for me. I feel a physical hunger for the tiny son she has given me. Women's lives are dangerous too. We lose as many wives in childbed as they do husbands on the battlefield. My turn to hold her close.

'You should go,' she says, over my shoulder. 'Ricsige wants to talk to you.'

I become the warlord again. Ricsige is standing patiently. Something about the stiff lines carved into his face always demands attention. He looks at me very steadily.

'My lord, I have a request to make.'

'Ask anything you like, except my kingdom, my honour or my wife.' The proviso is traditional, but he forces his face into a polite smile.

'This could be counted a part of your kingdom, your honour and your family, and so all the more valuable to me.'

'Name it, man.'

'Lady Hild, my lord.'

'You have her already. I made you handfast on the feast of the Trinity.'

'I know, my lord. And you gave me permission to marry her at the summer's end.'

'Yes, and I've seen the result. There are women busy all over the Queen's halls putting together what they think a married lady should have. There seems to be no end of stitching new tunics and re-embroidering old ones, and collecting enough shoes and knick-knacks to last for twenty years. Or so Hild complains. She says she'd rather jump on a horse and ride off into the dales beside you, leaving them all to it.'

'She's a noblewoman of the royal blood. She should be married with honour. But . . . I have this one wish.'

The request might have embarrassed another man and made him drop his eyes. Not this soldier.

'Speak it out, then. Have I ever refused you anything?'

'You have been all that a warrior could wish in his lord.'

'Well, then.'

'My lord, we're both soldiers. We know the risk.' He is speaking low. Ricsige will boast only of victory where the men can hear. 'I'm sworn to protect your life with my own. I'll do that gladly, and not for the gold you've given me and the lands you've promised us when I marry. I've never before gone into battle with anything but a high spirit, and never a thought of anything but glory and preserving your life. Marriage changes things.' And at last he does lower his head. His voice is gruffer now. 'For the first time, it's more than an idle dream that I could have a son of my own.'

He says no more. I understand. Only a few steps from where we stand, inside that hall, a small baby lies sleeping in his cradle or rocked in his nurse's arms. My son and Tata's, Wuscfrea. A tiny male life. Osfrith and Eadfrith will ride with me tomorrow.

Ricsige is single. He has no son, or none he can name his. Did this upright, disciplined man ever bed a country wench in the straw like the rest of us?

I find compassion softening my eyes to a dangerous wateriness. I hold his wrist. I love this soldier. I want to give him all I should have given Lilla, before it's too late.

'Take her,' I say. 'Enjoy her for one night. She's a healthy lass. Hild will give you what you want.'

'You'll marry us?' He cannot hold down the fire in his eyes.

'I'll pronounce you man and wife as soon as you can find her.

233

And Paulinus shall say a nuptial mass for the pair of you. Go on, man. Don't waste time staring. You have my permission.'

'Thank you, my lord.'

He has to put so much intensity into his quiet words. He cannot shout or fling his arms about or show delight in any normal way. I was brought up with the eloquence of the Welsh. Any of Cadwallon's bodyguard would have burst into a poetic flood of gratitude, comparing Hild to the beauty of Olwen, the giant's daughter, me to the generous King Arthur, and himself to the hero Culhwch, scouring all Britain on an impossible quest for the monstrous boar to win her. Ricsige is English. He hasn't drunk enough to make him shout, and he leaves poetry to skalds. Only in war I see the other side of him, furious as a berserker if anyone threatens me too close. In battle he shouts like a madman. What kind of lover will he make?

Hild cannot be found.

The tension in the palace yards is heightening. Scouts have brought news that the combined Mercian and Welsh warhosts are now marching down the Trent towards our boundary at the Humber. They say their spearmen have been seen spilling like a grey flood across the plain.

Excitement grasps my throat so hard, I think I may be sick. 'We move at dawn tomorrow. If blood has to be spilt and homesteads burned, let it be in Penda's land, not ours. We'll strike them south of the Humber, before they set their covetous eyes on York.'

A cheer goes up, and the yelling is taken on the wind, carried away to spark new flames of frenzy outside. In moments, the whole city's alight.

Wherever Hild is, she must be hearing this.

And here she comes, striding in through the gate with Hereswith, whose longer limbs seem to dance along beside her sister's. Their faces are ablaze with excitement, apprehension, hunger for information. Hild's eyes take in the situation at once. She doesn't need me to tell her that war is not only in the air, it has come.

'Have they crossed the Humber?' For weeks, Hild has obeyed her conscience, counselling me to make peace with my enemies. Yet now the spears are leaping from her eyes. Poor Hild. She would ride to battle with us if she could. She has a thinking head, but she is a woman for action.

I stretch a wolfish smile, enjoying the chance to shock her. 'Hild, how would you like to be married?'

She draws herself straighter, always slightly ridiculous in the dignity with which she tries to carry her short stocky body. 'I gave my word. I am handfast to Ricsige already.'

'I'm talking of more than formal betrothal. Penda and that devil Cadwallon have reached the floodplain of the Trent. We must move fast, to cut them off. Ricsige is asking for what you promised him, now. One night, Hild. A bodyguard's life is vowed first to his king, not his wife. But if he leaves you a widow, you can still be the mother of his child.'

She colours then, though not a pretty rose, as Hereswith's cheeks would. Hild's blush is more like dock leaves at the end of summer, mottled red. I read confusion in her clever grey eyes. Then she remembers what her name means, and who she is. Her voice is steady, her chin tilted so she can look me full in the face. She will respect Ricsige, but her first duty is to me, her king.

'I gave my promise. I am ready.'

And then she swings to smile at Ricsige. I swallow a lump of emotion. There is ten years difference between them. But in her smile this young woman is offering my hardened warrior confidence, reassurance, as she would with any of the boys she teaches. He grasps her hands.

'You honour a plain soldier, Lady Hild.'

I am a lucky man. All my life I have been upheld by loyalty around me, even when I was fleeing in fear of my life. These two are still staring at each other, as if they have only just realized the full extent of what they have committed themselves to.

I am not sure Tata quite approves of this, though she's laughing.

'Hild, we're not ready. Such a deal of sewing and furbishing for your wedding chest yet. We meant to marry you splendidly, in Paulinus's new stone church, and send you away with all the trousseau of a princess to the estate Edwin's giving you both.'

'That new church isn't going to be finished, even by summer's end. We've been to inspect it. Some of the wall fell down yesterday and there was a man crushed, who'll never walk straight again.'

'And Hild insisted on giving him her ring to feed his family.' Hereswith says this in mock despair. She is not sure whether she should scold her little sister for her impetuous generosity or boast of her.

Hild tosses her head. The plaits stay somewhat tidier now than when she was small. She is bringing herself under discipline. 'I didn't need that ring. And I don't need a fine wedding tunic. The clothes I have ready won't disgrace me or my husband.'

'The great-niece of Edwin would look a noble lady even in a slave's tunic.' Ricsige is doing his stiff best at courtesy. I'm tempted to tell him Hild will be royal gold even with her clothes off, but that would embarrass him more than her.

Hild is not beautiful, like Hereswith, but she is rooted, strong. She has a way of holding her fingers curled so that she seems to be holding a fistful of earth in her hands, the soil of Northumbria. She is part of this country. She carries it about in her heart, in her own flesh.

Tata and Hereswith sweep the bride away to prepare her. Outside, my men of war are readying themselves for a different sacrament. Ricsige at war is a different man from this taciturn courtier. I wonder if there will be passion in bed tonight.

The Britons tell a story of a man who mates with a woman uglier than plain, wise Hild, only to find she turns into a queen of fairy beauty who is offering him the sovereignty of the land.

I am startled out of this memory of my past by Paulinus. The bishop looks pale, tense, waiting at the door of the Queen's hall that leads to her oratory. This chapel will serve for Hild's nuptial mass.

'Will James sing?' I say.

'Of course, sire. Lady Hild shall be married with all the ceremony we can manage at such brief notice.'

He disapproves of this haste too. I understand. Status matters to us both. I never walk the streets, even a few yards, without my standard carried before me. I waited a long time to become king of Northumbria. Let everyone acknowledge it. Paulinus feels the same need of ceremony. He still longs to be archbishop of York.

'Sire . . . the queen. . . .'

'What of her? She'll be enjoying getting Hild ready for her wedding. It will take her mind off darker things.'

'But we are men. We must face every eventuality.'

'I'm the most successful warlord this island has seen since the English landed. I win because I leave no possibility uncovered.'

The bishop bites his lip. 'Sire, forgive me. All men, even the King of Northumbria, are mortal. Your people cheer you each time you go into battle because they know you are risking your life for them. God has favoured you so far, and I shall besiege Heaven with prayers that he continue to do so. But. . . .'

I glare at him.

'What is your wish for the queen if. . . .'

'Can you protect her?' I shout. 'If we lose, man, that's what you're trying to say, isn't it? I have loyal thanes who know what to do. She'll need armed warriors, not clergymen, if Penda and that vile monster Cadwallon break across the Humber. And my son will have even more need to flee to safety, as I did after Aethelfrith murdered my father.'

I am shaking again with that humiliation. I am still a four-year-old, torn from his mother's grasp, dumped down alone among the Christian Welsh, with Cadwallon for my brother.

Hild is coming back, transformed. The women of Tata's household are almost skipping alongside her. This is festival they never expected to enjoy in a camp of war. Hild looks unaccustomedly grave. She has put on solemnity, willing herself not to disgrace us, to do what is fitting when a noblewoman is wedded. With a rush of the ridiculous, I am reminded of that sunny day when Tata arrived in York, and Hild, with her crooked wreath of flowers, came stumbling out of the ranks of my Northumbrian women to make her disastrous curtsey. There are fresh flowers in her hair now. Will it happen again? Will the bridal wreath tumble over her ear and she fall sprawling on the chapel floor before Ricsige?

She manages it gallantly. Our hearts thrill to the bass throbbing of James's chants. Paulinus invests every word of the liturgy with a controlled passion. The bread and wine seem to have a more highly charged sacredness. Our nerves are stretched, knowing how fragile this joy is.

They have this one night. The women bear Hild away from the ale-feast early, because dawn will break too soon. She is laughing with them all, though awkwardly. We men make a play of holding Ricsige back, but not too long.

In my own marriage-bed I hold Tata tight.

Chapter Twenty-six

The first rays of the sun shoot into my left eye, making it blink and water. Over that eastern horizon it has climbed out of the North Sea, turning the grey whale-road rose and golden in the dawn. That was the way our ancestors came in the longships and made this land ours.

Mine. The fierce love of possession sweeps over me as I ride the road to the boundary with my warhost behind me. We shall cross the Ouse at Selby, and then the Aire. We shall pass out of my land, to meet them on Penda's. Now, in the early morning, the summer trees roll every way on the gentle slope of the Plain of York. They are like a host of women with their heads veiled in every shade of green.

The men are singing. It's a sound to lift the heart and carry us forward to victory. I do not join them. My lips feel set under my moustache. The cheek pieces of my helmet stiffen my face. I have to turn my head a little sideways to see my escort, riding close enough to demonstrate their watchfulness, yet leaving the space a king requires. Ricsige catches my eye and smiles briefly. He bore the jokes about Hild bravely this morning and they were soon over. If I turned round in my saddle I could still see York, the walls pale gold in the rising sun. But I shall not look back. Wives, children, homes are behind us now. We are going to war to protect them. That is all that can occupy my mind these next few days.

I have glimpsed enough on either side to satisfy me. Northumbrians: the bear-crested helmets of my officers, the metal and leather caps of the foot-soldiers, the bare, tousled heads of the peasantry plucked out of the fields to have a spear thrust in their hands.

At mid-morning we have to slow to cross the river. The host behind me is narrowing into two columns, crowding the bridge or splashing through the ford. There are dark stains on boots and trousers already, but today they are only water. The sun will dry them.

The heat is beating down on metal armour. My eyes are shaded by the fierce brows moulded into my helmet. I could take this off. The enemy will not be in sight yet. But I want my men to know me, not as Edwin the middle-aged father my family sees, but Northumbria's warlord, their land made physical in sinew and weaponry. A young lad is carrying my standard ahead of me. The winged globe bobs and rises to the pony's trot, as the dragon-heads of our English ships crested the waves.

Who shall I set to rule Mercia when I have killed Penda? Osfrith? That would be appropriate. He had a Mercian mother. The thought forces a smile to my lips. That will wipe out the humiliation I suffered at Mercian hands, when Cearl sent me running from Aethelfrith, but kept my wife and children.

I am the most powerful king in Britain, but the old hurts are still sore.

We cross the Aire. The ground begins to rise, though the bigger hills are still far off. Ricsige draws closer, glancing at me carefully to see if I'm willing to talk. I had better make it easier for him.

'We've got what we wanted. The battle will be inside their borders now. We shan't need to foul our own fields.'

He follows my gaze. The farms in the clearings here are ominously deserted. These border peasants have driven away what stock they could into the forest. All they have left we seize. My men are driving the half-crazed pigs and cattle in front of them, whooping at thoughts of roast meat tonight.

But Ricsige is looking ahead to where the landscape begins to fold itself into ridges, dipping and rising between tributaries of the Humber.

'It was near here you defeated him, wasn't it?'

'I've never met Penda yet on the battlefield.' Surprise confuses me. My wars with Cadwallon, too, were far from here, in north Wales and the islands.

'Not Penda. Aethelfrith.'

A start of realization jolts my heart.

'I never thought. We were marching north then, out of East Anglia. But yes, it was this side of the Humber, where the River Idle comes out on to the plain.'

I stare around me. The trees have been cleared from the lower ground. Which of these valleys was the site of that momentous slaughter? I cannot recognize it. Blood was in my eyes that day. I saw only the small space in which I fought, with Lilla and the rest desperately defending me. I didn't know when Aethelfrith the Ferocious met his end. I didn't witness how Redwald of East Anglia lost his son. Suddenly the present reality leaps across my picture of the past. I, Edwin, am now what Aethelfrith was that day, warlord of all Northumbria, king of the northern world, defending his power.

'The scouts are coming back.'

I hold my hand up and the columns halt. The sun is declining. We must have marched twenty miles and the men are still in good heart.

'We'll camp soon. Penda will have to turn west before he reaches the Humber, unless he intends his warhost to swim across. We'll cut them off tomorrow before they reach the first ford.'

Gyrth draws his knife across his throat, leading the laughter. These are warm-hearted companions, kindly men, but the war-light flashes in their eyes now, cold as the evening light on mail and weapons. We have banished mercy from our hearts.

Ricsige has been talking hurriedly with our scouts. He leads them towards me. 'You were right, my lord. They've turned away from the Trent. We'll meet them tomorrow between the River Idle and the Don.'

I scan the contours. We are still lower than I like. The ground is marshy here. Red-stemmed alders crowd round and the earth between has a black sucking softness.

'That rising ground beyond the next river? Is that well positioned to intercept them, should you say?'

The first slopes are patchily wooded, but the higher ground looks more open, with pines more common than oaks.

The scouts look at each other for confirmation.

'Hatfield Chase,' says one. 'Yes, my lord. You'll get a view of the dales on either side. They'll have to pass below you, to find a crossing place into Northumbria.'

'We'll make camp there. Sound the horn,' I call.

But before the lad can put the ox-horn to his mouth and blow the bellowing note to march on, Ricsige stops him.

'Forgive me, my lord. We may be closer to them than they think. Sound travels on the evening air. Even a flock of birds startled out of the trees could put them on their guard.'

I laugh like a dog barking. 'Fool. Do you think they don't have scouts, as we do? They'll know we're coming.'

The trees whisper more softly than the men muttering. We none of us know what they hide. I'm a careful man, but I don't like to move furtively. It admits my fear. Still, the horn stays silent. The word goes murmured from rank to rank. We move off. Damp earth squelches underfoot. The horses snort, ignorant of any subterfuge. Our voices are subdued. Owls sweep the air, like pale ghosts. The bats are making a faster, darker dance. There is just enough light to see us on to drier ground. This ridge seems to have gathered the last illumination of the day and its clearer light lets us pitch our tents or roll in cloaks under the misty stars.

We slaughtered the beasts back in the woods below, to silence them, but the plundered meat is hanging from the branches uncooked. There will be no fires on Hatfield Chase tonight. I feel in my guts this secrecy is futile. Cadwallon and Penda are marching to attack us. We have come to kill them. What is the point in pretending?

I have ordered my tent-door hung back. The summer night is still more grey than black. A large shadow darkens it. There is a brief word with the sentry.

'The deacon James, my lord. Do you wish to see him?'

I raise myself on one elbow. Bishop Paulinus does not march with the army. James is a warmer man. His English has taken on the burr of Northumbria, replacing the Italian accent with which he came north. James has a musician's ear. He sings our language lovingly, like a new-learned tune.

'My lord.' He stands like a physician by a child's bed, knowledgeable, reassuring.

'You're not asleep, Deacon? You'll need to be up early to give us God's blessing before the battle.' I wave to him to sit. The tent is low.

He squats comfortably beside me, with a sigh of satisfaction. 'A man of God learns to discipline his body, sire. I can keep up with your army as well as any warrior and still do my own work as well. And my work is prayer.'

'Aethelfrith slew the monks of Bangor because they were praying for his enemies.'

'I'll take the risk. I've no doubt Penda of Mercia will have the priests of Woden on his side.'

I can't stop the catch of bitterness in my voice. 'And Cadwallon of Gwynedd? Who'll be praying for him?'

'Aye.' The word falls heavily into the stillness. 'You'd hope, wouldn't you, that the followers of the Prince of the Peace might not go to war against each other? Our quarrels must make God weep. But you brought Northumbria to Christ, sire. The Roman Church will pray for you.'

'What did you want to see me about?'

'Exactly that. Prayer. Would you like to confess to me tonight, my son?'

James is younger than me. Our roles have changed. He is here as my confessor. When he has given me absolution, I will become the king again and he will call me 'sire'.

I stare, not into the silvered sky, but at the black shadows in the tent corners. It is not Penda I dread. Cadwallon has risen out of the west again. His shadow haunts me. He is the one I must meet tomorrow. I shall not know peace until Cadwallon is dead.

I must kill my foster-brother, my godfather.

My soul is being dragged downwards into black waters, like some pit where a foul beast lurks. Will I find in my despair a magic weapon to slay the monster, as the hero Beowulf did? Will I rise again, like him, to feast with friends?

I have not answered James.

'You may shrive me.'

It is not a long confession. I have still not acknowledged, even to a priest, the thing which shames me most.

The west of Britain knows. Cadwallon knows. A groan escapes me.

'Sire? Are you in pain?'

He thinks it's physical, or he'd call me 'my son'. Let him go on believing that.

'Just an old wound I got on Anglesey.'

Anglesey, not Ynys Mon. The English name. The past is gone. My fist is balling into a hard knot.

James blesses me. 'Sleep well, sire. Our future depends on you. That heathen Penda mustn't take Northumbria.'

He backs out into the starlight. I feel partly reassured. They all trust me. I must not fail them.

I close my eyes. Into that darkness comes the tall figure of Rhun the British priest. His face, with its more searching intellect, bends over me. Would Rhun give me absolution now?

The dawn is primrose yellow. We rise purposefully to find a mist is smoking out of the rivers on either side. Hatfield does not stand high. We are an island floating in a white field that seems to be gossamer light as dandelion seedheads. But the truth is that we are heavy with armour and shields and swords and spears. The earth is sandy here. It is shaking under the thump of hundreds of feet.

The lad has buckled my armour firmly, but Ricsige checks it. The linked mail knits itself over my muscles. I rejoice in my strength bearing the weight. I am not too old for this yet. I loosen the sword in its sheath to test it. The boy has my spear ready. My horse is waiting.

The sun stands judge over all of us. The mist is thinning and cries have broken out. From the distance comes a fainter shouting.

The enemy have seen us.

I stride through the gorse bushes and look down. The view is ragged. Swirls of cloud still weave between our armies. Then breath catches in my throat. I have heard tales of the strength of Penda's war-monster, but I've never seen it till now. It's a more fearsome beast than I dreamed. They seem to be all professional warriors. No matter where I look, I can't see the slouch of country folk, with forks and scythes snatched out of the fields. These are ranks of spearmen, with shields. Not all of them have helmets, but they're wearing stout leather jerkins.

Well, I can boast the two victorious warhosts of Northumbria. It's not Mercians I care about. I'm searching for the dragon standard of Gwynedd. I can't find it. Ricsige tugs my arm.

'Over there, on our left.'

My eyes widen. When we camped under the veil of dusk, we didn't know that we were already sharing this higher ground with the Welsh warband. The ridge of Hatfield curves away, more of it emerging out of the fog with every moment. Cadwallon's horsemen sit watching us. They will fight from the saddle. I have a vivid memory of Cadwallon and his friends galloping recklessly down the flanks of a mountain, laughing at us English who feared for our necks.

One of those riders is Cadwallon. With all the intensity of my being I long to charge him now. I fight on foot, like an Englishman, rooted to the soil. My spear would thrust to the height of his horse and bring him down to my level. Cadwallon is not tall. He wouldn't be able to scorn me face to face, with my bodyguard round me. I should smash the boss of my linden shield into his taunting face. I could watch the runes on my sword blade snake between his ribs. I'd silence him. I should wipe out for ever the memory of him standing above the pool where Rhun baptized me, holding wide his arms when I rose wet and naked. Kissing me, his eyes still mocking.

I cannot do that. I am Edwin the King. Penda's warhost commands the centre and I must ride to the brink of battle there, leave my horse under the last pines, march down, kill Mercians. Osfrith will lead the wing that deals with the Welsh. I glance around for Eadfrith. He's too young yet to lead his own warband.

'Stay close,' I order. 'Find out how the Northumbrian army wins.'

Under the edges of his helmet, Osfrith's light hair has taken fire as the sun rises. Eadfrith is less easily inflamed than his brother. He's frowning, trying to make himself look stern and soldierly. I can remember that feeling, the panic fluttering. Will he shame his blood by cowardice? Will he be brave and get killed?

I grin reassurance. 'Get a good grip on that spear, and keep the hilt of your sword loose and handy. If your bodyguard shout, obey them at once.'

I've given his escort the usual orders. It's allowable for a prince so young to be spirited from the field. Servants are holding his horse ready for escape.

Whatever happens, I shall not run from the field. This battle will end it. Either Cadwallon or I must die today.

Tata was shivering that this is a cold summer. She should be here, where the heat of battle is like a smithy fire.

No. Wipe out that memory. A spear comes lunging between two guards, aimed at me. Keep out all thoughts except my grip on Kingmaker, the twist and parry of my shield. Just stay alive.

Ricsige has finished that one. He never got near me. Let me not think of Tata.

What will happen to her if I fall today? What will happen to my baby son?

I have other sons. Where's Eadfrith in all this mêlée? Against common sense, I risk a glance to my right, over the swinging shoulders and the lifted blades. How can I hope to find him? How should I see anything but the dark sand, softer than I like underfoot, and the heave of men's bodies?

Concentrate.

Blood pounds as though it would burst out of my head where the helmet grips too tightly. The weight of the sword is dragging me forward stroke by stroke. Does Kingmaker wield me?

My lucky weapon. I beat Aethelfrith with this not many miles from here, half a lifetime ago. The blade is newer, of course.

A giant of a Mercian, with an axe in his fists. Kingmaker's blade feels suddenly slender. But Gyrth is here, aiming at his knees. The ugly brute topples like an oak. A second to grin at each other. We storm on over him and our shield wall forms again. I am the King. The rays of my army cleave a path through the darkness in front of me.

'Where's Penda?'

Ricsige has to pant through sweeps and parries of his own sword. 'Those ash trees . . . over there. . . . Could be . . . his standard.'

The swirl of iron in the air is too fast for more than a glance. There's an angry swarm between us and that knoll. It's too much to hope for the accident of both kings coming face to face.

Just thrust. Shield carried forward by shoulder, grinding an enemy's face to bloody blindness. Shove in the sword, like a fork into hay. My muscles tell me I've met iron, leather, wood, steel, bone, over and over. I'm not young now.

How long is this day? The sun has left my eyes and is beating on the back of my helmet now. We've gained that advantage. But another fire is burning in my brain. My sinews are red-hot. I feel the next Mercian stroke will bend them into submission, like the smith's hammer on hot metal.

But my will is cool iron, defying the limping body and the panic fear in the heart at each new attack. Success in war is throwing myself into the flailing fury of flesh and blood and holding the mind cold and steady.

I could be out of this. I could stand on the hill with my herald at my side. By signalling for the lifting of my standard and the braying of my horn I could direct death for thousands.

I could watch Osfrith charge Cadwallon.

I feel the tug to the left. It is not Penda I want to meet.

Cadwallon fights on horseback. Osfrith's men will have rushed the Welsh cavalry on foot. I imagine the screams as they drag them out of their saddles and butcher them on the ground. I wish I could see Cadwallon die.

Another spear-point, a dragon's venomous tongue almost in my face. Fear leaps in my throat. I must defend myself.

I have not lost the art. Grey brains spill on the greying face between channels of red. No time to wipe Kingmaker. Let it bite through another leather jerkin to buff it back to brightness. My gauntlets are slippery with blood. I don't think it's my own. I'm so weary I hardly know if I'm hurt. There's darkness, like skeins of gnats before my eyes. Perhaps I'm losing blood. From where?

'My lord.' Ricsige's voice is urgent, as though as he has said this before. He's holding my elbow, with his sword slack in his left hand, trailing on the ground. It's unpardonable madness to let his guard slip like that. We could both be dead in another moment.

'My lord, it's getting too dark to see if we're stabbing Mercians or Northumbrians. The lines are separating.'

I feel weakness rolling over me in a huge breaker. My knees are giving way. Gyrth and Ricsige both catch me. Gyrth is older than I am. He was with me when I fled to Ynys Mon.

'Have we won?'

Here on the lower slopes, trampling through alder bushes and willows, I've lost all sense of this day. Whom has the sun carried away with it? They exchange looks.

'The Welsh have regrouped on the end of the ridge. The word is Cadwallon's dragon was still flying.'

'Penda?'

'He's lost men. But so have we.'

We struggle back to our camping ground. The servants have come out of their safe retreat. There are fires tonight, in full sight of each other. No point in secrecy now. I stand, tearing at a hunk of Mercian beef and try not to think how similar it looks to the muscles of men butchered by sword or axe.

'Osfrith?' I say. 'Eadfrith?'

My eldest son comes limping towards me. There's a wound in his leg heavily bandaged and bloody, but he's bearing it proudly. It's not dangerous. He'll be able to boast about it.

'I'd never want to fight on horseback. It's all show and yells. They've nothing to brace their feet on to put enough weight behind their swords. The horses do more damage than their riders.'

I grasp his hand, too tired for praise. If I can't be the one to kill Cadwallon, let it be young Osfrith.

'Where's Eadfrith?'

The silence is too long. Terror rises. He can't be dead. They carry the noblest casualties off the battlefield. My son would have been the first.

'No one's seen him,' Ricsige says quietly. 'Some of his bodyguard were found dead.'

'His horse?'

That's it. Penda's warriors must have harried him too closely and his escort thought it time to remove the lad. Their mounts were ready. They'll have galloped him away to safety, till they saw how the day went.

He may be wounded.

'The horses were found where they left them. Eadfrith didn't leave the field.'

I gaze down into the dusk clotting the battlefield. It is heaped with shadows that will prove to be more solid in daylight. Tomorrow, the two warhosts will have to advance through this evidence of our mortality to close with each other again.

'He didn't leave the field on this side,' Gyrth says at last.

Is that meant to give me hope? That Eadfrith may be Penda's prisoner?

Or Cadwallon's.

The food chokes in my throat and I am sick.

'Rest, my lord. Tomorrow's another day.'

Ricsige is steady as an oak. He's a younger man. Perhaps he's truly not as weary as I am.

Just now, sleep seems more urgent than grief.

I must lead my warhost. I'm the King only because I win battles. It's not for nothing my sword is called Kingmaker.

I now have a son to rescue or avenge.

I've hit my second strength. I feared when I woke I wouldn't be able to crawl out of bed. But I find I can still fight like a man half my age.

We must be winning. We're forging forward, long past the ash grove where Penda took his stand yesterday. I can't see his standard now.

As we swing to the east I suddenly see the Welsh horsetroop. The silver tide round them must be the British infantry with the morning sun behind them. We're fighting blindly, into the shadowed faces thrusting towards us. My armour is burning. Well, then, let its brilliance dazzle them. My arm is locked against an opponent's shield-guard. I have to force myself on him. Somewhere the energy surges that bears him down. He's under my feet. Someone else is spearing him through so I don't need to stoop and drop my guard.

Through the brilliance between us I can still see the silhouettes of those horsemen. Light dances on either side of them, seeming to carve the flesh from their flanks and leave them slender black ghosts. So may the sunset find them. Osfrith must finish them.

I cannot get it out of my head that one of them is Cadwallon. A standard twists in the sun, a painted board. In a brief flash of insight I know what it is. The figure of Christ, haloed in glory.

Cadwallon, my godfather.

I'm flaunting the cross on my own banner, to taunt Penda's Thor-hammer.

Cadwallon's face, smashed into a thousand fragments, reflected in the pool where Rhun baptized me.

'My lord, look out!'

I've been striding towards that ridge, veering away from the course that ought to carry me against Penda's strongpoint. Cadwallon is drawing me, like a colt on the end of a schooling rope.

Ricsige forces me back to the danger bearing down on me. We battle on almost in silence, save for the grunts as weight shifts to gain advantage over nimbler-footed opponents. Elbows are thrusting shields, lifting spears, swinging swords. My shoulders ache with the pressure and rejoice when the cut drives home. I'm good at this. I hear the wounded scream as I hack my way to glory.

That line of horsemen has dissolved. He must be down there at the foot of the ridge, lost at this distance among Osfrith's spearmen. A horse rears. The warrior's hair streams as the daylight shows between him and the saddle and he grips the reins for his life. I'm convinced it's Cadwallon.

I must get to him. I must swim my way through this sea to where he's fighting. I'll rip back the cheek-guards of my helmet, uncover my forehead, throw back these beetling iron brows. Let him see the blue eyes of English Edwin one last time. Let him taunt me now if he dares.

My hand tightens round the sweaty hilt of Kingmaker. I can feel it slide under his ribs. If I have to tear the armour from his lithe body with my own hands, I shall bare his flesh for my last stroke.

My last stroke. I see nothing but darkness after that.

'My lord!' Ricsige is angry with me.

I turn back to the Mercian warhost and do what I must. It no longer seems important to stay alive, to beat Penda. I still have a grown son left. Let Osfrith inherit Northumbria.

If I might only kill Cadwallon.

Would that give me peace? I can feel Rhun's arms, strong even in old age, hauling me out of the watery grave into the sunlight of the waterfall. I look up into his humorous face and watch it change.

Cadwallon, my brother.

'*Edwin!*'

I've stumbled against an obstruction. I look down in surprise. Riscige is doubled at my feet. I can't see his face. He's dropped his sword and his hands are cupped in front of him where blood and bowels spout.

There's no time for pity. Suddenly I'm aware that the shield-wall round me has thinned. When did my guards fall? I've a sense that the tall shadow behind my right shoulder may still be Gyrth. But the shield-fence is broken to pieces. The hostile pack of the Mercian army is crowding round us. There are so many of them. Grim-faced under iron caps, swinging axes, sweeping swords. The ones who press behind them still have their spears.

There's no end to them. No time to wonder how close Penda himself may be. One dangerous glance to my left, but the towering crests of English warriors black out my Welsh brothers. I can't see what damage my son is doing, how Cadwallon may be killing my son.

There's a screeching groan beside me, like a door wrenched on a stiff hinge. Gyrth is down.

I'm alone.

Just for a moment my eyes flick up to the pure blue sky. I see only ravens. I thought there should be angel wings gold with glory.

A Mercian wrestles with me. I must attend to his death. The years of youthful training, a career of conquests, have all narrowed down to this tussle.

He's not even noble. 'Haa!' I hear myself laugh in exultation as knowledge distorts his face. He has realized he's fighting Edwin, King of all the Northumbrians, Bretwalda of Britain. I drive the sword home.

Something has changed. I did not expect the first sensation would be surprise. I'm still driving on, and the impetus is forcing the spear further into my body through the rent where the chain-mail has broken. Didn't my smith sit up half the night repairing it?

Red pain now. I'm angry at the irreversibility of what's happening.

I am quite alone. There are hundreds of helmeted warriors all around me, not one Northumbrian. They're all grinning now, fighting each other to get at me. Each of them wants to claim the blow that kills King Edwin.

I've lost Kingmaker.

White pain. I lift my eyes and the sky is pale over the battleground where I last saw Cadwallon charging my son.

Are you still alive, my brother? Can you see this?

Then triumph soars. Is this how I beat Cadwallon after all? Yes! I have won. I shall die on this battlefield with my honour high and my name will go down in glory. Edwin, the great Christian King of Northumbria.

One flash of sweet memory as the darkness swoops. Hild's

young face, walking into St Peter's at York, where I set her free for baptism. Joy shining in her eyes.

I have done this, if nothing else. I gave Hild to Christ, and all Northumbria after.

Black pain.

Pray for my soul, Hild. Hold fast to Northumbria.